MARVEL

AVENGERS

THE EXTINCTION KEY

GREG KEYES

TITAN BOOKS

MARVEL'S AVENGERS: THE EXTINCTION KEY
Print edition ISBN: 9781789092066
E-book edition ISBN: 9781789094244

Published by Titan Books
A division of Titan Publishing Group Ltd
144 Southwark Street, London SE1 0UP
www.titanbooks.com

First edition: August 2020
10 9 8 7 6 5 4 3 2 1

FOR MARVEL PUBLISHING
Jeff Youngquist, VP Production and Special Projects
Caitlin O'Connell, Assistant Editor, Special Projects
Sven Larsen, VP, Licensed Publishing
David Gabriel, SVP of Sales & Marketing, Publishing
C.B. Cebulski, Editor in Chief

FOR MARVEL GAMES
Loni Clark, Operations Coordinator
Tim Hernandez, Executive Producer & Vice President
Dakota Maysonet, Creative Assistant
Becka McIntosh, Director of Operations
Haluk Mentes, Vice President, Business Development & Product Strategy
Eric Monacelli, Director of Production & Project Lead
Jay Ong, EVP & Head of Marvel Games
Bill Rosemann, Vice President & Head of Creative
Tim Tsang, Creative Director

Cover Art by Steve Epting

Avengers created by Stan Lee & Jack Kirby

Marvel's Avengers developed by Crystal Dynamics

This is a work of fiction. Names, characters, places, and incidents either are the product of the author's imagination or are used fictitiously, and any resemblance to actual persons, living or dead, business establishments, events, or locales is entirely coincidental. The publisher does not have any control over and does not assume any responsibility for author or third-party websites or their content.

A CIP catalogue record for this title is available from the British Library.
Printed and bound in the United States.

For Jack Simmons

PROLOGUE

THE Sorcerer Supreme danced on the wind, her bright-pinioned wings beating beneath the blazing noonday sun. Through dark syllables, arcane gestures, and the force of her will, Shaushka bent the elements to serve her fury, striking lightning through the Aegean skies as she descended toward the gathering below. There were twelve of them, assembled around a circle of nine monoliths standing on the rocky surface of the Isle of Penthos, a dot in the turquoise expanse of the sea.

Her target was Pabil, the Archer, but her thunderbolt dissipated before it reached him. His response was swift. Arrows as bright as the sun flashed from his bow with unnatural speed. Shaushka invoked Raggadorr, and seven cyan rings of energy enveloped her, shielding her from the deadly missiles, but even through the Eldritch Bands she felt the impact and heat.

The light blinded her for an instant.

In the middle of that heartbeat, something wrapped around her arcane defenses and yanked her from the sky. She beat her wings harder, but to no avail; she slammed hard into the rocky isle.

She struggled to stand, but as the spots faded and vision returned she saw the lash of energy that had pulled her down. A powerfully built dark-eyed woman held the other end of the whip. Shaushka knew her by reputation: Ab-Sin, the Maiden of the Stellar Knout.

"Oh, goddess," the Maiden said. "How you have fallen."

The rings still protected Shaushka from the searing weapon, but it was tightening. Sparks flashed, and she knew the Rings of Raggadorr would soon collapse. She implored dread Ikthalon, Lord of Stagnation, and long tendrils of intense cold curled from her fingers. The air itself condensed about the strands and then wrapped around her enemy. At their touch, the Maiden became rigid, encased in frost. Her glowing whip sputtered and vanished.

As Shaushka leapt up, a huge man appeared, with bull's horns curving up from his skull. He charged her. Laughing, she danced and vaulted over him, recalling her days posing as a priestess in Knossos on Crete-that-was. As she whirled through the air, she bound him in Cyttorak's Crimson Bands, so he fell heavily to the rocky soil, struggling against his mystical imprisonment.

As she dodged more of the Archer's arrows, she felt a sharp prickling on her face—or at first she thought so. But then as the barbs sank deeper her thoughts became confused. She realized that her mind itself was under assault, and her psychic shield slammed down as she turned to the culprit, a man whose skin looked like the armor of a sea-creature. His black eyes bulged from his skull and antennae protruded from his cheekbones. *Dub*, she guessed. The Pincered One. Whirling through the air she struck Dub in the face with the blades of her wings, slamming him into one of the standing stones, and the attack on her senses faded as quickly as it had begun.

The distraction cost her.

A bolt of energy appeared in her peripheral vision. Shaushka turned almost in time to deflect it. Almost. Everything went white as maleficent force surged through her nerves and sinews. A human would have been slaughtered on the spot, but Shaushka was born of the immortal Enna, a more ancient race. Still, she was staggered, and her limbs trembled.

A numinous shield around each hand, she deflected the next bolt, more arrows, a blast of heat from a woman with ram's horns. But her foes closed in now, totally encircling her.

She flapped her wings and rose above the ground, beginning a terrible and irrevocable invocation to Dormammu. Before she could finish, the element of Air itself attacked her, beating her back to the stony earth. There the Earth also defied her will, gripping her feet like manacles. Holding her fast. The power was astounding. She felt the first creep of terror in her soul.

But she was *Shaushka*.

She pushed down the fear. Panting, she faced her enemies, turning as best she could to see all of them.

They parted ranks, and one stepped through.

He had changed since she had last seen him, but she would recognize him in any guise.

"Atherwan," she said, and spat. "Traitor."

He smiled.

She had known him as a tall, pale man with narrow features. He had styled himself as a magus from the distant northern land of Bakhlo, and found favor in her court in Nineveh. Now his skin was bluish-black, and appeared almost rigid, like the armor of an insect. His hair and beard had fallen out, and in his eyes, otherworldly stars gleamed.

"Goddess of Nineveh," he said, mockingly. "Queen of Heaven. Sorcerer Supreme. How can I betray someone I never served?"

"You were my vizier," she said.

He shook his head. "You believed that," he said, "but everything I have ever done, every word I whispered into the ears of the mighty—into your ears—has all been for this."

In his hand, he held a gleaming golden object. It was shaped much like an ankh—a cross with a loop on one end, but with the shorter part of the cross curved like horns. Power emanated from it, more raw energy than she had ever felt in a single object. Yet Atherwan wasn't drawing her attention to the thing—he was using it to gesture at the sky.

It was almost noon, the sky was at its brightest, but along the ecliptic stars were appearing. Constellations, outshining the sun itself.

They were growing larger, brighter—closer.

"That is what I serve," he said. "The *Mulapin*. The Shining Herd." As she watched his fingers fused into pincers. A gleaming black scorpion tail rose from behind him and curved above his head, the wicked, venom-slick sting threatening her.

The others were changing, too, their human bodies distorting. The Bull was free, and nearly twice the size he'd been just a moment ago. Energy shivered from his horns as his legs shortened and arms lengthened so his fists rested on the ground.

She nodded her head at the object in Atherwan's hand.

"That's it?" she said. "The Key?"

"You know of the Key?" he said, his face darkening. "And you knew of our gathering here. You know about *us*. How?"

She lifted her chin. "I am Shaushka," she said. "Mistress of Love and War, Queen and Goddess, Mother of Sorcery, Empress of Heaven. Sorcerer Supreme by right and by trial. Did you really believe you and these other fools could plot beneath my very nose? In my own city? On this world I *protect*? I don't know all of your so-called herd, but I know of them. The cat, there. The Lion. A magus in the court of Mycenae, come there from the distant Kuru Kingdom. Ab-Sin, the harlot with the whip, a mistress of that doddering idiot Il-Keshub in Karkemesh and not at all the virtuous maiden whose title she usurps. Guanna the Bull, hitherto a royal scribe in Kolkhis. All of them—like you—worms in the apple of civilization. Like you, little schemers, playing at being the powers behind the throne. For what? Discord for the sake of discord, Atherwan?"

"I am not Atherwan," he said. "I am Gir-Tab, the Clawer, the Cutter. The Scorpion. And if we seek discord, it is only to bring order, and an end to the vanity of human rulers. Freedom from the whims of self-styled gods and goddesses like yourself. And you are half right—in the past, our ultimate goal eluded us. But no longer. Now we have this."

He brandished the Key in his claws.

"Yes," she said. "That I can see."

"You thought too little of us," he said. "You were too slow to act, and even now, in your pride, you believed you could defeat our combined might—by yourself. It is your final misjudgment."

He frowned. "Why are you smiling?"

"I've made mistakes," Shaushka admitted. "Coming here alone was not one of them."

His face was still human enough to show puzzlement.

Fist of Khonshu, Shaushka thought. *Now.*

Her answer was a rush of air above her. All eyes turned up as her champions appeared and hurled themselves down on the Shining Herd. Ares, war god of Olympus, resplendent in his armor and horse-comb helm, hurling his javelin at Guanna the Bull before his feet even hit the ground. Brunnhilde of Asgard, golden locks flowing from beneath her steel cap, her mighty sword Dragonfang cutting toward the Ram. The Black Panther from the Hidden Land of Libia dropped toward the Lion, who leapt to meet him, massive claws raking at the lithe warrior.

And Kandé, the Fist of Khonshu, who had brought the others from Shaushka's palace by the arts of the Moon God. She now drifted down in front of Shaushka, her bone-white cloak billowing in the wind, her features masked in darkness. The earth released Shaushka's feet and the air her arms, and with a cry of triumph she blasted Atherwan—Gir-Tab—with an eldritch bolt.

The battle began.

Caught unaware, Gir-Tab was knocked from his feet. Kandé sprang forward and grabbed the Key. Shaushka felt a surge of power as the Fist of Khonshu attempted to teleport away with it, but it didn't work—Gir-Tab still gripped it tight. He and Kandé faded for a moment, but then snapped back to solidity. Shaushka added her effort to Kandé's, but the Key was like a short, unbreakable tether. It would not be teleported—not without its master.

The Fist of Khonshu shrieked and her hands flashed through the colors of the rainbow. They seemed to vibrate like the plucked string of a lyre, and a high-pitched hum cut through Shaushka's skull.

Gir-Tab snarled and thrust the Key forward.

"Away!" he shouted. A sphere of expanding force slapped the Fist of Khonshu and Shaushka back.

Gir-Tab swung the Key again, and a burning wind entered Shaushka, parching her from the inside. Her throat closed and her chest heaved, seeking breath that was not there. Kandé moved to help, drawing her crescent-shaped sword, but the Maiden had recovered from Ikthalon's tendrils. She lashed at the Fist, who vanished before the whip could touch her. Shaushka saw Kandé reappear above the Maiden, but before she could retaliate a fist of water leapt from the Aegean Sea and enclosed her.

It didn't hold her long; she might have failed to destroy the Key, but the Fist of Khonshu was no mere mortal, her weapon no ordinary metal blade. The sword bit into the water as if it were a solid thing, shattering it like ice. The bits flew apart, then came back together and reformed into a human shape. Shaushka recognized Gula, the Great One, the Waterlord. The Fist of Khonshu did not relent, but struck again and again with her sickle-shaped blade.

Then Shaushka had to return her attention to her own battle. She sent the Maiden hurling back and cast the Flames of Faltine upon the Scorpion. The ball of fire engulfed him, burning not his flesh but his soul, his spells, the powers contained within him. The Key combusted with a clear azure flame, and an unholy scream escaped Gir-Tab's inhuman lips.

Ares came thundering between them, grabbing the Bull by the thigh and neck, lifting him, and slamming him down to earth. In the distance, she saw the Lion swiping clumsily at the Black Panther, while the Libian cut him mercilessly with his metal claws. Brunnhilde was beset by four foes at once, and doing well enough, but Shaushka blasted one of them, a woman with scales like a fish and the horns of a goat. Howling a battle song, Brunnhilde the

Valkyrie put her blade through the Pincered One; the spray of blood was not red, but blue.

They were stronger than Shaushka had anticipated, but the tide was turning. She felt it in her ancient bones.

Then Gir-Tab raised the Key high, and thunder rocked the island—thunder with no flash of lightning. The Flames of Faltine blew off of it as in a high wind, flickering for another few heartbeats before extinguishing for good. He twisted the Key in a strange, intricate pattern. Shaushka felt space and time swell, like a wave building and then breaking, pulling her under…

○————————○

SHE was alone on the island.

The sky dark, the sun further south—another season, another year…

"No!" she shrieked. She sent her senses scrambling up and down the timelines, through day and night and the seasons, until again she saw the battle at the moment she was ejected from it. She tried to open a portal to the same instant, but was denied re-entry by whatever force powered the Key.

Moving ahead an hour, she found a way in.

From just outside of time she studied the tableaux beneath her, trying to understand how the battle had gone. Was going. Gir-Tab had been right. Shaushka hadn't taken the Shining Herd seriously enough. When their silly games had come to her attention, she had watched them almost with amusement, certain she could turn their antics to her own purposes.

Now they had the Key.

What it was exactly she did not know, but she could see what it was doing. The twelve constellations of the ecliptic were descending into the Mortal Realm, infusing the Scorpion and his comrades with nearly unlimited stellar energy. She knew from her studies that when the descent was complete, the world would be theirs—perhaps for eternity. A world thus created would have no room for her, any of her champions, or any of their like.

What she saw emerging from that frozen moment was an Earth wiped clean of Enna, Annunaki, Asgardians, Olympians, Heliopolitans—all the gods of old. Heroes and champions, villains and demons, all stillborn not just in their mother's wombs, but within the time stream itself. In the place of all of that potential—the power and greatness for good, evil, and everything in between—there was just these twelve for eternity, tending an utterly predictable world bereft of chance, of choice, of volition.

This could not be allowed.

Yet the battle was not going well. The Watery One seemed to be out of the fight, along with the Lion. That left ten of the Mulapin to her four warriors. Ares wrestled with the Bull, the Olympian's sword and javelins broken, his face bloody. The Maiden's whip was wrapped around him, wracking his immortal frame with stellar energy. Brunnhilde was also bloodied and on one knee, fending off the Crab and the Goat, one arm hanging uselessly at her side.

The Fist of Khonshu grappled with a hazy figure that phased in and out of existence. One of the Archer's darts had struck Kandé; parts of her skeleton were showing through her skin as the uncanny energy penetrated her body. The Black Panther was setting his strength against two identical women who were in the process of merging into one. Where they fused, stellar energy shone like a star being born. The Ram was charging toward him, head lowered.

Gir-Tab stood alone, the Key lifted to the sky. Very little sign of humanity remained within him, but his chiton-armored body shone from within. He had grown gigantic, larger than an elephant.

Shaushka directed all of her attention to the artifact. It still warped space and time, unlocking the power of the constellations, but it was also feeding—absorbing power. It was hungry.

In that, she saw a possibility.

She returned to time, and to the ground.

The battle snapped back into action.

The Scorpion, she sent to her champions. *The Key. We must have it. Ignore the others.*

As she dispatched the message she went to work, summoning bindings for the Bull, the Goat, the Ram, and the Crab, raining the Fires of Raggadorr on the others so her champions could break free and assault the Scorpion.

He saw them coming.

The remaining members of the Shining Herd came for her. Shaushka summoned shields mystical and diabolic, calling on the Vishanti and even more ancient, less trustworthy powers. Against the assembled Herd even those defenses would not last for long, but she set that aside, and ignored them as they strove to extinguish her. She focused on the Key, until only it existed for her.

The Key could control the elements. It fed on their energy.

Let it gorge itself sick on them.

Drawing into the hollow of boiling rock beneath the island, on the storm forming in the air, on the crushing depths of the ocean, she sent it all streaming into the golden ankh.

And it drank. It grew brighter, spilling into adjacent dimensions and pulling energy from there. As if alive, greedy and insatiable. The Scorpion didn't notice; he repelled his attackers with wave after wave of stellar energy. Even so, Ares managed to reach him, only to be impaled by the venomous black sting. Immortal though he was, he stumbled and fell as the toxin worked in his blood. The Black Panther followed him, slashing off the sting with his metal claws, only to be batted aside by a pincer.

The Bull broke his bonds and charged back into the fight. He stood twenty feet tall at the shoulder, and his eyes blazed like suns. Brunnhilde met his charge. They collided; thunder clapped. The battered Valkyrie was hurled high into the air.

The light of the Key began to creep into the Scorpion's claw. It spread, moving faster. Gir-Tab looked up at her, puzzled.

The Key was powerful, but on one level it was a receptacle, and a receptacle could only hold so much. It had been using energy as fast as it had been garnering it. But not any longer.

It was full.

The Scorpion understood now. She could see that, and felt his panic.

Kandé, she thought. *Get them out of here.*

The Fist of Khonshu was reeling, only half conscious. For a moment Shaushka thought she would fail, but then Kandé and her champions vanished from the field.

As her shields shredded around her, Shaushka kept directing her energies at the Key. She couldn't leave, not until it was done.

An arrow of light struck her, and then a bolt of stellar energy. Thoughts that were not hers crowded into her mind. A titanic wave rose up from the sea, towering above her. The Scorpion's tail darted down. The sting had grown back, but her last remaining shield deflected it. She screamed as she wrenched open the stony gate of hellfire beneath her feet.

Then she felt the Key—*break*.

Where the Scorpion had stood was nothing but white energy, expanding. Time had slowed, creating the illusion that she could escape, but it wasn't possible. She was injured and spent. If she tried to flee, she would die all the sooner. Even in this state of hindered time, she had only a handful of heartbeats remaining. She was immortal in the sense that the years had little effect on her, but her body could be destroyed, and this would surely do so.

But she had triumphed. There was no better way to die.

And then…

○————————————————○

SHE was elsewhere.

"You're welcome," Kandé said.

Shaushka was with her battered champions, on a spit of land

facing a broad sea. In the distance, it looked as if the sun was rising from it, but far too quickly, pulling a black column of ash and smoke behind it.

The stone beneath them groaned and shook.

"There will be earthquakes," the Fist of Khonshu said. "Tidal waves."

"More than that," Shaushka said, as the light of the explosion rose so high it was hidden by the vast plume of ash. A secondary explosion expanded from the first, this one of boiling white clouds. *Steam*, she thought. The sea was pouring into the lava-filled heart of the island. But that wasn't what she meant. The constellations of the Shining Herd were fading, but much of their energy had been released. Waves of terror, fury, and discord spread out from the explosion even faster than the physical shockwave.

Ares sensed it too. He laughed.

"There will be war," he said. "Everywhere. War and chaos. The world is changed."

"And that pleases you?" the Black Panther asked.

"Immensely," Ares said. "Things have been quiet for too long. It's been boring."

"I must return to my people," the Black Panther said. "To protect them from what is coming."

"I will take you home," Shaushka said, "and then I must return to Nineveh. I fear Ares is right, and I do not take pleasure in it as he does."

Brunnhilde pointed out to sea, where the horizon lifted higher and higher.

"I suggest we all depart," she said.

"Agreed," Shaushka said. The airborne shockwave was even closer than the tidal wave, carrying steam, smoke, ash, and stone on its crest. Even for immortals, that would be painful.

○———○

DAYS later, from her palace in Nineveh, the Sorcerer Supreme left her physical body, traveling in astral form to the site of the explosion. The Isle of Penthos was gone, no stone of it remaining above water. The sea still bubbled and boiled. The sky there was dark, the sun a pale lemon sphere barely able to pierce the black clouds.

Every trace of the Scorpion's Shining Herd was gone.

Or was it? She sensed something familiar—feeble, but real. A trail, a future. Something—or someone—had escaped, leaving only the faintest trace in passing.

Had the Scorpion survived? Was the Key actually destroyed?

She had to know. And so she began the search.

But Ares' prediction proved prescient. In the months and years that followed, famine and war swept the land. The kingdoms of Mycenae, the Hittites, Babylon, and Egypt all collapsed. Barbarians swept in from the seas and plains, threatening even her own city of Nineveh. Finally she abandoned the search and returned to her beloved palace where, after much struggle, she managed to keep the kingdom from completely falling apart. Even so, it became a ghost of its former self.

Years after the battle, Kandé, the Fist of Khonshu, returned to Nineveh, seeking aid in a cause of her own. She came in mortal guise, without veil and cloak. Unmasked, she was as beautiful as a goddess, with eyes like black opals gleaming in her deep brown face. Shaushka had likewise withdrawn her wings from sight. They sat—to all appearances—as two mortal women on the willow-shaded terrace of the crumbling palace, listening to the nasal croak of a sacred ibis rooting in the weed-choked canals below, to the nightingale singing in its ornate cage, the trickle of water from the garden pool down the stepped sides of the royal dwelling. They sipped the strong red-black wine from Kaptara.

"This is good," Kandé remarked. "It is difficult to find good wine these days."

"Enjoy it," Shaushka told her. "This is from the last amphora of a lot I bought twenty years ago. That art of making it has been lost, and the vines now only a memory."

"Like so many things," Kandé said. "Was it worth it? We prevailed, but the cost was terrible."

Shaushka thought to share her suspicion—that the Key might have survived by slipping into some other dimension. But she had never found satisfactory proof of that, and saw no reason to dampen further her guest's spirits.

So instead she sipped her wine, and then nodded.

"This is only one corner of the world," she said. "The East was untouched. The Shang Dynasty thrives. Cities are rising on the Western continents. Civilization has fallen before—you know this as well as I. We have lived much, seen much. Atlantis and Mu were destroyed long ago, but life continued. People die, more are born. Cities fall. Cities are built. The humans go on, pursing their own often violent, twisting paths. If we had allowed the Shining Herd to descend, there could only have been one path—theirs. I have seen it. That would have been far more terrible, and it would have been permanent. In time, humans will rebuild these lands. They will lay brick and stone, bring crops from field and desert. One day there will be a wine to match and even surpass this one."

Kandé nodded. "I am the Fist of Khonshu, but before the moon god chose me I was born human. The Kingdoms I knew have fallen, my people slip into ignorance and darkness. I do not know those cities across the oceans, beyond the mountains. I know these places. And now I mourn them."

Shaushka shrugged. "I have some affection for this corner of the world, as well," she replied. "I have lived among these humans for centuries; I have been priestess, queen, sorceress, goddess— sometimes all of them at once. I have descendants among them. But as Sorcerer Supreme my view must be broader. Sometimes sacrifices must be made."

"I suppose," Kandé said.

"Now," Shaushka said. "Tell me why you have come, and I will tell you if it is a matter which interests me."

"It will," the Fist of Khonshu promised. "But even if it does not, you do owe me a favor, yes?"

ONE

BY the time the plane took off, Bruce Banner remembered how much he disliked commercial aircraft. He despised the crowded, claustrophobic space, the plastic smell of the air, the thoughtless behavior of the other passengers. He itched to get up, get out, be free. Alone.

How could he have forgotten how much he detested this?

Granted, it had been a long time since he had traveled by passenger plane. Not since before the accident. In fact, now that he really thought about it, he remembered his first flight: his delight as the plane rolled out and swept into the air, the fields and rivers dwindling with distance, even as the greater dimensions of the earth were revealed.

No, he thought. *I hated it even then.*

There was some sort of kerfuffle going on a few seats up. He had noticed the guy staring at him earlier and tried to ignore it. Now the man was standing in the aisle, having a furious whisper-argument with the flight attendant.

"…in the front," Bruce heard him say. "As far as possible from that thing."

"Sir," the attendant said. "I'll do what I can…"

Now nearly everyone was looking at Bruce. Including the person in the seat next to him, a professional-looking woman in a black suit with dark hair that was cut short and touched here and there with gray.

He tried to pretend he was reading his book, but she kept glancing at him.

Reluctantly, he looked up.

"Hi," he said.

"You *are* him, aren't you?" she said. "The Avenger. The one who…"
She trailed off, smiling uncomfortably.

"Let me help you out," he said. "I'm the one who turns green."

"Yes," she said. "Doctor Bruce Banner, right?"

"Umm—yes. I don't usually get recognized like—this," he said.
He looked around. "At least, not until lately."

"Oh," she said. "I read your profile in *Rolling Stone*. About how
you're a scientist, not just a… an Avenger."

The profile. They'd asked to interview him, but he had declined.
They went on with the story, pestering everyone from his childhood
friend Randy to General Thaddeus Ross, who had very little good to
say about him. Or so he heard. He hadn't read it, but he remembered
the cover: a picture of him from his college years superimposed over
the Hulk's face.

He nodded. "Okay," he said. "Well, I promise to stay a scientist
on the flight. No green guy." He hoped that was an end to the
conversation, but as usual, the world cared little about what he hoped.

"I'm Andie Strain," the woman said.

"Nice to meet you," he replied.

There was a little pause, and he started to let his eyes wander back
to his book. Maybe she would get the message.

"So you're in coach," she said. "Shouldn't you be in the Avengers'
jet, or—I mean, can't you fly?"

He laid the book face down in his lap.

"No," he said. "No, I can't fly. What I can do is jump—really,
really far. But I have to be the green guy to do that, which would
destroy my suit, and I've only got this one suit. I could pack a bag, I
guess, but he would probably throw it away or rip it open and scatter
my clothes from New York to San Francisco. I'm on my way to a
meeting where I figure clothing is… if not required, at least desirable.
And the Avengers' jet—the Quinjet—is really just for—well—special

stuff. This is more like a business trip. And first class seems sort of... I don't know. Unnecessary. So here I am in coach. And you?"

"I'm going to a job interview," she said. "I'm a copyright and trademark lawyer. I can't afford first-class. One day, maybe." She glanced at his book. "Sorry," she said. "I'm bothering you. I'll let you get back to your book."

He tried to smile. "It's okay," he said. "You're not bothering me. But, you know," he lifted the book back to reading position. The guy who had been arguing with the flight attendant seemed to have won his case. He was headed toward the front of the plane.

Andie noticed.

"That guy," she said, when the agitator was out of earshot. "Don't worry about that guy." She looked away, as if embarrassed, but then met his gaze squarely. He tried not to flinch. It felt threatening at first, that direct stare, but then he realized it was just sincerity, which was in some ways more difficult to accept.

"Look," she told him. "I'm a New Yorker. You guys have done so much for our city, and that thing that went down in Brooklyn, a couple of years ago? Without you, there's a good chance I wouldn't be sitting here right now. My brother was a first responder, and I *know* he wouldn't be with us. Some people say the bad guys come to fight you—that if you weren't headquartered in New York, we'd be better off—but I know better. A lot of people do. It's good to know you're there. Maybe you turn into a big green monster, but you're *our* big green monster." She nodded up the aisle. "Guys like him—I wonder what he's done for anyone."

"Oh," Bruce said. "That's... Thanks. I appreciate it."

"Any time," she said.

He turned back to his book then. He still felt confined and irritated, but—a little better. Almost enough to continue the conversation, see where it might go.

Almost.

It made him wonder. Had he really always felt this way about flying? Was he remembering it right, or was that the Hulk in him bleeding through? He'd been more social once, hadn't he? More adaptable around people? He remembered having a long talk with a complete stranger on a flight to a conference in Iceland. Nothing unpleasant then. Before that, his first time as a kid, watching the world below unfold like a topographic map. He had actually *loved* that, hadn't he? He'd written about it in a notebook he kept.

So why had he just been thinking he had hated it?

Was the Hulk in him revising all of his old memories? The Hulk didn't like people, or crowds, being confined, controlled in any way. What if every time he changed, more of the Hulk came back with him? What if eventually there was no difference between them but how much weight they could bench press?

He tried to concentrate on his book, but it wasn't easy, and halfway through the flight he gave up in favor of watching the landscape change beneath the jet's wings, trying to remember what it had been like to be eight years old.

o⸻o

MONICA Rappaccini met him at the gate, holding a placard with his name on it.

He first met Monica in grad school in New Mexico and the first thing he noticed about her was her eyes. Not what color they were or how they were shaped but how she used them, how she scrutinized everything around her, deconstructing everything she saw and putting it back together, all in the space of seconds. She never just observed the surface of anything, but always the structure, the components, the operating mechanics, the theory inherent in its design. She'd been a brilliant student, one of the smartest people he'd ever met, and one of the kindest. He'd really been impressed by her. He'd even had a little crush on her, although he'd never done anything about it. He'd been too busy.

And then—years had passed. Life intervened, in a very big—very green—way. He hadn't forgotten about Monica; he had read a lot of her publications, often because they coincided with his own interests, sometimes just because he liked the way she thought, how her ideas scanned on paper.

Six months ago, they'd met again, in San Francisco, at a pitch meeting with a fellow named George Tarleton. Monica and George had a start-up, a little company named Advanced Idea Mechanics—or as they called it AIM—and some very big, very exciting ideas. Monica had approached him about a meeting with Tony, mostly on Tarleton's behalf. She had seemed a little embarrassed about playing on their very old, very thin acquaintance, but he had agreed to talk to Tony.

He'd felt a little intimidated seeing Monica again, unsure how to handle himself. But she was still just Monica—smart, driven, focused perhaps to a fault. Flirty, but not that practiced at it.

Tony had been a bit of an ass, as usual, and Tarleton had been a little prickly himself. Bruce and Monica had become instant allies, trying to keep the peace and move forward toward an agreement.

Afterwards, he'd invited her to coffee; she had upped the ante to dinner, and things had moved on from there. Stark had gotten involved with AIM, and he and Monica had gotten involved with each other. He'd offered her the use of his lab in New York a few times, but now her lab in San Francisco was about as well equipped, so she didn't have much reason to come that way anymore.

When she had asked him to come out to San Francisco, he hadn't argued. He didn't mind taking things slow—in fact, he preferred it. But for a while now, it had felt to him as if he and Monica were, well—moving along. About as well as they could, long distance. It felt like something was maybe about to change—for the better.

But here she was, holding a sign with his name on it. That was a little weird.

"Doctor Banner," she said, letting her hand drift out for him to shake. "I trust your flight was alright?"

He had been starting toward her for a kiss, but that put him on pause.

"Umm—what?" he said.

She smiled.

"It's a joke, Bruce," she said. She held out her arms. "Come here."

○————————○

"SO how have things been?" he asked as they drove north along the Bay, beneath low gray clouds.

"Great," Monica said. "The new lab is—I can't wait for you to see it. Amazing."

"Well, you can thank Tony for that," he said. "He's pretty excited about what you guys are doing."

"Yes, I can tell," she replied. "He's always checking in. I can't believe he didn't come with you."

"He wanted to," Bruce said. "But he'll be over next week. My idea. I told him we needed a little alone time."

"You and AIM, you mean?" she said. He thought it was probably meant to be a joke, but something sounded a little funny about the way she said it.

"You know," he said, "I may have misinterpreted your invitation. I kind of thought—"

"That I wanted to see you for personal reasons?" she said. "No, you didn't misunderstand me. I've missed you, Bruce. I wish we had more time together, and not just so I can pick your brilliant mind. I've been thinking—there's a whole continent between us. Why?"

"Yeah," he said. "I've sort of been wondering about that, too."

"Really? I don't mean to be pushy. It's just—you and I, we have similar research interests. We're good together. You've been kind enough to let me use your lab in the past. Now that I have one to equal it—or almost, anyway—I wonder if maybe I can return the favor."

"You mean move out here?" he asked.

"I mean at least stay for a while. Stark has made a huge investment in AIM He's been talking a lot lately about having a liaison here." She glanced over at him. "I… may have suggested you."

"He said something like that," Bruce admitted. "I thought it came from Tarleton."

"And now you stand corrected," she said.

He cleared his throat. "I'd—uh, I'd be lying if I said I hadn't thought about it."

"But?"

"It's just—for Tony my moving out here— it's part of something bigger. Something I can't talk about right now. And something I'm not sure I'm on board with."

She nodded. "Let me give you something to think over, then. Did you read my last paper?"

"The one on mutagens and intra-cellular toxicity?"

"That's the one."

"Of course," he said. "Brilliant."

"It was inspired by you," she said.

"By my—condition."

She nodded. "I know how you feel about the accident, about the Hulk. I don't blame you. I can't even imagine what it must be like for you. And I know you've tried—tried to find a way back. A cure."

"That's no secret," he said.

"Well, I have some ideas," she said.

"Really?"

"Yes. Just ideas. But if you were around more, if you were willing to cooperate—"

"I— That's great," he said. "I'm grateful you want to help. But you're talking about figuring out the Hulk. And that—that could really be dangerous. You're not the first person to ask."

"But that's why I want you *here*, Bruce. So you can oversee everything I do. So the instant something doesn't feel right to you, you can shut it down. Think of it as if we're doing the research you are already doing yourself—but with a partner who might think of things you haven't. A partner who cares about you."

He had to admit, it sounded good. Really good.

"That's what you asked me out here for?" he said.

"That's part of it. The rest is purely selfish."

He smiled. "Okay."

"Okay as in 'yes'?"

"Okay as in I'm willing to be convinced."

"Perfect," she said. "I'm willing to convince you."

TWO

NATASHA Romanoff accepted the flute of champagne. She sipped it, wrinkled her brow slightly, and set it down.

"Is it not to your liking?" the man in the blue suit asked.

"It's fine," she said.

In fact, it was very good wine. Expensive. It went with the nineteenth-century Persian rug, the Grecian vase in the corner, the Mayan stele imbedded in the floor, the lapis lazuli necklace hung on a headless bust on the wall, and the jade statuette of an Olmec jaguar man on the end table where she rested her champagne.

And the guards, of course, the men who had patted her down before she entered, and now stood at roughly each cardinal point of the room.

"You are the buyer?" the man in blue asked.

"The buyer? Of course not. She does not do—errands—but I represent her. I've been authorized to make an offer. A generous offer. After I've seen it."

"I understand," the man said. "Ms.?"

"Smith," she replied.

"Of course."

He peered at her, and for a moment his eyes narrowed slightly. Did he recognize her? Her hair was dyed black with a streak of gray, and she wore brown contacts over her naturally green eyes. Her cheeks were sprayed with temporary freckles. Her accent was that of

Ghent, in Belgium. She wore a black three-piece business suit over a white shirt.

It had been easier in the old days, before all of the television exposure. She'd taken this assignment as a challenge, as much as for any other reason. To prove she could still go undercover. Now she worried they should have sent in someone else.

"Do I know you?" he asked.

"We have done business before," she said. "I sometimes work for a certain successful businessman on the West Side. I'm sure you remember." In fact, she'd never met the man in blue before. If he called her bluff, asked for details, she was screwed.

But he didn't; he backed down, just as she thought he would. He knew which businessman she meant. Few were interested in getting on his bad side, or showing disrespect for anyone who worked with him.

"Oh," the man in blue said. "Of course. My apologies for not recalling you immediately."

"No matter," Natasha said. "I am not here to discuss history, but to see it."

"Of course."

He stepped behind a long, low hardwood cabinet. His hand worked for a moment out of sight, and then he pulled out a wooden tray with a glass lid, of the sort in which jewelry was often kept. He walked to where she sat and tilted it in front of her so she could see its contents.

The tray was far bigger than it needed to be to contain the object it held, which was no larger than the palm of her hand—a rectangular tablet inscribed with the elongated wedges of cuneiform and a peculiar diagram that might be some sort of map. It displayed a central circular object with rays, with eight smaller circles ringed around it.

"One of the few such tablets known to be inscribed on metal rather than clay or stone," he said. "And the language—"

"—is undeciphered," Natasha said. She reached into the sleeve of her shirt and pulled out her phone.

"I'm sorry," the man in blue said. "That won't work in here—and if you take pictures, I shall be forced to confiscate it."

"I'm not taking pictures," she said. She tapped in a code and watched the screen until she was satisfied. "It's the real thing."

"Of course it is," he said. "But—"

"How do I know? Because this was stolen from a special collection of the Smithsonian five days ago. By a crime lord in Taiwan."

The man in blue took a step back. Balancing the tray with tablet in one hand, he drew a pistol from his jacket. The guards pulled theirs.

"Who are you?" he demanded.

"Like I said, I'm on an errand."

She grabbed the jade statuette and kicked the tray as she flipped backward over the chair. The tray slammed into the man in blue's face as she added a half gainer to the flip, slinging the heavy jaguar man at the guard farthest from her and landing in a crouch two yards from the nearest guard in the back of the room. He fired his pistol as she sprang forward, but she was to the left of where he thought she was going. She clotheslined him with a spinning roundhouse, then tucked and came down as two bullets *panged* into the wall above her.

The guard at the far end collapsed, clutching his face where the jaguar man had hit it. The remaining two were busy trying to put holes in her suit.

Scooping up the gun of the man she'd just kicked, she ran toward the next closest guard and shot him three times in the chest. He had body armor, but the shots dazed him long enough for her to break his arm and take his weapon. Now she had two guns. She crouched behind the Mayan stele as shots from the final guard and the man in blue chipped the ancient stonework, rendering illegible the ancient glyphs that had survived acidic rainforest downpours, excavation, and rough transport.

She leaned low and shot the remaining guard in the knee. Then she came out from cover, both guns blazing, hitting the man in blue in the right shoulder. He dropped his gun and scrambled backward.

"Don't," he said. "Don't kill me. Tell Capricorn I can make it good!"

Capricorn? That rang a bell. A very old one. She'd told the man in blue she knew the theft had been commissioned by a man in Taiwan, and that was all she'd known. She didn't have a name to go with the information. Now she did. Capricorn. *Put a pin in that,* she thought. There were more guards downstairs. They should be arriving in about three…

o———————————o

WHEN it was over, she propped the man in blue up in a chair. His eyes were glazed, and he clutched his hand to his bleeding shoulder.

"I know better now," he said. "I won't do it again. I'll do anything. Anything he wants."

"Capricorn, you mean," she said.

He nodded. "It's just like you said. His men took it from the museum, but you can't take a thing like that in this city without me knowing, right? So I took it from *them.* This is my town. If he'd come through me, none of this would have happened. You have to believe me."

"Uh-huh," she said, cocking her gun. "And how will you make this up to him?"

He gestured at the tablet. "There's another piece like that," he said. "I can get it for him. Gratis."

She shook her head. "He's not the forgiving sort."

"I just didn't know, okay? I heard the rumors, sure. They said not to mess with them, but I thought they were a myth."

Them? Natasha thought.

"What do you know about the others?" she asked.

"Some sort of syndicate," he said. "They used to be a big deal, but nobody's heard anything out of them for years. I don't even know what they're called. Only that Capricorn is one of them."

"And what do you know about Capricorn?"

"He's a businessman, a boss. Works out of Taiwan, like you said. That's all I know."

She nodded and uncocked the gun.

"I'm going to take you along anyway, so we can talk about this in a more comfortable setting."

"You're not going to kill me?"

"Not today." She gestured. "Get up."

As he rose shakily to his feet, Natasha felt a pulse of hot air. Time seemed to slow as her instincts kicked into high gear and her senses expanded, taking in the whole of the room. The guards were all still down, and she was sure there were no more left in the building.

Yet someone was here, in her blind spot.

She spun away and hurled herself to the side. Heat and force clipped her, sending her off-balance. There was the smell of burning hair and she realized it was her own. At the same time, cramps ran up the right side of her.

Sonics, she realized.

Natasha hit the ground, half paralyzed, squeezing off shots with her left hand. She saw a blurry figure holding up both fists in front of his face, knuckles out. She rolled as another blast of sound and heat roared past her, setting the Persian rug and a scattering of papers aflame.

Then one of her bullets found him.

The figure staggered.

She rolled back to her feet as her metabolism fought off the sonic paralysis, launching herself toward her attacker.

He vanished in an implosion of air.

Then the man in blue screamed, and she turned just in time to see that someone else was in the room—a male wearing some sort of body armor. With one hand he had the man in blue gripped by the neck, and held the metal tablet in the other. When he flashed a very white grin at her, his eyes looked like welding arcs.

Then he was gone, just like the other guy, along with the artifact.

The man in blue lay on the floor, gasping. His face was turning cobalt to match his suit.

He stopped breathing before help arrived.

THREE

THE AIM labs were in the San Francisco neighborhood known as Dogpatch, less than a block from docks on the San Francisco Bay. From the outside it looked like one of many old red-brick warehouses, long relative to its width with a peaked roof that made it look a little more charming than industrial. Even so, Bruce could see that the windows had been refitted for security and new high-tension power lines strung to accommodate the equipment inside.

The front door was an airlock, and the moment they were inside he smelled the cool, slightly metallic scent of processed air. Just beyond the door stood a security station where a big, very fit-looking fellow with dirty blond hair and a slightly receding hairline watched them enter. His gaze flicked up and down Bruce's frame. Sizing him up.

"Doctor Bruce Banner," Monica said. "This is Emil Blonsky, our head of security."

Bruce shook Blonsky's hand.

"Pleased to meet you," the man said. He had an accent Bruce couldn't identify.

"Likewise," Bruce said.

Blonsky nodded. "Doctor Rappaccini," he said, "I haven't been informed of Doctor Banner's security status. No offense, Doctor Banner."

"He takes his job very seriously," Monica said.

"No… he should," Bruce said. "It doesn't bother me. And it's Bruce."

"That's an oversight," Monica told the security chief. "He should have clearance. Check again."

"Of course," Blonsky replied. He tapped on a screen for a few moments.

"There it is," he said. "It wasn't activated yet. You're good now, Doctor Banner. I'll print you an I.D. and have it to you in a few minutes."

"That's great," Bruce said.

"Meantime, I'll give him a tour of my lab," Monica said. "When George gets in, send him over, will you?"

"I'll do that," Blonsky said.

Inside, AIM was a work in progress, but it had come a long way since Bruce had first seen it a few months ago, when a lot of the space stood empty. Now, most of the building had been converted to labs and offices. Monica's lab was the same size as he remembered it, but before it had been a bit under-furnished. Now it was full of brand-new equipment. Most of it was in keeping with Monica's biochemical interests, but one piece in particular was a little more puzzling.

"That's a gamma projector," he said.

She nodded. "I told you I've been busy. Low dose, nothing too powerful. But over time, I've had some really interesting results."

"'Interesting' is a word that's come to make me very suspicious," Bruce said.

She chuckled, low in her throat. "I don't blame you," she said. "In general, the effects of gamma radiation are unpredictable, and the suite of mutations, if left to chance, are rarely beneficial. But using new gene-editing techniques, I think it's possible to isolate specific mutations that might be beneficial."

"That's... interesting," Bruce said.

"But?" Monica said, turning.

"But it's still gamma radiation."

"And who knows more about gamma radiation than you?"

"So this isn't just about—my condition."

"Bruce," she said, taking his hand. "It is about that. But it's about more. That amount of radiation you absorbed should have killed you, but instead it made you stronger. How long since you've been sick, with even so much as a cold?"

He considered. "Not since… then. I've thought about this, too."

"And when you're… him, your healing rate must be unbelievable."

"Sure," he said. "But… um… no offense, but you're not the first person to think there might be some way to exploit the green guy. To make more of him, or use his blood to become immortal, or—"

"I don't want to make more Hulks," she said. "I want to make people healthier. Cure cancer. Counter toxic reactions. Without the… side effects. And repair damage or mutated tissue, if that's what's wanted. To reverse the effects. But I still have a long way to go. Your firsthand experience, your intimate knowledge of gamma rays, is invaluable to this project. Just let me show you some of what I've been doing. If you don't approve, I'll shut the whole thing down, I promise. I've got plenty of other irons in the fire."

○————————○

THE next few hours passed in the blink of an eye. He found he wasn't becoming just interested in her work, but excited about it. She had sequenced the DNA of low-dose gamma-mutated cells, and had begun isolating the various traits coded in that genetic material. She seemed to think some of those traits could be used for gene therapy, without transferring the whole collection of gamma mutations to the recipient. If true, that could lead to a lot of things, all of them good. And from what he saw, she was onto something. Of course, there was only so much she could do with the low-dose cells she could create with the equipment she had. But down the road, with better equipment, he had no doubt she could accomplish miracles. There were possible pitfalls, to be sure, but—well, it seemed promising.

So absorbed was he by their discussion, he didn't realize anyone else was in the lab until he heard a low cough.

"George," Monica said, rising from the table at which they were sitting. "Come in. Bruce and I were just talking."

"Doctor Banner," Tarleton said. "So good to see you again. I hope your flight was okay?"

"It was fine," Bruce replied. "How have you been?"

"Very well," Tarleton said. "You can tell Mr. Stark the new equipment has been put to good use. I've made more progress in the last week than in the previous three months."

"You can tell him yourself in a couple of days," Bruce said. "He's planning on dropping in."

"Checking up on us?" George said. "Of course, it is his money. And of course, I value his opinion and expertise. Yours as well."

"I appreciate that," Bruce said. "He may not have shown it, but Tony really is blown away by your work."

"Terrigen Crystals," Tarleton said, sounding steadily more excited "That's what I've settled on calling them. I'm convinced they're going to revolutionize—well, everything. As a source of power, I believe they could rival anything we've discovered so far. And I believe their power can be transmitted without wires."

"That's great," Bruce said.

Privately, he was a bit more reserved. Tarleton had been running an experiment designed to detect geomagnetic anomalies when he turned up strange energy readings in the San Francisco Bay. He had managed to pinpoint the readings and recovered a number of crystals from the depths of the Bay. He had realized he had something of potentially immense value, but didn't have the capital to investigate them properly. That was why he'd sought out Tony. The two of them were working on processes to extract and use the energy stored—or perhaps *generated*— by the crystals.

And that was all well and good. But exciting new sources of power—from oil to nuclear fission—rarely came without some sort of cost. So far these "terrigen" crystals seemed too good to be true. Bruce was worried that they probably were. But at least, with Tony involved, security was tight. The existence of the crystals was known to only a handful of people, and just under half of them were now standing in Monica's lab.

"If you would like to have a look now—" George began.

"Perhaps that can wait until morning?" Monica asked. "It's getting late, and I'm sure with the flight and time change, Bruce must be exhausted."

"Oh, yes—of course," Tarleton said. "First thing in the morning, then?"

"I'm looking forward to it," Bruce said.

Tarleton nodded, then headed off toward his labs.

"So what now?" Bruce asked.

"I thought you'd like to get cleaned up for dinner."

"That," Bruce said, "sounds like an excellent idea."

FOUR

STEVE Rogers watched as Maria Hill tapped on a keyboard and molecular diagrams appeared on the holographic cube in the middle of the conference table. He glanced over at Natasha. She rarely showed emotion without purpose—he had long ago decided never to play poker with her—but today he sensed a certain rawness in her demeanor as they followed what the SHIELD operative was saying.

"They killed him twice," Hill said. "He was injected with a neurotoxin at five points in the neck." The outline of a human bust appeared, with the five punctures marked as little red pins.

"His fingers," Natasha said. "The attacker was holding him by the neck."

Hill nodded. "The toxin is fast-acting, and lethal in far smaller doses than what he was exposed to. It would certainly have killed him, except he was essentially already dead."

"How's that?" Steve asked.

"His cellular structure had been disrupted," Hill replied.

"Disrupted?"

"Each cell in his body had the moisture sucked out of it," she said. "Violently, rupturing the cell membranes. He was murdered cell by cell."

"What does that?" Steve asked.

"We don't know," Maria replied. "If you freeze-dried someone and then thawed them, you might get a similar result."

"He wasn't cold," Natasha said. "In fact, his skin was hot to the touch. But I didn't see any steam."

"Forensics is still working on it," Hill said. "Hopefully they'll come up with some answers."

"Hopefully," Natasha said.

"This tablet," Steve said. "Was it that valuable?"

Maria shrugged. "Valuable? I mean, it was weird. We didn't think it was all that special. There are hundreds of artifacts around the world that SHIELD has flagged as exhibiting odd radiation or energy signatures. We can't curate them all, and if we tried, it would just generate unwelcome interest. We hold onto the ones that seem to represent clear and present danger. The rest we keep tabs on.

"That tablet has been squirreled away in a special collection since 1921," she continued. "The archaeologist who found it concluded it was probably a fake, and said so in the only published article that refers to it. When it was stolen last week, it set off a low-level alert. We contacted Romanoff." She pulled up a diagram of the building.

"We had a team waiting downstairs," Hill said. "For all the good it did us. Whoever launched the assault teleported in and out. No enhanced individuals were involved until that moment. None of us was expecting that kind of force to be brought to bear on what we thought was likely a simple antiquity theft. The deceased trafficked primarily in high-end artifacts. He had no previous affiliations with any of the organizations on our radar."

"I think he may have done business with Wilson Fisk in the past," Natasha said.

"We didn't know about that."

"What about this Capricorn?" Steve asked.

"I checked some of my sources," Natasha said. "He's a shadow who works with other shadows, supposedly part of an organization so secret both the KGB and CIA concluded it never existed, or ceased to exist a hundred years ago."

"Utter secrecy," Steve said, "and yet they killed someone in a very visible way."

"Maybe," Hill replied. "Or maybe it's all a smoke screen for something else—a distraction from another operation. We've got our feelers out. If there are shadows out there, something is casting them."

"What's our next move?" Steve asked.

"We know that Capricorn is in Taiwan," Natasha said. "Or was, anyway. I'd like to start there. See if I can track him—or her—down."

"We've got people on that," Hill said. "Less… conspicuous people. When we think this is an Avengers-level matter, we'll let you know."

Natasha frowned slightly, but then nodded. "Makes sense," she said. "But if you find anything out, I'd appreciate it if you let me know."

Hill nodded. "Of course," she said.

FIVE

"SIR?"

"What is it, JARVIS?" Tony Stark asked absently. He was in the middle of reconfiguring the life-support systems of the Iron Man suit. The cooling unit had dropped to twenty percent in the last fight, which could have been deadly. The suit generated a lot of heat; shedding the excess was absolutely essential if it was to operate for extended periods. The next time he had to put the thing on, he didn't want to come out like a lobster entrée.

"*Something is approaching Stark Tower,*" the computer said. "*It is moving at supersonic speed.*"

"Interesting," Tony said. "Do you have a profile?"

"*The object matches no known missile or aircraft configuration.*"

"How big is it?"

"*It's small, just two meters in length but quite dense. It will reach us in eighty-three seconds.*"

Tony didn't look up, but continued soldering.

"Power source?"

"*Of alien origin,*" JARVIS replied. "*I am preparing countermeasures, sir.*"

"Excellent," Tony said. "What do you think it is? A flying saucer?"

"*No, sir. It is roughly cylindrical in shape and seems to be mostly organic in nature. Locking on target.*" There was a pause. "*Update—it is beginning to decelerate. Sir, I believe it may be a person.*"

"Is it Thor?" Tony asked.

"*Analyzing,*" JARVIS said. Then, "*Yes, sir. It is, in fact, Thor.*" JARVIS was a computer, and shouldn't sound embarrassed, but Tony nevertheless thought he heard a touch of mortification.

"It was a natural mistake, JARVIS," he said.

"*The error was in my programming,*" JARVIS replied. "*I've now corrected your error.*"

"Good for you. When he gets here, invite him in."

"*Happily, sir.*"

○────────────●────────────────────●────────○

THOR always entered the room as if he expected fanfare—literal fanfare. The blowing of trumpets and tubas and alphorns or whatever the band played in Asgard. When Tony offered him a seat, he settled into it and made it look as if it was a throne, even though the chair was too small to pull it off.

"You really ought to use that transponder I gave you," Tony said. "JARVIS was on the verge of shooting you down."

"Ah," Thor replied. "My apologies. The device was destroyed in combat."

"So you found someone to fight on your cosmic walkabout," Tony said. "Anything I should know about?"

"A conflict far from here, of concern to my father—but not, I think, to Earth."

"Maybe, maybe not," Tony said. "SHIELD reported an uptick in extra-solar presences in our system. Nothing overtly threatening, but it's got them on edge. They've been calling in whatever sources they can, so they'll probably welcome your report, even if it doesn't directly concern them. I've been trying to help them track Captain Marvel, but so far without any luck. She—"

"Oh, her," Thor said. "Our paths crossed. She's battling off-planet, as well. That may continue for some time."

"Any details you can offer?"

"She didn't provide any information," he said. "I didn't ask." He shifted in his chair. "She asked a favor of me, though."

"What was that?"

"To return here," Thor said. "To protect the Earth. In her travels the Captain encountered... many things. Dangerous things. She wanted to make certain her home planet was as well defended as possible." His hand strayed absently to the grip of Mjolnir. "I agreed, out of respect for her warrior's intuition," he added.

"That's why you're back?"

Thor shrugged his massive shoulders. "In truth, she only asked that I indulge my heart's desire. I have been torn, Stark, since my brother's crimes brought us all together. My duty as a son of Asgard is to my home, and to my father, her king, yet my heart lies here, on this planet, with these mortals. That bond was forged centuries ago, but in my arrogance I grew contemptuous of this place. Only later, when I was humbled, did my heart open again."

Tony noted Thor's earnest expression.

"So, let me see if I'm reading you right," he said. "You're saying you're back."

"Verily."

"Great," Tony said. "We can always use you—and the press loves you, which doesn't hurt. There are some folks out there who really don't like the Avengers."

"Who says this?" Thor said, his voice becoming louder. "Have we not battled for humanity?"

"Sure, we've done that," Tony said, "but here's the thing. These cosmic beings with powers beyond what most mortals can imagine—these threats that endanger our very existence, this is all new to most people. It makes life... uncertain. Then they see us. A guy in a metal suit, a Viking space god, a reformed assassin, a big green monster—"

"But—Captain America. Surely they trust him."

"Yes," Tony said. "Steve's in the plus column. But my point is, we're also part of this new, scary thing. People wonder, what if we turn on them? What if we decide *we* know what's best for humanity, and decide to impose our will on the world?"

"That is not the way of the Avengers," Thor said.

"You know that," Tony said, "and I know that, but people are suspicious—and not entirely without reason. They've been betrayed in the past by leaders they trusted, by corporations that claimed to have their best interests at heart, by the very technologies intended to make their lives better."

"Yet not by us," Thor insisted, leaning forward and causing the chair to creak. "Captain America would never—"

"Sure. Everybody's fine with Cap. He has a track record. He was vetted by their grandfathers and great-grandfathers. He's not a monster created by radiation, or an alien from another world—"

"I thought you said this 'press' liked me."

"You have good looks and charm," Tony said, "and you come off as honest and unironic. You take a hell of a good picture. So right now, you're good."

"I strive to be." Thor sat back again.

"Right, that's for the best," Tony said. "Look, I'm glad to have you back. Why don't I call in the rest of the team, and you can brief us on your adventures out yonder? You may be right, it may have nothing to do with us, but more knowledge is always better than less."

"Except when it involves the mating habits of Asgardian sewer lizards," Thor said. "That's best left unknown—and definitely unseen. Properly they're from the Realm Below but some were brought as pets to Asgard, and—"

"Good point," Tony said quickly. "Maybe not that. But in general…"

○———————○

BRUCE was used to waking up wondering where he was, how he had gotten there, and what sort of damage he had done in the preceding hours or days. So it wasn't without a little panic that he took in his unfamiliar surroundings. A small room, plain except for a bookcase and an end table with a clock and his phone. A strange bed...

Well, a bed was a good start. The Hulk didn't usually seek out a mattress on which to pass out, and nothing looked broken. Also, he wore a t-shirt and shorts, neither shredded nor stretched out. All good signs.

Then it came back to him. Dinner with Monica—oysters, salmon, crème anglaise. A pleasant walk in the night air, good conversation. Eventually bed, and a deep, guilt-free sleep.

Someone moved around in the apartment; it was probably what had wakened him. He rose, tugged on his pants, and exited the room.

The apartment was tight: the small bedroom, a toilet and shower, a galley kitchen that opened onto a modest living room with a view of a building with green-tinted windows reflecting the morning sun. Monica was already up and dressed, sitting at the kitchen table and staring at her phone. She glanced up and put it down as he entered.

"Oh, good," she said. "You're up. I was beginning to wonder if I was going to have to wake you."

"Did I oversleep?" he asked.

"No," she said. "We have time, if you want to shower and such. I thought we would get breakfast on the way."

"Sounds good," he said. "I'll be a minute."

○————————○

BREAKFAST was pastries and coffee, of course, in a little hole-in-the wall run by a blue-eyed woman who chatted with Monica in Italian. They sat outside at a small round metal-mesh table. People and cars appeared and vanished like ghosts in the morning fog, so that it felt like only the two of them were real.

He smiled as he bit into his croissant, thinking of another time, another morning meal.

"You're remembering that time I served you cookies for breakfast, back in New Mexico," she said.

He paused with the pastry halfway to his mouth.

"God," he said. "How do you do that?"

It had been a long time ago, and it hadn't even been a date. Just a morning meeting to go over lab notes before a huge exam. She'd put down coffee and a plate of cookies and hadn't noticed his puzzled expression for several moments.

He'd thought about asking her out that morning, but he hadn't.

Maybe just as well. Even if she'd said yes, what relationship could have survived what happened to him a few months later?

Better that this was happening now, when he was finally coming to some sort of—well, not peace, exactly. But at least a truce with the green guy. *Now* something was possible. What, exactly, he still wasn't sure.

"Just a guess," she said. "I wondered, why would that pastry make Bruce smile? I entertain a hypothesis…"

"You couldn't find any decent pastries, you said."

"Yes," she replied. "I was devastated when I realized you thought it was odd. I had hoped to make a better impression on my brilliant lab partner."

He smiled, watching her sip, thinking again how close to normal this all felt. How he wanted it to keep going.

"Can I ask you a question?" he said.

"Sure."

"Why did you go in with George on AIM? You could have been in one of the big labs, with unlimited funding."

"Well, I have that now, thanks to you and Tony," she said. "But I see what you're getting at. I think it's that I liked the idea of working with like-minded people. A place where I wouldn't just be a cog in a machine I didn't design. And look where I am—with George, with you, with Tony—doing exactly what I want. Making the world a better place." She put her cup down and her eyes drifted a little.

"I mean, it may sound corny, but that's what I always wanted." Then she looked up. "And to get my share of the credit. I don't think that's asking too much."

"Wow," he said. "You never really got over that science fair thing from when you were a kid."

Her eyebrows drew together.

"I invented a programmable robot knife!" she said. "*He* had a cheese volcano! That his father built for him! How is that fair? In what world—"

"Hey," he said, fending her off with one hand. "I shouldn't have brought it up."

Her frown vanished, and she chuckled. "You see, I sometimes take myself too seriously. You were always able to ground me, Bruce. I like that about you. I think I kind of need that, to stay balanced."

He studied her for a moment, saw she was serious.

He took her hand. "I like that," he said. "Look, I get it. You deserve to follow your own path. And I don't doubt it will take you to even more amazing places than you've already been."

"Thank you," she said, setting her cup on the small table. "That means a lot to me, coming from you."

"And I'd like to… be with you for it. For the whole thing."

"Of course," she said, softly. "I'd like that, too."

EMIL watched Rappaccini and Banner approach on the monitors, waiting to see if the bot recognized them and applied the appropriate security measures. The system had been buggy for the first week or so, but he finally seemed to have tamed it. The two showed their IDs, the bot scanned them, then gave the greenlight to enter. Emil switched it to auto, and allowed it to let them in.

Emil knew who Banner was, of course. If the Avenger *really* wanted to come in, he could, and nothing they could bring to bear would stop him.

That was a problem. Even as a child back in Zagreb, Emil had known that the only way to keep someone out was through force of arms—not just the threat of violence, but the ability to deal it out.

The defenses here were all passive, and that had profound limits. AIM needed more… aggressive measures.

He had started out with AIM when they were a tiny start-up. He'd been protecting them from scams, cyberattacks, and run-of-the-mill burglary. But now there was millions of dollars' worth of equipment within these walls. That increased the threat of an organized break-in considerably, and that had to be reckoned with. But with Stark and the Avengers involved—with the Hulk actually here—he worried more than a little about his own job. He had to show that he could protect this place as well as any so-called super hero.

But he needed the okay, and a budget. Tarleton seemed interested, but he was always busy, and hard to pin down. Rappaccini had told him to run a cost analysis, which he had begun doing.

Emil wanted to do well here. He was good at what he did, and he meant to prove it. Coming to the United States, he'd hoped to start over, rewrite his history. He didn't talk about his past, the war, his years in the military and as a mercenary. It kept people from knowing the worst about him, but it also prevented him from becoming close to anyone. Inevitably potential friends or lovers sensed the gaps he wouldn't speak of.

Add to that the natural suspicion Americans had of immigrants, and he'd found a lack not just of personal prospects, but professional ones.

America wasn't the land of endless opportunity even if you were born there. When you came from a place like he was from, you were starting in a hole to begin with. Over the years the optimism which had brought him from his war-torn country had soured. He had been lucky to get this job. He intended to keep it.

SIX

BRUCE made a final solder, inspected the workmanship, and sat back, regarding the scattering of parts from the gutted projector. Monica, hard at work on her side of the lab, glanced his way. She had tied her long dark hair back, to keep it out of the way, but little wisps strayed from the tie here and there. He found it endearing.

She noticed him looking at her.

"You're sure you can put that back together?" she asked.

"Pretty sure," he said. "Do you still have the instructions?"

"Considering what Stark paid for that thing, you'd better be a little more than 'pretty sure.'"

"It'll be as good as new," he said. "Better, actually. It should project at about twenty percent greater efficiency."

"That… will be impressive," she said, "when I see it."

"Oh, you'll see it," he said. "Don't worry about that, Doctor."

She smiled at him, and dark eyes seemed to gleam, and for a second he wanted to drop everything, cross the space between them, and just—

He realized that the tumblers in his heart and mind had stopped. The combination was lined up, and he'd decided.

"You know what," he said. "I'm gonna take that as a challenge. I'm going to go outside, and when I get back, I'll put this thing back together—with no distractions."

"You're going outside?" she said. "Have you taken up smoking?"

"No," he replied. "I need to make a phone call."

"Ah," she said. "George's cell-jammer. Annoying, isn't it?"

He shrugged. "It's a sensible precaution, I guess."

○———————○

ONCE beyond the range of Tarleton's jammer, Bruce tapped Tony Stark's private number.

"Hey, Bruce," Stark answered immediately. "How's it going out there?"

"It's going really well," Bruce said. "They've got their labs up and running. Very impressive."

"You've seen Tarleton's work?"

"Yeah, this morning. It's moving along. He got a thirty-percent reaction from the crystals, but he seems certain he can get it to ninety or even higher."

"Without any pesky explosions, I assume?"

"Right."

"That's good," Tony said. "I've got some ideas myself. An ion-permeable filter—"

"That's kind of what he's doing," Bruce said.

"Oh. Well. I've got other ideas, too. That's not my only idea."

"I'm sure it's not," Bruce said. "Look, Tony—that thing we talked about. The West Coast thing."

"You can say it," Tony said. "Don't be afraid. Just say it."

"I—it makes it sound like a franchise," Bruce said. "Like some kind of burger joint."

"It is a franchise," Tony said. "That doesn't mean it's not important. It's America. Say it. You want to talk about what?"

"The, uh… the West Coast Avengers thing," Bruce muttered.

"See? Was that so hard?"

"My mouth hurts," Bruce said.

"Just—what about it?" Tony asked.

"The idea… it's growing on me."

"Growing on you. I like the sound of that. I don't suppose a certain Italian genius had anything to do with that... uh, growth?"

"That is really not your business, Tony," he said. "Do you want to hear what I have to say or not?"

"I'm all aflutter," Tony replied.

"I'd like to stay out here for a while, that's all. So if you really want to do this thing—"

"This thing?" Tony interrupted. "You mean the West Coast Avengers?"

Bruce closed his eyes. "Yes, fine, that. I think... we might start the process."

"We might," Tony said. "If I hadn't already. Been looking for a location for months now. I've narrowed it down to two..."

"So I'm okay to stay out here?"

"You have my blessing, my son."

"Great," Bruce said. "That's great, okay."

"Bruce?"

"Yeah?"

"We're gonna do this."

"Yes," Bruce said.

"What are we gonna do? Say it."

"Goodbye, Tony," he said, and hung up.

He stood there for just a moment. As easy as that.

He knew he had a goofy smile on his face when he went back into the lab. He didn't care.

BRUCE reassembled the projector and then ran a test on it. He was pleased to see that it outperformed his expectations. Slightly. He glanced over at Monica as she was tidying up her work area. A look at his watch showed him it was almost nine o'clock.

"Calling it a night?" he asked as she approached.

"Maybe," she said. "Are you finished up?"

"For now, I've got some ideas for a few adjustments…"

"Tonight?" she asked.

"Tomorrow," he said.

"So you'll still be here tomorrow?"

He liked the look on her face. Confident, like she already knew what he was going to say, and was glad about it.

"You should probably tell Blonsky I need long-term security clearance."

"Long term?" she said. "How long term?"

He allowed a little smile. "I called Tony," he said. "I've let him know I'm going to be staying out here for a while."

There were those eyes again, taking him apart in the gentlest way imaginable. She nodded and stepped closer.

"Good," she said. She leaned. He leaned.

When they finished the kiss, he realized they were holding hands.

"Perhaps," Monica said softly, "we ought to call it a night."

"That sounds good to me," he said.

"Just let me shut down a couple more things and lock up," she said. "I'll meet you by the security desk." She squeezed his hand. "I won't be long."

He tidied up his workspace, and then went to the foyer, trying not to put too much on what had just happened. It felt like he'd made the right choice, but he knew it didn't guarantee anything. He wasn't sure exactly what Monica wanted. Hell, he wasn't sure what *he* wanted. But now they had the space—the time—to explore that.

Another, more worrying thought had been lurking for a long time. Now it pushed its way forward.

What was the Hulk going to think about this?

Bruce knew the Hulk was part of him—had always been, even before the accident that gave him the power to come into the world—but it helped to think of the green guy as something… separate. Apart from Bruce Banner, both as a practical matter and as a way to stay sane. In reality, though, if he and Monica were together, he was going to be sharing her with the Hulk. Sometimes in a very literal sense. It was something he had to think about, however weird and unfun those thoughts might be.

It was a measure of how distracted he was that it took him a few minutes to realize he was alone in the room. Blonsky was nowhere to be seen. Maybe he was on patrol. Although Tarleton's lab was locked down, and he'd just come from Monica's lab. There was storage space, but that was mostly out in the open. There weren't a lot of places the security chief could be.

Maybe he was outside, on the phone. That made sense.

But something about the situation made Bruce feel uneasy.

He took a step to peer out the window, but didn't see Blonsky out there. Shrugging, he turned back to the kiosk, and noticed a booted foot sticking out from behind it.

"Blonsky?"

The man was on the floor behind the desk, unconscious. Bruce bent down beside him and was relieved to find that he was still breathing. He might have fallen, or fainted, or had a stroke, but Bruce didn't believe it. Something was wrong here. He felt his pulse quicken and begin to throb in his temples.

"No," he said. He stood up, sweeping his gaze about the room as he dialed 9-1-1. Nothing looked out of place. He gave it a second pass and saw—something. A distortion in the air, like a piece of warped glass—or an energy field.

"What the..." The phone told him it didn't have a signal. Of course...

The blurry patch moved, fast, and in it he saw a sort of misty outline—a person, or at least a humanoid. A woman.

Coming at him.

"Hey!" he shouted. "No!" He stumbled back, but she came on. A spectral arm plunged *into* his chest. He felt a tingle... and then white-hot pain detonated in his entire body. Through a haze of agony he saw his attacker, looking a little more solid. Wearing a blue outfit, she had sharp features, a thin nose, blonde hair cut short...

His legs crumpled, but already he felt the presence pushing back against the pain. The jittery, awful exhilaration of strength flowing from the depths to the surface as he—Bruce—was dragged down below, caught in the undertow of the approaching tsunami...

"Whoever you are," he said just before he lost control of his lips, "you just made a big mistake. Huge."

Then the anger overcame everything.

SEVEN

THE mist-woman stuck her hand inside of Hulk and hurt him.

Roaring his rage, he hurt her back, swinging one of his bunched knuckles into her. It was almost like hitting air, but he did feel something—like water, or a curtain. The woman flew in the direction of his punch. She vanished through the wall.

He went after her.

The difference was, when she went through the wall it was still there. When he followed her, it smashed to pieces. She flew through another wall, and he went through that, too, getting madder with every second. He didn't know her. Why had she hurt him?

Something to do with Banner.

Soft, weak Banner.

Banner, who thought he was so smart. He thought he knew everything, but when Banner went away, Hulk could really *think*. He knew what was real, and he knew what to do about it. Banner just thought and thought and thought, filling his head with clouds of suffocating nonsense—guesses, maybes, might-have-beens. Banner couldn't concentrate. Not like now—now everything was clear.

The mist-woman hurt Hulk.

He would hurt her.

Hulk was outside, now. The sun was gone from the sky, but there was a little bit of yellow left in the clouds. He remembered the street as if in a dream, but it was real, something he could put his hands on.

He dug his fingers into the pavement and ripped up a chunk of it to throw at his antagonist. She faded through another building before the mass smashed into it. With a growl, he prepared to spring.

There was motion, something coming at him, and he turned to meet it—but it was already there, hurtling toward him feet first from above. Claws slammed into his shoulder, digging in and pushing him down with enough force that he almost fell to one knee. Another one! Why didn't they just leave him alone? Why was someone always attacking Hulk?

Hulk swung a backhand, but the guy flipped over it and slashed him in the face. Sharp claws cut into his skin; the pain was surprising, and so was the blood that spurted. His skin was usually hard enough to protect him against anything. Bullets and missiles bounced harmlessly from it, but this man-lion—or whatever he was—his claws looked like they were made of light, or lightning.

Screaming his fury, he caught his attacker with a left, sending him hurling through the air. The punch felt solid, and good, and he didn't think the guy would get up again.

But he did.

The man-lion was big, for a human, with long golden hair. His eyes were yellow, too.

"Stop cutting Hulk!" he shouted, charging.

The man with the yellow hair opened his mouth. He yelled, too, and Hulk saw a light so bright it blinded him. The light came right out of the lion's mouth and hit him so hard it felt like he had been knocked half out of his own skull. He crashed into a building and sailed through it, tearing through walls like they were tissue paper, before he finally broke through another brick wall and skidded down the street.

The weird thing was, even though the light had hit him, *hard*, he felt stronger than ever—although still furious and confused. The cuts from the lion's claws were all healed. He jumped up, just in time to see that the mist-woman was there again. She flew right through his chest, and all of a sudden he felt like he'd swallowed lightning. His arms and legs jerked and cramped as if they didn't belong to him.

Then the woman was laughing at him, stoking the fury within him like a raging flame. She ran and he chased her, punched his way through another building in pursuit. He would make her stop laughing. On that he was absolutely clear.

The man-lion was there again, charging him. Hulk stamped on the ground, cracking the pavement and sending yellow hair up in the air, where he swatted him like a bouncing ball. He watched with satisfaction as his attacker slammed into a building, but just like before he jumped back up. Hulk braced himself, ready to pound the cat-man flat into the pavement, but then the woman was at it again, flying through him, snatching him off his feet and into the air.

He swung his fists like crazy, but there was nothing to hit as the street and buildings below grew smaller and smaller. Then once again a flash of light surged inside of him, and he was falling.

o———————o

EMIL remembered a young woman staring at him, reaching out to touch him. Then a sharp pain like an electrical shock, and after that— nothing.

He regained consciousness to the sound of approaching sirens. Gagging, he reached up to the security desktop and used it to pull himself to his feet. Everything was hazy, still spinning, but he managed to stand. What had she hit him with? A Taser? A drugged dart?

Emil found himself staring at a gigantic hole in the wall.

"*Šta je ovo?*" he grunted. Unsnapping the holster of his sidearm, he drew the pistol out, checked to make sure he had one in the chamber, then groggily walked through the gaping hole.

Where he nearly fell into a big hole in the street. Bricks and concrete rubble were strewn everywhere, and half of the nearby buildings looked as if they had been blasted with dynamite. The air was full of dust; sparks sprayed and cascaded from torn wiring. Had the woman who touched him done all of this?

No, there was an easier answer.

Banner.

Yet the Hulk was nowhere to be seen. In fact, Emil didn't see anyone, except a long-haired blond guy without a shirt gazing up at the night sky.

California, he thought.

His vision focused better as the man turned to look at him. The fellow's eyes had a weird glow to them, and he had shards of lightning for fingernails.

"Hey," Emil shouted, raising his pistol but not quite pointing it at the guy. "You. Get down on the ground."

The shining eyes focused on him. Then the man began to run toward him.

Seriously?

"Last warning," he shouted.

He'd seen it before. Men so pumped with adrenaline or drugs or holy zeal they didn't recognize death staring right at them. Emil had hoped all of his killing was behind him, but sometimes there was no choice. This wasn't his fault.

His first shot was at long range, and although he aimed to hit, he figured he wouldn't, and it would serve as a warning. To his mild surprise, the blond man stumbled slightly. Grazed maybe, but he wasn't stopping. The man was stupid or crazy, and Emil didn't have the luxury of trying to figure out which.

Taking careful aim, he squeezed off two, three more shots. The first missed, kicking up dust from the pavement. The next two hit; he saw the impacts. The weird thing was that both of them flashed white, as if they were detonating rounds or something. Too late, he understood. He should have gotten it earlier. If the Hulk was involved, other monsters couldn't be far behind.

And this was a monster. His exposed torso was thick, banded with muscle, and did not taper at the waist. His shoulders hunched forward and his arms came out more like forelegs, bent and terminating in those road-flare claws. He was much bigger than he looked at a distance. His nose was both flattened and protruding; his teeth were sharp.

Lav, Emil thought. A freaking lion.

The charging beast-man leapt. Emil tried to sidestep and club him with the butt of the gun, but he was still woozy. The creature tackled him, hitting him below the waist and lifting. Emil dropped the gun to shield his head and neck as he was smashed into the pavement. His instincts kicked in, and he tucked and rolled out of it, but a hand slapped his chest and he felt claws score across his skin. His breath sucked in and he fell back, watching in shock as blood appeared and quickly began soaking his shirt.

The lion kicked him, hard, and then turned and trotted off.

No, Emil thought. That wasn't the end of it. He wouldn't be so easily knocked aside. This was his *job*. He pushed himself up on blood-slicked hands and stumbled over to his gun. He picked it up, but thought better of using it. It hadn't worked before. He needed something more powerful.

The answer was obvious, and parked only a few feet away. His truck. He dug out the keys, trying to ignore the blood soaking his shirt, crawled in, and started the engine.

The lion didn't notice him until he was almost there.

It was like hitting a concrete pylon, and Emil was glad the old vehicle didn't have airbags. The impact knocked the lion off his feet. Emil threw the machine in reverse, backed up, and hit him again, knocking him further down the street toward the docks.

Screw you and your super-powers, he thought.

The lion was standing back up. He hit him again.

This time, things didn't go as well. The monster sank his claws into the hood and hung on. Emil gunned it, aiming toward a warehouse next to the dock, but the lion planted his feet, dug into the concrete, and lifted.

It happened so fast, Emil didn't react at first. He and the truck were in the air, and then the monster hurled it. Emil felt the light belly of free fall, and then the car slammed into the water, hard.

○————————○

THE pavement cracked under him as the Hulk crashed into it. Roaring, he swiped at the mist-woman, who danced just out of reach. Taunting him.

Beyond her he saw the lion-man toss a car into the water. He wouldn't have thought much of that, except that in the streetlights he could see a man was inside the car. Probably someone who had nothing to do with the fight. Someone just in the way.

That made him even madder. Why did they have to hurt someone like that? He was like Hulk—he hadn't done anything. Didn't deserve to get hurt. But they were trying to kill him!

Raging, he leapt toward the car.

The yellow-hair met him in midair, and they both went sprawling. He rolled, limbs swinging, blasting fragments from the asphalt as the lion flipped and wriggled maddeningly out of reach.

Hulk almost caught him, but then the stupid mist-woman was there again. She grabbed him and everything went funny—he felt light and heavy at the same time. Something sucked at him, pulled him right down until he couldn't see anything but darkness. He'd sunk into the street like it was quicksand.

Then it was solid again, and he was inside of it, where he couldn't breathe.

○————————○

BLONSKY knew he must have blacked out again. He was still in the car, and for an instant, he didn't understand why it was so dark outside. The headlights were shining, but nothing much was visible except little bits of stuff, as if he was in a midnight snowstorm. And he had the feeling he was facing *down*.

And he was wet up past his waist.

Then he got it. The lion had tossed him into the water. The truck was sinking, quickly. The weight of the engine had already turned the vehicle nose-down.

He didn't usually panic easily, and he didn't now. The truck was already completely underwater, so he knew trying to open the doors was no use; the pressure was too great.

Taking off his seat belt, he hit the electric window opener; it whined a little, but nothing happened, which meant he must already be pretty deep.

That left breaking the window. He slammed it with his fist, but it was like hitting a wall. He tried his elbow, with no better result. The cab was filling up quickly, and his head was spinning, either from lack of air or blood loss or both.

Then he remembered he still had the gun. It was wet, but it might still work. He unholstered it, placed the muzzle against the glass, and pulled the trigger.

The pin clocked on an empty chamber.

Swearing, he pulled back his hand to hit the glass with the pistol, but at that moment, the truck crashed into the bottom, hurling him down and into the windshield. He heard something snap as once again his skull filled with darkness.

○━━━━━━━━━━○

HULK heaved and flexed at the concrete and rebar in which he was embedded, trying to howl. His huge lungs heaved against his ribs, feeling red, angry that they could no longer suck in breath. He pulled in on himself, trying to roll up into a ball, and then flexed out with every fiber of his muscle and bone. Something cracked, then shattered, then exploded as he burst up from his entombment.

The lion-man was there, roaring. Blazing argent light struck Hulk point-blank, sending him hurling through the third story of an old brick building. The lion came right after, slashing, biting, but as before, Hulk felt revived, full of energy. They grappled, crushing their way through that building and the next, the lion-man's strength failing beneath his onslaught.

Then they fell, turning...

Until they hit the water. The lion opened his mouth, and again the white light shone. The water exploded into steam. Hulk yelled and thrashed, trying to land a blow on the guy, but he struck only water until he hit the bottom, where he braced his feet and *pushed*.

He erupted out of the bay and came down on the docks. Yanking his head this way and that, he searched for either of his attackers, ready to pound them into pulp.

Then he remembered the man and the car. There was no sign of them, but he remembered where they sank. Diving back into the bay, he swam downward with broad strokes until he dimly made out twin beams of light in the murk, and found the car resting on the bottom. Hulk clenched his fingers into the grill and hauled the car up with several kicks of his powerful legs, pushing against the weight.

Breaking the surface, he dragged it up onto the dock, yanked the door open so the water flooded out.

There were flashing lights everywhere. He knew what that meant. These people had come to help the others, but he knew from experience they might shoot at him. He also knew the people who came with the flashing lights were people he wasn't supposed to hurt—and he didn't want to.

He wanted to hurt the mist-woman and the lion. He would find them and make them sorry they had ever messed with Hulk. Roaring a challenge, he swept his savage gaze around and saw the lion-man, perched on a building above.

Stamping so hard that the street beneath his feet shattered, he leapt toward him.

The lion stood as still as a statue until Hulk was almost there, then dodged to the side, sinking his flashing claws into Hulk's arm and twisting, using his momentum against him, hurling him to the side and slashing at his chest with the other hand.

Once again, Hulk felt the shock of having his skin pierced; only the bones protecting his heart stopped the deadly blow. He caught onto the lion's arm and hurled him at the ground. An instant before he crashed into the broken streets, however, the mist-woman appeared and grabbed the lion's hand.

They both vanished in a puff of air.

Hulk leapt down after them, swiping at the space they had just occupied, but they were gone. Landing with a loud impact, he howled his frustration.

Humans were everywhere now, many of them screaming. He heard gunfire and felt the sting of a bullet on his skin. It didn't hurt that much, but it made him mad, mad enough he almost forgot he wasn't supposed to hurt these people. He had to leave. Get away. They all hated him anyway, no matter what he did. Hurt someone, save someone. They didn't care. Banner was too stupid to see that, but Hulk wasn't.

As a second shot struck him, he bent his knees and leapt, rushing into the foggy sky and leaving the rest behind him.

EIGHT

TONY thought Maria Hill looked impressed. That was difficult to achieve, but to be fair, blowing a hole through a block of Vibranium-laced titanium was, well—impressive.

"I've been playing with some of the energy profiles you dropped on me," he explained. "You know, the ones from the really 'out there' sources."

"To good effect, I'd say," Hill said.

"It meets your required metrics, and then some," he pointed out.

"It does," she replied. "Good work, Stark."

"Which begs the question, Commander Hill. What the hell do you expect to be shooting with this thing?"

Hill turned a gaze on him as inscrutable as the *Mona Lisa*'s.

"Oh," she said, "you never know. They say too often generals are gearing up to fight the last war, right? But we can't afford to be behind the curve. Not with everything we know is out there, and even more because of everything we *don't* know about. We're trying to get ready to fight the war-after-next."

"I thought that was what the Avengers were for."

"Never hurts to have a plan B."

"I guess not," he said. "Wait. Are *we* plan B, or—?"

"Is it true?" she interrupted. "What I hear about Banner?"

"He's taking a little 'me' time in San Francisco, if that's what you mean."

"So he's unsupervised," she said.

"Well, he's a grown man and a brilliant scientist," Tony replied. "But if you want to look at it that way—"

"It's the only way we *can* look at it," she said.

"Well, I suggest you go tell him that, then," Tony replied. "Anyhow, we've got our Norse god back. That should make you happy."

"Overjoyed," she said. "If he stays, which isn't a given."

"How was the interview?"

"It went well enough. We tend to agree with him that the objects of his latest adventure probably don't pose an immediate threat to Earth—not least because if he's telling the truth, he and his pals beat the living snot out of them. Frankly, I'm more worried about what Captain Marvel has gotten into."

Speaking of mysterious subjects, Tony thought. From what he knew, Danvers could probably handle the Hulk and Thor at the same time without working up a sweat. But she wasn't usually around. He wasn't sure if that was good or bad.

"You've talked with her?"

"No," Hill replied. "Not for a while. That's what worries me."

"So," he said, "there's a recent uptick in the alien activity in our solar system. A big one. Does SHIELD have any theories as to why?"

She pursed her lips. "It coincides neatly with the rise of enhanced individuals on Earth, don't you think?"

He'd noticed that, of course, but he already knew what *he* thought. What interested him was what Hill thought, or *knew*.

"As in the aliens are responsible for the growing number of superhumans," he said, "or as in we're starting to draw their attention? Chicken or the egg?"

"Amniotic eggs started with reptiles," she said. "Hundreds of millions of years before chickens."

"You're evading the question."

"I'm not," she replied. "I'm telling you—it isn't the first time something like this has happened."

"What do you mean?" he asked. "You mean like when Thor used to pal around with the Vikings? Because sometimes he goes on about that, and he won't shut up." Tony rolled his eyes.

"It's way bigger than that," she said. "We're still putting it together, but whatever happened back then, we went a long time without interference from... out there. Some of us think the break is over."

"But again, why?" he asked. "Why now, and not fifty years ago?"

"Well..." she said, but she let it hang.

"Oh, come on."

Hill shook her head.

"Enough of that," she said, pointing to the weapon. "Tell me about this."

"Pulsar tech," he said.

"Like your repulsors?"

"That's proprietary," Tony said, "so I'm going to say no. Also, because the principles really aren't the same. Any other questions?"

"How well does it scale up?" she asked.

"You want a bigger cannon than that?"

"If a bigger cannon is more powerful, yes."

He looked at the demolished block of metal. "What did you say you were planning on fighting?"

"Like I said—"

"Right. You're not sure. No idea." He shrugged. "But your specs seemed oddly specific."

"This isn't your first dance, Stark. Are you going to let me lead, or do I find a different partner?"

"Nope," he said. "You can lead all day, so long as you pay me."

She sighed and folded her arms.

"Just give us the prototype, the specs, the blueprints—we'll take it from there and let you know if we need anything. Sound good?"

"I'm happy to oblige," he said. "And we already have a legally binding contract, so—"

"What's that?" Hill asked, looking off to one side.

"Are you trying to distract me?"

"No, but I think your security system is."

She was right. He'd turned the volume down for the meeting. "JARVIS," he said. "What is it?"

"*It's Doctor Banner, sir,*" the computer said. "*I'm afraid there's been an incident.*"

"What? Define 'incident.'"

"*It's the Hulk, sir.*"

Hill's phone made a noise. She pulled it out, scrolled, and frowned a little.

"Yeah," she said. "No kidding. Better get on that."

"He's in San Francisco," Tony said. "Does SHIELD have a base out there?"

"No." She shook her head. "Our nearest Helicarrier is halfway around the world. We could probably have a team there in five hours, but it's the Hulk, so—"

"As fast as your floating fortress may be, it's still a big ship, and takes time to get from one place to another," Tony said. "We can be there quicker."

Hill continued scrolling on her phone. "There's not much information, but it looks like enhanced individuals are involved. Nobody we've heard of."

"Wow," he said. "Nat's enhanced assailants were new, too. Now more? These guys are really coming out of the woodwork. JARVIS, prep the Quinjet and alert Nat, Cap, and Thor."

○——————○

THE Quinjet, wonder of engineering that it was, had its limits. Its maximum speed topped out at just over Mach 2, which meant that by the time the craft was prepped, everyone was on board, and they reached maximum airspeed, nearly three hours had elapsed before they reached San Francisco.

As the craft settled onto the debris-strewn street, Cap spotted Thor striding up to meet them, cape billowing from the blow-back of their underjets.

"He beat us here," Tony said. "Son of a... Bifrost."

"You owe me twenty bucks," Natasha said.

Cap surveyed the wreckage, wondering exactly who or what the Hulk had been up against. They'd heard reports on the way that there had been a few injuries, but no fatalities; it looked like the area didn't have much in the way of residential population. An ambulance and at least eight squad cars were parked around the damaged buildings, and a crowd of reporters was gathered at the edges of the police tape that surrounded several city blocks.

○———————○

"NO sign of Banner," Thor said when they arrived. "Witnesses say he jumped away and headed north, but I couldn't find him. He could be a thousand miles from here by now, but I'm willing to make another attempt."

"Can you give me a read on the situation first?" Steve asked. "We heard a little on the way, but you've been here a while. How bad is it?"

"The area was mostly deserted when the fight began," Thor said. "Some bystanders were mildly injured by flying debris. One man was more seriously wounded. All before I got here, I'm afraid. The Hulk and those he battled were gone when I arrived."

Behind Thor, Steve saw a group of men and women approaching the Quinjet—some uniformed, some not.

"The person that was hurt," Steve said. "Did the Hulk—was he responsible?"

"His car was knocked into the water by some sort of 'lion-man,'" Thor said. "I'm not sure what is meant by that, whether it was a lion with a man's face or a man with a lion's, some sort of costumed warrior, or something else altogether. There was once a race named the Tyanna, I've heard, an ancient lineage—"

"So the Hulk wasn't involved?"

"No," Thor said. "You know Banner. As the Hulk he is a brute, but even then he is mindful. In fact, he saved the wounded man from drowning. The villains here were the attackers—the lion-man and some sort of ethereal spirit, by the sound of it. Banner was defending himself, and others." He looked around. "He did make a mess, though."

Steve knew he shouldn't feel relief. Someone had been hurt. There was no good to be found in that, but it could have been far worse.

So far, as Thor said, the Hulk had never crossed the line, never murdered an innocent. Even in his darkest rage, Banner was still in there, hidden in the brutish body, having his say.

If that ever changed, heaven help them all.

"Hey, Cap?" Tony said.

"Yeah?"

"Can you handle the press this time? I've got something I need to check out right away."

"Sure," Steve replied. "Not my forte, but I'll do what I can."

○────────────○

FOR most people, waking from a nightmare was a good thing. For Bruce Banner, the real nightmare began after his eyes opened.

This time waking revealed no small, neat room in a friend's house, no promise of a good day, of coffee and conversation. Instead, he found himself trying to piece the nightmare together, images in his mind—more like a sequence of still photos than a movie, and a woefully incomplete series at that, wrapped up in such rage that everything he remembered was suspect.

Had there really been a lion? A woman who could walk through walls?

Why had he been fighting them? And the man in the car. Something familiar about him. He'd pulled him out of the water, but had he lived? Had he knocked him into the water in the first place?

Another flash of memory—yanking the car door open, water pouring out, revealing the man.

Blonsky.

He closed his eyes. *Please don't let him be dead,* he thought. But that limp figure...

Monica! He hadn't seen her during the fight, but she'd been there, in her lab. He didn't remember the fight going that way, but chunks of concrete and asphalt had been flying all over the place. What if she'd been hurt, or worse?

He had to get back. Now.

But where the hell was he?

He was in a forest, lying on his back, staring at the trunks of trees that seemed infinitely high, vanishing into a mist above. It was quiet, peaceful. He understood why the green guy had liked it and decided to rest here, where it felt calm and safe. But which woods? It was an evergreen forest, but there were evergreen forests in Alaska, Chile, China, Russia...

These trees looked familiar. Were they redwoods? If so, he might not have gone far. He might at least still be in California, and maybe no further than just beyond the Golden Gate Bridge.

He grabbed what was left of his clothing and began the familiar routine of trying to piece together something to wear from what the Hulk had left him, trying not to rush, to become impatient. He couldn't just run in any direction; he might end up deeper in the woods.

A little hunting found a well-used foot trail, which he began to follow; it would come out somewhere, hopefully somewhere he could get directions and maybe hitch a ride.

○————————○

GEORGE Tarleton was in his lab when someone knocked on his door. Security in most of the building was down, of course, but the door to his own lab was miraculously intact. The monitor wasn't though, so he had to crack the door to see who it was.

"Mr. Stark," he said.

"George," Stark said. "Are you okay?"

"Yes," George said. "I wasn't here when it happened. I arrived an hour after it was all over."

"And Monica? Where is she?"

"She was here," George told him. "She's the one who called me. She wasn't hurt, thank goodness. She talked to the police. I think now she's in her lab."

"I heard someone got hurt?"

"Emil Blonsky, our head of security. I wasn't here, but Monica was. He... tried to stop them. He's expected to recover."

"I'm glad to hear that," Stark replied. "And I'm glad you and Monica are okay."

"Thank you," he said.

"Uh-huh," Stark said. He looked around. "So it looks like your lab didn't take much of a hit."

"No," George said. "The equipment you so thoughtfully provided is mostly intact. The attackers don't seem to have come in here."

"Well, that's good," Stark said. "So the crystals—"

"I know what you're thinking," George said. "I thought the same thing; that someone broke in here to steal the crystals. But I checked the vault, and they're still there."

"What do you think they were after, then?"

"I still think it's the crystals," George said. "There's nothing else as valuable in the lab. I think Bruce ran into the intruders before they could get what they came for."

"I thought the crystals were a secret," Stark said. "How did anyone even know they were here to steal?"

George found he couldn't quite meet Stark's gaze.

"I don't know," he said. He thought he would be questioned further, but instead Stark shrugged and patted him on the shoulder.

"Look, I'm just glad you're okay," Stark said. "If those guys came to steal the crystals, they might be back. If they do, we need to be ready for them. First and foremost, that means getting the crystals into a secure location."

"They're in a vault," George said.

"Yeah," Tony said. "I think we want them in the Quinjet for the time being. It will be easier to set up a perimeter there. I want you and Monica out of here, and not at your apartments. I'm putting you in a hotel with a security detail."

"You think that's necessary?"

"Until we find out what's going on, I think it's a good idea. Just enjoy the room service and don't steal the towels, okay?"

"Mr. Stark, this is my business. I should be here to defend it."

"I hear you," Stark said. "But these guys went toe-to-toe with the Hulk. There's no reason for you to risk your life while we're here. This is what we do."

George started to protest, but thought better of it. He didn't like it, but Stark was right. He nodded.

"Very well," he said. "But I must be involved."

"Of course you will be. Now let me go set all of that up."

George watched him go, realizing he was growing angry. He had been angry since Monica's call, of course. Just as he'd finally thought everything was going well, it was all suddenly set back, threatened.

He should have known becoming involved with Stark and Banner might bring them to this—attract the attention of so-called super-powered beings. Banner had only been in San Francisco for a few days. Could it be coincidence that his lab was suddenly attacked by beings with more-than-human capabilities? The Avengers attracted things like that.

He'd had his eye on them. Watched the faith people placed in them, as if they were gods, as if they could lead humanity to a better future than the deities of the ancients. As if it had gone so well back then. It was all backward—gods took the place of reason, of understanding, of science. They held humanity back, *always*. The last thing the world needed was a whole new race of them, whether they were self-made like the so-called Iron Man, or freaks of uncontrolled technology.

Like Banner.

He knew it was uncharitable. He owed both Stark and Banner a lot. But they were scientists, like him. They should know better. They should know that science should lead the way—not government, not talking heads, not so-called super heroes. Science.

But as much as he wanted the Hulk to be at fault for all of this, deep down he feared it was something else. That *he* was to blame. He couldn't tell Stark that. Not just then, not now. Not until he had checked a few things and thought it through.

Right now he needed them, these super heroes. He hated to admit it, but it was true. But they were a means to an end. One day he wouldn't need them, or fear them. He would be beyond them. And so, too, would the rest of the world.

The Avengers and their kind were not the future. Science was the future.

He was the future.

○————————○

EMIL sat up in his bed in the ER. One of the nurses saw him and hurried over.

"You shouldn't move," she said. "Those wounds could open right back up."

He glanced at the bandages where the lion's unnatural claws had cut him, at the IV in his arm. She was right, he was sure. He nodded at her and lay back. The attack was over, and he had survived. He should feel safe now.

But he felt—exposed.

He remembered one time, when he was a boy. He'd lived in the fifth story of a blocky, Soviet-era high-rise, surrounded by almost identical structures. One day a sniper set up in one of the buildings and began shooting people in the street. He could hear the shots and watch through the window as the bodies on the street multiplied. They needed food and milk, but his mother dared not go out of the apartment. It went on all day and through the night. Early the next morning, someone kicked their door in, and soldiers barged into the apartment. His mother begged for her life, and for his, but they ignored her. After searching the apartment, the men departed, leaving the broken door behind them.

Half an hour later he heard gunfire. Not the single, high-pitched whine of a sniper's rifle, but the percussive chattering of automatic weapons. An hour after that, soldiers began clearing the dead bodies from the street.

The enemy sniper had been in their own building, a floor up and six apartments over.

Every step Emil took after that, he imagined the crosshair of a sniper's scope on his head. It had been a lousy way to grow up.

Now he felt that way again.

He had mastered the sniper's rifle himself, and the automatic rifle. He had made himself intimate with weapons of war and murder; he had become a weapon himself. And he had been a good weapon, an efficient one. That feeling of helplessness he'd had as a child—that he was merely a target for the predators around him—had been erased by his own competence at killing and not being killed. By the body count he left behind.

But in the face of these—monsters—he was again like that little boy, hiding in his mother's apartment. All of his skills, all of his training, were nothing in the face of that kind of power.

Banner's kind of power.

It had been the Hulk, not Emil the security chief, who had driven off the attackers. The Hulk had pulled him from the bottom of the bay, wrenched off the car door as if it were wet cardboard, rescued him as if he was a helpless infant.

He knew he should be grateful for his life. Grateful to the green monster.

But he wasn't. He had no close friends, no lovers, no one he cared for or who cared for him. He had sacrificed all of that to become who he was. But at least he'd *known* who he was. That he was good at something. That if nothing else, he would always survive.

Now he didn't even have that. The monsters had taken the only thing he had left.

NINE

FOR Cap, the next few hours blurred past as he talked with the police, the feds, and finally the media in a hastily cobbled together press conference. The chief of police started, laying out the facts as they were known: that two enhanced individuals attacked the start-up known as AIM; that Banner got caught up in the attack and became the Hulk; that there were fortunately no serious casualties. The investigation was ongoing.

Then it was Steve's time at the microphone.

"I just want to make it clear," he began, "that we're not here to get in the way. The San Francisco police know what they're doing, and we see that. The Avengers are here to support them in any way we can."

"Aren't you here because one of your own went berserk and tore up half of Dogpatch?" a young woman asked.

"What's your name?" Steve asked.

"Sona Jahal, *Golden City Chronicle.*"

"Thank you, Ms. Jahal," he said. "Of course, we're always concerned by the actions of one of our own. As Chief Landau just informed all of us, Doctor Banner wasn't the aggressor in this situation. He was acting to prevent the activities of two bad actors."

"Cap, what was Doctor Banner doing in San Francisco in the first place?" another reporter asked.

"He was here visiting a friend."

"So he wasn't representing the Avengers?"

"If you're asking if Bruce came here looking for a fight, the answer is no," Steve answered. "But when innocents are attacked, the Avengers are always on duty."

"Who were the two super-powered attackers?" Jahal asked. "Enemies of yours? It seems strange they would show up in the one place in San Francisco where they would run into the Hulk."

"Not only were we not aware of them," Cap said, "they don't match the descriptions of anyone we've ever heard of. Who they are and why they chose to terrorize this area is as much a mystery to me as it is to you."

"Do you know the current whereabouts of the Hulk?" Jahal asked.

"No," he admitted. "I'm sure he'll turn up soon on his own, but in the meantime, we're doing our best to locate him. I wish I had more answers for all of you, but at the moment I really don't have anything more I can tell you. Why don't we meet back here in a few hours, and I can let you know if anything new has turned up?"

That didn't shut them down, but it gave him a chance to politely beg off after another five questions.

○────────────────○

BACK at the Quinjet, they got their plan together. Thor flew north to look for Banner. That was the direction he'd been headed when last he was seen, and if he was still the Hulk he wouldn't be that hard for the Asgardian to spot. Even if he wasn't the Hulk, he might have left an obvious trail.

The others were setting up for a siege. Tony and Nat had moved Tarleton's crystals out of the lab and into the Quinjet. They debated moving the jet, too, but decided to stay put in case Bruce showed up. That was taking a bit of a risk if the attackers returned, but on the other hand, if they did come back they would be facing not one Avenger but three, along with the Quinjet and all of its considerable resources.

Since they were going to stay, Steve decided to do a little looking around. The boys in blue might have missed something. Anyway, after all those hours in the jet followed by standing at a microphone, he felt the need to move, if only a little.

The morning sun gave the thick persistent fog a rosy glow, restricting visibility considerably. He might have thought it beautiful, in a way, but it reminded Steve of Italy—the Po Valley—back during the war. That had been a really nasty business. The enemy had dug a maze of trenches, reminiscent of the Great War decades earlier. Many of them had probably been using some of the same weapons as their grandfathers. Dense fog had rolled in during the night, hiding everything—every gun, bayonet, mine, and artillery emplacement.

It had been like fighting in a cloud.

This was half a world and three quarters of a century away, but he still felt as if the fog was hiding something. Something dangerous. The soldier in him hated it.

Cap didn't have any idea what he was looking for. He tried to recreate the fight in his mind; he knew it had started in the lab building, then moved into the street. From there it was a matter of following the direction of the destruction—which way the rubble was strewn.

Whoever the attackers were, they had given the Hulk a fight like he rarely saw. The one described as being like a lion seemed to have gone toe-to-toe with him at times, which implied a great deal of strength and mass. In places he found scorches and melted stone that must have come from energy weapons of some sort, including a series that looked like claw marks. Had the Hulk's opponents been wearing suits, like Tony, or were their abilities innate?

Either way, why were they using such impressive powers for a breaking-and-entering? It reminded him of the guys who had attacked Nat. It felt like overkill for a situation that could have been handled by regular bad guys with ski masks and silenced guns.

The trail took him a considerable distance, as he knew it would—

the damage had been visible coming in from the air. The Hulk's battles tended to range. At what looked like the furthest engagement, he guessed he was probably between quarter and half a mile from the start. Two buildings lay in ruins, and the street was cluttered with rubble.

The sun was higher, the fog starting to burn away. Visibility was still terrible, but his other senses were tuned in. He could hear cars in the distance, airplanes overhead. Someone was hollering commands over on the docks.

He was set to turn around and work his way back when he noticed something in the rubble, something that gleamed a little brighter than the dim sunlight ought to allow. Bending, he touched it experimentally, then picked it up.

It looked like a bracelet or a wristband made of some lightweight red-gold metal. Odd markings were inscribed on it, reminding him of hieroglyphics of the sort he had seen in museum exhibits. The metal was bent; it looked as if it had been twisted off of someone's wrist, but exerting a little strength on it proved it wasn't all that flexible. Considerable force must have been applied to deform it like that.

Perhaps it was nothing. When he was a little boy, there had been a huge fad for all things Egyptian, spurred by the discovery of Tutankhamen's tomb and the fabulous objects found within it. He remembered upscale ladies in "Egyptian" dresses and buildings with a papyrus motif. President Hoover had named his dog King Tut. There was one building on West 70th Street in Manhattan that was all pharaohs and sphinxes. It had seemed pretty impressive and exotic when he was young. Doubtless over the years he'd spent in the ice there had been dozens of such crazes based on ancient civilizations. What he held might be nothing more than a piece of costume jewelry that had gotten mixed up in the rubble.

But still—that thing Nat had been involved in. The metal tablet with a weird energy signature. Hadn't that had symbols on it sort of like these? If so, it might be more than coincidence. He'd best hold onto it just in case.

Then the thing began to vibrate, and the inscriptions flared into fitful light.

Maybe this is *something,* he thought.

There was a thudding sound, off to his right. He strained his eyes into the mist, but still saw nothing...

Something flashed from the fog.

Cap instinctively threw himself to the side and backward as a long, glowing tendril curled past him. Twisting, he landed with his left hand down and finished the turn, vaulting to his feet. The lash licked back into the fog and he saw, emerging from the mist, the woman who was connected to it. Slightly built, she moved above the street with nearly blinding speed. Her outfit was mostly deep brown and green, tight like his own; an eight-pointed star glowed on her sternum. She wasn't holding the whip, though; it emerged from her hand, a glowing, crackling strand of energy.

She came to ground and danced toward him, long brown hair flowing behind her as if she was underwater. Her whip flicked toward him. He raised his Vibranium shield, and sparks flew.

"The bracelet," she said, in a soft accent he couldn't quite place. "Drop it, for we have no quarrel with you."

"You just tried to bushwhack me," Steve said, hooking the object on his belt. "I think we have a quarrel."

Wait, we?

He spun in time to see the other one, also a woman, charging out of the fog. This one was big, tall, probably twice his mass. He couldn't tell if she wore blue body armor or if that was her own physique showing through, but whichever it was, she looked nearly as muscular as the Hulk. Two glowing projections curved from her head like horns. She had her head lowered, too, like a bull, but she didn't finish her charge. Instead she stamped her booted foot on the street. Pavement cracked and jumped up in a line racing toward him.

An instant earlier, *down* had been where he'd left it, beneath his feet. Now it was suddenly behind him, as if gravity had suddenly shifted ninety degrees. He "fell" backward, kicking at the earth to try and slow himself, watching the grinning woman dwindle with distance until he smashed into the wall of a brick building. It knocked his wind out, but he didn't have time to get it back.

The whip was slicing toward him.

As he twisted aside, gravity returned to normal and he fell back onto the street. He rolled, came to his feet, and hurled his shield at his muscular antagonist. Above him, the strands of energy sparked against brick.

Who were these people? Bystanders of the Hulk's fight had described a lion-like man and some sort of intangible apparition, not a bull and a woman with a whip. These two were new. Were all four a part of the same gang?

Halfway to its target, his shield crashed into the pavement as if yanked down by an unseen hand. Cap hadn't been standing still, though. He somersaulted over the flashing knout, weaving around its coils and launching himself at the wielder. His blow landed hard in her ribs, and she staggered back with a gasp, then fell. The whip flickered and went out. She wasn't so tough, once he got past her weapon.

"Ab-Sin!" the other woman shouted. She stamped again, and Steve suddenly felt incredibly heavy, as if he was in an aircraft pulling multiple Gs. His legs quivered with strain and then refused to hold him—he fell to his hands and knees.

The extra weight didn't stay with him long, but as he recovered the bull-woman crashed into him, headfirst. It wasn't exactly like being punched by the Hulk, but it was damn close.

Letting his body go loose, he rolled with the blow as best he could. Momentum sent him past his shield, which he snagged and hurled at her. This time she didn't have time to react, so it clocked her in the face and sent her tumbling back. He caught it on the return and threw it again, striking her on the chin as she tried to get up, and came along right behind it.

Cap was getting real tired of being a punching bag for these two.

As she heaved up his first punch landed in her gut, and then his second on the chin. It was like hitting a sack of cement, but she felt it, grunting and falling back before his attack.

Light flickered in his peripheral vision like the flash of tracer rounds. Then Ab-Sin's whip wrapped around him. White-hot pain struck him to the bones as the lash lifted him above the ground. With a flick of her wrist, Ab-Sin sent him crashing to earth, then whipped him again, the bright strands curling around his arm. He tore free and staggered to his feet, but the bull-woman rammed into him, and he was chewing pavement.

Darkness closed in as his vision dimmed, and he tasted blood, bright and metallic. He struggled to get back up, but his body was too heavy. Ab-Sin leaned down, smiling, and took the bracelet from the belt.

"You should have just given it to us," she murmured, "but your end was inevitable, eventually. None may oppose our purpose for long. Finish him, Guanna."

The bull-woman loomed over him. He was so heavy his lungs wouldn't take in air. Her horns blazed brighter, and her eyes became like flame. His pulse pounded in his ears, pumping far too quickly. She bent, pointed the horns at him…

There was a distant shout, and suddenly glowing rings appeared around him. At first, he thought it was something one of his attackers had done, just another nail in his coffin, but then he saw that Ab-Sin and Guanna were looking up, startled.

"Another time, Captain," Ab-Sin said. She glanced at Guanna. "Go!" she commanded. She touched her wrist, and he noticed a bracelet there. At this distance it was hard to be sure, but it resembled the one he'd found. As soon as she touched it, she vanished. Guanna smiled at him grimly and then did the same.

Suddenly Steve was no longer heavy.

The glowing rings vanished.

He picked up his shield and turned around.

There was a man floating a few yards away. He wore a billowing red cloak, dark leggings and a tunic, and sported a neatly trimmed mustache and beard.

"Doctor Strange," Steve said. "This is a surprise."

"Captain America," Strange said. "It's good to see you again."

Steve winced as he took a step, glancing back toward where his recent antagonists had vanished.

"Good to see you, too. I've got a feeling I'm lucky you showed up."

"Don't be so sure," Strange said. "Help was already on the way." His eyes shifted. There was the sound of something whirring through the mist. Steve spun.

Thor. The Asgardian touched down a few yards away.

"I thought I heard combat," he said, standing ready to fight, eyeing Strange suspiciously.

"Yes," Steve said, "but not with him. He saved my bacon. The other guys took off."

"As you say." Thor nodded and put his hammer in his belt.

"Do you know Stephen Strange?" Steve asked.

"Earth's Sorcerer Supreme?" Thor said. "I've heard of you, but we've never met. Good day to you."

"And to you, Asgardian."

"Those who attacked you, Captain," Thor said. "Have they gone far?"

"I don't know." Steve shook his head. "They disappeared. Whether they're just invisible or went someplace else, I can't say. They have these bracelets…"

"The same two villains as attacked Banner?" Thor asked.

"No," Steve said. "Not unless they did a costume change. And I got the names of these two—Ab-Sin and Guanna."

"I suspected as much," Strange said. "Although I take no pleasure in being right."

"You know these people?" Steve asked.

"Not personally," Strange replied. "I know *of* them. Perhaps, now that Banner has returned, we should join the rest of your companions to discuss this in depth."

"Banner?" Steve said. "We haven't—" He broke off as a disheveled, half-naked figure appeared from a side street and stopped to stare at them.

"Cap? Thor?"

"Bruce. You're okay?"

"Yeah. Listen. Monica—Monica Rappaccini. Have you seen her?"

"Not personally," Cap said. "But I'm told she's okay. She wasn't hurt in the fight."

Bruce nodded, closing his eyes. "Good," he said. "Thanks, Cap."

Steve nodded at the sorcerer. "Doctor, we'd all love to hear what you have to say."

TEN

NATASHA and Tony were waiting in the damaged building. He didn't see Tarleton or Blonsky. But Monica was there. Before Bruce could react, she rushed into his arms.

"You're okay," he said. "I—"

"Of course I'm okay," she said. "You made sure of that. And you? Are you hurt?"

He shook his head, then held her.

"You shouldn't be here," Bruce said. "Two more of those guys just showed up. For all we know there are fifty of them. Tony said he arranged hotel rooms for you and George."

"He did," she said. "But I had to wait. To be here when you got back. I brought you some clothes from the apartment."

He nodded and followed her back into her lab, which thankfully was untouched by the fight. She handed him a stack of clothes.

He pulled on the pants and unfolded the shirt.

"I'm sorry," he said.

She turned around. "For what?"

"Everything," he said. "For the damage here. Blonsky…?"

"He survived. You saved his life."

He sighed. "What about Tarleton? How is he?"

"He's upset, of course," she said. "But his lab was hardly touched. You ran them off before they had a chance to get past the security post.

If it hadn't been for you, things might have been much, much worse. I may owe you my life."

"I don't know about that," he said. "But when I was up there in the woods, and I didn't know... Monica, the thought of something happening to you is hard for me to take."

"It's the same for me," she said. "It's natural when you care about someone to try and protect them. But no one is ever entirely safe. This company is part mine. If you're going to discuss what threatens us, I should be here. After that I'll go to the hotel. Maybe."

Then she pulled him in for a kiss.

When they backed up a little, he gazed at her for a moment. She didn't have superpowers, but Monica didn't need protecting, and he had no business suggesting that she did.

"You're right," he said. "Come on."

○———————————○

STRANGE settled cross-legged onto the floor. No, he was floating just slightly off the ground. It made Steve uneasy. He'd once thought most of the odd things he'd encountered in his life could be accounted for by science and technology. Back in the old days, there had been few things that made him question that.

Then again, a hundred years before he was born, folks would have thought an airplane or a radio amounted to black magic. Just because he didn't know how something worked didn't mean there wasn't a logical explanation for it. Yet some of the stuff he'd seen Strange do didn't seem scientific at all, no matter what your perspective.

Like levitating without wires or what-have-you.

"I've been following a series of thefts," the sorcerer began. "Art and history museums, private collections, curio shops, government repositories, and so forth. The objects stolen were of an eclectic nature. Most investigators—even those versed in such curiosities—wouldn't notice a pattern. Even I didn't at first, but in the past few months I have felt something... rising. An arcane power of an order I have not encountered before. A power not strictly of this world. It led me to consider these thefts with fresh eyes, and to develop a theory." He turned his gaze. "Widow, your latest adventure proved quite fruitful for me—a turning point in my investigation."

Natasha frowned.

"The tablet, you mean," she said. "It had a weird energy signature."

"Yes," he said. "That, and the one who commissioned its theft, a man who calls himself Capricorn."

"How did you know about any of that?" she asked.

The sorcerer shrugged. "I have my ear to the ground, you might say." He paused, as if gathering his thoughts.

"The Captain was attacked by two women styling themselves as Ab-Sin and Guanna," he said. "They are also known as Virgo and Taurus."

That sent tumblers clicking in Steve's head.

"Capricorn?" Steve said. "Virgo and Taurus? Why does that sound familiar?" Then he remembered. "Constellations, right?"

"Or Zodiac signs," Tony added.

"Like in the newspaper," Steve said, snapping his fingers. "The *Daily Bugle* used to run a column. A fortune-telling thing, right? My aunt read mine to me right before I went off to sign up for the army."

"What did it say?" Natasha asked.

"Not to hold my breath, if I remember right," he said. "I figured it was hokum, or maybe my aunt was making it up. After all, *no one* thought I would get in. Nobody needed magic to predict that I'd be rejected."

"It *is* hokum," Strange said. "At least the column in the newspaper is—but the Zodiac itself was known in Sumer and Babylon, and ages before those places were built. At that time it was known as the Mulapin, the Shining Herd, and it was very real indeed."

"Hang on," Tony said. "Are you saying these nutjobs that attacked Bruce and Cap believe they're signs of the Zodiac?"

"It's more complicated than that," Strange said, "but the short answer is yes. From the description in the news, I believe the two who attacked Banner were Zibaana and Urgula."

"Not that I check my horoscope every day," Tony said, "but those don't sound familiar. Are either of them compatible with Pisces?"

"The Greeks renamed everything," Strange said. "The Shining Herd became the Zodiac. They renamed the signs, too. Zibaana and Urgula are now known as Libra and Leo."

"One was like a lion," Banner said. "I remember that much. Libra is scales, right? The kind you weigh things with? That doesn't sound like what I saw. She was more—ghosty."

"The portrayal of Libra, as justice holding the scales, is relatively recent," Strange said. "Based on a misunderstanding of her true nature. In Baxol, where the constellation was first worshipped, it represented the aether, the unseen forces beneath the face of reality. You should not judge these beings based upon what Captain America so aptly called 'hokum.' These are ancient and terrible beings, gods in their own realms."

"I am not familiar with any of this," Thor said. "I know of stars, of course, and constellations, the shapes people see in the stars. They named one after me, you know, back in the old days – Thor's Wagon. I used to have a wagon." He looked a little wistful. "But of this thing you call the Zodiac, I know nothing."

Strange shifted his regard to the god of thunder.

"The Zodiac is seen on Earth as a series of constellations," he said, "found in the part of the sky known as the ecliptic—roughly the path of the sun through the heavens. The ancients instinctively worshipped the power that was represented there, though without understanding it. But later, the followers of the Shining Herd—the Zodiac—believed that those constellations embodied the cosmic order.

"They looked around at the Bronze and Stone Age kingdoms of their world and they saw disorder," he continued. "War, chaos—nations ruled by the strongest, the most violent, not the wisest. They wanted something more—better, from their point of view. They desired to impose the cosmic order of the Zodiac upon all of the world, to create a sort of utopia. They believed the way to do this was to manifest the power of the Shining Herd on Earth. The twelve cosmic powers would occupy twelve human avatars, and each would cede control to another as the sign they represented became ascendant.

"They searched for a way to execute their plan, but could not achieve the method of bringing the Zodiac powers to Earth. So they went to a 'plan B.' The human worshippers of the Zodiac spread themselves throughout the world. They became magi, counselors to the powerful. When they saw a chance to move their agenda forward, they would do so, but subtly. If they could not, they would foment unrest and bring about the collapse of kingdoms, hoping to pick up the pieces and remake the new states founded in the principles of cosmic order.

"It went that way for a long time," Strange said. "The members of the Zodiac lived and died, passing their positions to their heirs. They remained a secret disease within the body of civilization. But then, around 1210 BC, they made a breakthrough. Led by one known as Gir-Tab—Scorpio—they created or discovered the instrument by which to accomplish their goals. It was an object known simply as the Key. It held the power to warp time and space, but more significantly it could allow the power of the Shining Herd to descend from the heavens and become incarnate on Earth—if it was used at the right time, and in the right place.

"Fortunately, one of my predecessors, the Sorcerer Supreme of that era, caught wind of their plot. Shaushka discovered that the Zodiac had re-taken the site of one of their ancient temples on an island named Penthos, and were preparing to consummate their plan.

"Shaushka assembled a company of heroes and did battle with the Zodiac. She was nearly too late; the constellations were in perfect alignment, and the Shining Herd descended. The human members of the Zodiac partook of the stellar energy released in the transition, becoming exponentially more powerful as the descent neared completion. In the end Shaushka and her champions prevailed. To an extent."

"What do you mean?" Thor asked. "Did they win or not?"

"Shaushka prevented the Zodiac from reaching its ultimate Earthly manifestation. She denied the Zodiac the ability to impose their 'order' upon the world, but she defeated them by destroying the Key. Doing so unleashed terrible forces. Earthquakes shattered cities and raised tidal waves. Ripples of arcane energy triggered discord, war, and madness. The results were catastrophic. Civilization in Europe, the Middle East, North Africa—all collapsed. A dark age followed that lasted centuries."

"Wait," Thor said. "Was Ares of Olympus involved in this? He used to go on about some sort of battle against the 'very stars themselves.' Talked endlessly about it, and about how he and Valkyrie..." He trailed off. "I'll have to ask her about that, the next time I see her. I always assumed he was making it up, or at the very least exaggerating."

"Ares was involved," Strange confirmed. "As was Brunnhilde of Asgard."

"You didn't get in on that action?" Natasha said to the thunder god.

Thor frowned. "I don't think I was asked," he said. "I was very busy in those days, you know. Battling. Far from here."

"This is all fun history," Tony said, "but if those guys all got blown to kablooie three thousand years ago, who jumped Banner here?"

"My research suggests that the organization survived," Strange said. "Without their Key, they went back to their old tricks. There is good evidence that they poisoned Alexander the Great, and they played a major role in the fall of Rome, but without the Key their higher aspirations waned. By the early part of this century they had become little more than a crime cartel, albeit a secretive one. Lately, however—in the last year or so—they have resurged. I believe they have learned once again how to draw upon the power of the Key."

"You said the Key was destroyed," Tony said. "It's really hard to 'draw' upon something that doesn't exist."

Strange nodded. "So Shaushka thought, at first, but soon after the battle she began to suspect it had somehow survived the explosion, and that its bearer—Gir-Tab, Scorpio—survived as well, at least for a time. Long enough to hide the Key and leave clues that would enable later versions of the Zodiac to find it."

"You believe they have the Key?" Steve asked.

"No," Strange said. "No, because if that were so, things would be much worse. I believe they have made a tentative connection to it, enough to allow them the powers you've witnessed. And I think that they are on the trail of it. The constellations approach the same alignment as when they last attempted to bring the Shining Herd to Earth. If they find the Key before the conjunction, they might succeed. With or without the Key, their powers will grow stronger until the constellations align."

"Which means the guys that set Banner, Natasha, and me back on our heels are going to get even stronger," Steve said.

"With each passing moment," Strange said.

"Then we must act now," Thor said.

"Agreed," Steve said, "but where do we start?"

"Capricorn," Nat said. "We know he's in Taiwan. We check with SHIELD and see if they've narrowed that down."

"Good idea," Steve said. "Strange? Any other thoughts?"

The sorcerer nodded. "I have a meeting with a colleague this afternoon. He has information that he believes is relevant to the investigation."

"This sort of thing is your area, Doctor," Steve said. "Are you just dropping this on us, or do you plan to stick around?"

"I'm charged with protecting our world from threats of exactly this nature," Strange said. "I came here to ask for your assistance, or to be of assistance to you, however you want to see it. My predecessor was wise enough to know she couldn't handle the Zodiac alone. I hope I am at least as wise."

"Is Ares busy, then?" Thor asked.

"I don't know," Strange said. "I haven't approached him."

"Well, he *is* better at bragging and talking than fighting," Thor said, "but I would gladly lend my hammer to this battle."

"How do the rest of you feel?" Steve asked.

"I could go for a little payback," Natasha said.

"I'll let you know after I consult my astrologer," Tony said.

"One thing," Cap said. "What did these Zodiac guys want in George and Monica's labs? As far as I know, there aren't any ancient tablets here."

"I'm not sure," Strange admitted. "I suspect they are in need of a power source, something beyond what is readily available. Perhaps they thought to find something along those lines here."

Tony and Bruce kept their poker faces, as did Steve. He knew about the crystals Tarleton was experimenting with, and he also knew that their existence was supposed to be a secret.

Tony broke the uncomfortable silence.

"Monica?" he said.

"I think I can speak for George," she replied. "If you trust this man…"

Cap thought about that for a moment. Did he? Strange was a character, mixed up in a lot of weird things. But in his experience, the sorcerer was one of the good guys.

He nodded.

"Yeah," Tony told her. Then he added, "Strange, maybe you should have a look at something."

Cap noticed one member of the group had been conspicuously silent.

"Bruce?"

Banner shook his head. "No, Cap, I'm sorry. I'm out."

"May I ask why?"

"Someone needs to be here in case those guys come back. Besides, Monica and George could use some help cleaning up."

"Okay," Cap said. "So, the rest of you—suggestions. What's our plan of action?"

"I'm going to show Strange the stuff," Tony said. "Let's reconvene in a couple of hours. Strange, do you have any of that Zodiac business on file we can have?"

"A computer file?" Stephen said. "No."

"Can you put something together?"

Strange sighed. "I have a colleague who might be helpful."

ELEVEN

IN the Quinjet, Strange reached to touch one of the crystals, and then seemed to think better of it.

"Extraordinary," he murmured.

"Aren't they?" Tony said. "They're really off the charts."

"Not of this world," Strange said. "Not strictly, at least."

"That's what I've been thinking," Tony replied. "Is there anything else you can tell me about them?"

"It would require more study," Strange replied. "But they would certainly supply the power the Zodiac needs."

"For what?"

"My research suggests that their Key is locked in an extradimensional space," he replied. "They would need considerable raw power to liberate it. One of these, I think, would do the trick. Are you certain that they didn't take any?"

"It doesn't look like it," Tony said. "They never made it into the lab where they were kept."

"One of the attackers was Libra," Strange said. "She can move through material objects."

"Yes," Tony said. "But—" He realized suddenly he'd been following the assumptions Tarleton had laid out. He hadn't actually checked. "You know what?" he said. "Let me get back to you."

STEVE found Tony in the Quinjet, very busy at a terminal.

"What's going on?" he asked.

"Just checking something," Tony said. "The witnesses—including Bruce—said this 'Libra' could go right through walls."

"True," Cap said, "but if she was busy fighting the Hulk…"

"I pieced together available camera footage," Tony said. "Enough to create a timeline of the fight. There's a gap. Libra takes off while the Hulk trades punches with the big kitty. When she returns, they go *poof.* Want to guess where she's been?"

"So now you're—"

"Hacking into their security systems," Tony said. "Ah, here we go."

The computer screen split into eight video feeds. He began moving through them.

"Did you ask George or Monica about this?"

"Nope."

"Pretty sure breaking into their computer isn't legal."

"Looked it up," Tony said. "Totally legal."

"Really."

"Do your own internet search on the topic if you don't believe me."

"I'm still struggling with e-mail," Cap said, "but I think I understand the law. Without resorting to a computer."

"You don't need a computer—you can do it on your phone, just so you know," Tony said. "I'm a major investor in the business, so… Wait—look here…" He pointed.

At first Steve wasn't sure what he was seeing, but then he made out what could only be described as the ghostly figure of a woman coming through the wall. She sort of ebbed and flowed between almost invisible and fully there.

Blonsky, the security head, noticed her too. On screen he stood up, reaching for his sidearm. The woman darted forward, stretched out her arm, and pushed it *into* him. There was a flash of light, and he dropped to the floor, spasming.

The woman started toward Tarleton's lab, but before she could go more than a few steps Bruce came in. She tried the same trick with him and ended up with a Hulk. A few seconds later, he was watching the green guy make a hole in the wall.

"She never got in there," Steve said.

"Wait," Tony said. He sped the recording ahead, then stopped it. The spectral figure returned. This time she slipped through the lab door. A few minutes later she came out again.

"And there we go," Tony said. "She must have taken one of the crystals."

"Why?" Cap asked.

"Strange says the Zodiac guys need one to do their thing," Tony said. "My question is, why didn't George mention a missing crystal? He must have known."

"Can you tap the feed inside of the lab?" Steve asked.

"I thought you were dubious as to the whole legality of—"

"I am," Steve said, "but, since we're already here…"

"No," Tony said. "It's a separate system from the other security feeds. Whatever he's got blocking cell phones also makes it impossible for me to link in there—at least not with the tech I have right now. Anyway," he said, pointing to one of the Quinjet's external monitors. "Here he comes. Why don't we just ask him?"

Steve caught the motion on the monitor, too.

"That might be best," he said.

TARLETON'S gaze jumped around the interior of the Quinjet.

"Like it?" Tony asked.

"It's a beautiful machine," he said.

"It suits us," Tony replied. "How are you doing?"

"To be honest," Tarleton said, "I'm concerned."

"I am too," Tony said. "Maybe we're concerned about the same thing."

Tarleton pursed his lips. "Possibly," he said. "I would have mentioned this to you earlier, but I wanted to check some things first."

"Okay. And have you checked?"

Tarleton nodded. "One of the Terrigen Crystals was stolen," he said. "I wasn't sure at first, but I've taken inventory and watched the security feed." He paused. "The same security feed you just watched. I get a silent alert when someone breaks in."

"Ah," Tony said. "About that—"

Tarleton shook his head. "I'm not pleased you went behind my back," he said. "But I see why you might. I was not altogether forthcoming. About the crystals—and about something else."

"You've got my attention," Tony said.

"When I first discovered the crystals and understood their potential, it occurred to me that no one would take me seriously. I've had bad experiences like that. I needed backers, investors who could help me realize my dream. That's why I came to you."

"Yes," Tony said. "And you were right. So of course I took you seriously."

"But initially I…" He trailed off, frowning. "You were not the first one I approached with my discovery. It was before I partnered with Monica, before I had an… in… with you."

"Who did you approach?" Tony asked.

"Actually, they approached me, and a lot of other start-ups in the area. A scientific investment firm, MetiTech."

"You showed them the crystals?"

"No, but they saw some of my data. I was trying to convince them to take me on. They weren't interested."

"And then you came to me."

Tarleton nodded.

"Is that it? No one else knows about Terrigen?"

"Not from me," George said. "It might be nothing. Maybe there is no relationship between the break-in and MetiTech. But considering how much you've invested here, I thought you should know."

"I appreciate that," Tony said. "MetiTech. I'll check them out."

"Very well," Tarleton said. "Well, then, if you'll excuse me."

They watched him leave.

"JARVIS?" Tony said.

"*Yes, sir?*"

"Can you give me everything you've got on a company named MetiTech?"

"*Yes, sir. There isn't very much, I'm afraid. They were registered as an investment firm.*"

"Were?"

"*Yes, they ceased to exist as a company last year.*"

"They went bust, huh?"

"*Apparently. I can't find any record of them having ever invested in anything, despite having existed for four years.*"

"They never invested in anything," Cap said. "I'm not a businessman, but—"

"No, you're spot on," Tony replied. "That doesn't make sense. Probably a cover for some other company, or even another country. Industrial espionage. You find out what's out there, and if you want it, you steal it."

"Any way to trace them back to whoever really runs MetiTech?"

"We'll see," Tony said. "But I think we can safely assume they were connected to the Zodiac. They have the power source Strange says they need—it's probably about time to get this party started."

"I think you're right," Steve said.

"But before we go all in—I've been thinking, how the worst of this might have been prevented if Bruce hadn't been by himself."

"We can't keep him on a leash," Steve said. "He's his own man."

"Not my point," Tony said. "It took us too long to get here, and there's no one out here prepared to deal with... this sort of thing. These Zodiac guys. And it's not just them: there have been incidents all along the Pacific Rim, and as far as I can tell, this is all on an uptick. SHIELD is starting to get nervous about little green men—if we had a base over here, just think how much we could cut our response time. It's started to get a little crowded in New York, anyway. And with all the tech being developed out here it might be good to have a closer, on-the-ground perspective. We've got plenty of prospects for new additions to the team, and if Bruce is really gonna stay out here, it might be good to have a little oversight of that, too."

Steve shrugged. "You don't have to convince me. I thought it was a great idea the first time you brought it up. Bruce wasn't thrilled, though."

"He's had a change of heart."

"We should run it past Nat and Thor, but I don't think they will object," Steve said. "The West Coast Avengers it is."

"Thank you!" Tony said. "I'm glad somebody is on board with the name."

"But," Steve said, "right now, we need to deal with what's in front of us. The Zodiac. Let's not give them a lot of time to breathe. SHIELD came through with some intel about this Capricorn character in Taiwan. I say we check that out first—"

"There you go," Tony said. "We're closer to Taiwan here than if we were in New York. In fact, it's easily within range of my suit—"

"I don't think it's wise for you to go alone," Steve said. "By now, I'm sure they know we're on to them."

"Look, just because they cleaned *your* clock—*hey!*"

Stephen Strange appeared on the other side of the cabin.

"I'm sorry to interrupt, gentlemen," he said, "but there's a bit of an emergency, and I'm afraid I might need your aid. If you could meet me outside, with the others, I would appreciate it."

○————————○

AS they stepped out of the Quinjet, Natasha and Thor were waiting with Strange. Which was weird, because Tony hadn't seen the Strange *inside* go anywhere.

"What is it?" Cap asked.

"The friend I spoke of has arrived in New York," Strange said, "but he fears he is in imminent danger of attack."

"And you want our help?" Thor said.

"Given the circumstances," Strange replied, "it might be prudent. I can teleport us there, to my Sanctum Sanctorum."

"Cap?" Tony said. "How do you want to handle this?"

"I'll go," Cap said. "Who else?"

"I will also accompany you," Thor replied.

"Nat?" Cap said.

"The three of you can take care of yourselves," she said. "I'd like to pursue the Taiwan angle. Tony, I could use your help on that."

"That's fine," Tony said. "You guys have all the fun."

"Oh, don't worry," Nat said. "I'm pretty sure we'll have fun, too."

"I don't wish to hurry you," Strange said, "but I believe there is very little time."

"I stand ready," Thor said.

"Any time," Cap said.

"Very well," Strange said. He lifted his hands, and a circle of light appeared around Cap, Thor, and the Sorcerer Supreme. Then they were gone.

"Neat trick," Tony said. "I'm gonna have to figure that one out. JARVIS, remind me to invent teleportation."

"*Yes, sir,*" his phone said.

○━━━━━━━━━━○

STEVE felt a flash of dizziness as the light changed from outdoor to indoor. They were in a house—strike that, a mansion—with wooden floors laid out in weird, angular patterns, stairs and bannisters filling a space that rose up several stories to a dome above, a big round window, weirdly partitioned…

That was all the time he had to take in the grand scheme of his stationary surroundings, because there was way too much happening on the kinetic front. Strange had abracadabrad them straight into the middle of a brawl.

Steve had always been pretty good at managing more than one thing at a time, even when he was just a scrawny kid from Brooklyn, but since the Super-Soldier Serum first entered his bloodstream, he'd become *really* good at it. It was as if time slowed down to let him absorb everything going on around him, and allowed him to react. So what was happening didn't overwhelm him—but it did tax him a bit.

There were five people in the room besides those he had arrived with. A cloaked man with white markings and mostly exposed musculature was locked in battle with four others, three of whom he recognized immediately as the Zodiac members Virgo, Taurus, and Libra. The last—a massive man with a mane of yellow hair—had to be Leo.

Spectral energies emanated from the dark-skinned man and formed a sort of cloud. Things moved there, forms with dark, hollow eyes and inhuman shapes. Virgo's whip slashed into the murk and stuck fast, and the ephemeral Libra seemed paralyzed on the edge of it, a phantasm grappling with spirits. But the wizard—or whatever he was—was against the wall, bleeding and having difficulty standing. As a result his summoning—it seemed like the right word—was faltering, the dark vapors attenuating and shrinking.

"Strange!" the man gasped raggedly.

"Hold fast, Drumm!" Strange shouted.

Leo was quick. It took him only an instant to understand the changed situation, pick Steve from the crowd, and launch himself across the room, his claws flickering with actinic light like ten finger-mounted arc welders.

Cap's shield stopped the slashing claws, but the impact was still considerable. Instead of meeting Leo's bulk straight on, he deflected the huge figure to the side. Yet for all of his mass, the fellow was nimble. He tumbled in the direction of his fall, turning quickly when he came back to his feet. As his own fight narrowed, Steve remained aware of the others.

Virgo's whip—free again—lashed out at Strange. Taurus stamped the floor, splintering floorboards, so that the god of thunder was thrown from his feet. That made him feel marginally better about his own encounter with her—if she could knock an Asgardian down, maybe he hadn't done so badly.

Libra phased up through the floor behind Strange. Did the sorcerer know?

Then Leo demanded most of his attention.

o———————o

THOR reeled back in surprise as Taurus followed up her first unseen blow with another.

"Well met!" he bellowed. "There are few who can—" He was cut off as the ceiling suddenly became the floor, and his body quadrupled in weight. He grunted as plaster and wood splintered from the force of his upward "fall." It slowed him for an instant, but then he crashed through another ceiling, and finally the very shingles of the house itself.

Twisting around, he watched in astonishment as the roof of the mansion dwindled below him and the familiar skyline of New York became his distant horizon. Gritting his teeth, he whirled Mjolnir and hurled it back down, holding onto the strap as it pulled him against the strange reversal of gravity.

An instant later, down was suddenly toward the earth again, and Mjolnir carried him back through the building, shattering tiles and roof beams. He had a brief glimpse of the others as he knocked a hole in the floor of the room where they'd appeared, and then he and Mjolnir rammed into the basement and dug a crater into the bedrock beneath.

"By Odin," he growled, looking up through the hole he'd created. "That will not go unanswered."

He leapt back up into the fray.

Captain America was squared off against the lion-like one. Strange was down on one knee, caged in magical bands, fighting off the ghostly Libra and whip-wielding Virgo.

"Work together, everyone," Captain America shouted. "Keep them contained."

Then Thor was struck from behind. Searing pain shot through him, as if he'd been stabbed by burning daggers. He bent his knees and dug his heels into the floor, then turned violently and swung Mjolnir with all of his might. The blow struck Taurus as it might a mountain. She shuddered under the blow, but did not move even an inch. It was as if her feet were planted in the planet's very core.

"Ouch," she said. He thought she sounded sarcastic.

Enraged, he swung again, but this time she dodged, turned and ran, head down, roaring. A section of the mansion's wall suddenly exploded. Taurus charged through, out into the street. There she turned and taunted him with the one-finger sign humans seemed to love so much.

With a war-bellow, Thor went after her.

"Thor!" Captain America shouted after him. But it was too much. He could not allow his horned foe to escape, much less insult him in such a manner. Once he was done with her, he would return to help the others with the rest.

He flew at Taurus with the force of a storm, but she did her trick with gravity again, bending it so he flew astray of his intended path and struck a building across the street. He didn't hit it hard—really just enough to dent it and dislodge a few stones—but it abruptly came apart around him.

Suddenly it was as if he was the center of the universe, the still place to which everything else was attracted. The building seemed to share the same opinion—it fell at him from every direction, and an instant later he was cased in a prison of rock and twisted steel. He strained, but it continued to contract, crushing him in its center.

CAP leapt high and slammed his shield down on Leo, then spun and sent the disk arcing toward Virgo, whose whip had cut through Strange's defenses. She noticed, but not in time, and the metal disk clipped her off of her feet. The glowing lash vanished in a spray of sparks, dropping the half-conscious Sorcerer Supreme to the floor.

In the same instant, Leo bounced back into the fray. Steve braced for the impact, but the maned man set his feet—and howled.

As Steve dove from his path, aiming to retrieve his shield, a blast of light and heat singed where he'd just been. Using the hardware on his arm, he summoned the disk and clipped it magnetically into place. He caught a motion from the corner of his eye and turned, bringing his shield up defensively.

A face appeared, coming *through* the shield. He tried to scramble back, but it was too late—he saw stars as energy jolted through his entire body. It hurt, a lot, and his muscles threatened to disobey him, but he managed to hang on, hurling the shield again. This time he had the satisfaction of seeing it strike Leo directly between the eyes.

But Libra was still there, like smoke—there was nothing to hit. He tried anyway, dodging her next jab at him and throwing a roundhouse at her head. There was a little resistance, but it wasn't worth the new shock that numbed his arm and set his lungs on fire. Whatever he needed to fight this one, he didn't have it.

He backpedaled, trying to think.

Suddenly eldritch light flared, encasing his opponent. He looked up and saw Strange, appearing a little punch-drunk, but still in the fight.

"I've got this one," the sorcerer said. "Outside…"

Steve followed his gaze through the hole in the wall. Beyond it, a building had collapsed in on itself, forming a swirling cloud in the air.

"Thor!" he shouted.

Leo seemed to be down, and Virgo, too, although the latter was struggling to rise. Doctor Strange had Libra gummed up in some sort of force field. Still shaking off the effects of Libra's shock-blast, Cap dashed out into the rubble-strewn streets.

The wreckage of the building contracted into a sphere about thirty feet above the ground and then suddenly exploded, sending debris in every direction. That was bad—not just for him, but for two dozen onlookers gawking from the sidelines.

It took him less than a millisecond to set his course of action. He threw his shield to deflect a chunk of stone and mortar flying toward a young boy, while he sprinted forward to carry a young woman and her child from harm. Flying debris banged into his back, hard, and sent him sprawling, but he scrambled up, trying to reach the next two in harm's way, a young man walking with an older one, just now seeing the doom descending on them.

A yard short of his goal, the falling stone blotted them from his vision. In that last instant, he saw the older man's face: dark-eyed, a beard shot with gray, and a look of determined resignation as he folded his body over the younger man. Then a stone struck him in the side of the head, and the pavement came up to meet him.

○————————○

THOR managed to twist his hammer through the debris compacted around him, straining his muscles to their limits. He accomplished one full rotation, then another, picking up speed, until the interior of the stony sphere was whirling like a centrifuge.

All in a moment, the stony prison came apart and he burst free. He saw Taurus in the distance and hurled his hammer, but never saw if Mjolnir connected. The threads of Virgo's effulgent whip wrapped around him, searing him through his flesh to his very bones. He grabbed the burning cable with his bare hands and—unmindful of the pain— yanked as hard as he could.

The shining lash vanished.

So did Virgo, as Thor fell heavily to the street, landing in a crouch just as Mjolnir came whirring back to his grip.

Virgo was gone, and he didn't see Taurus, either—or any of the Zodiac for that matter. What he did notice was a steadily growing crowd of humans. The police and emergency crews had arrived and were trying to keep the crowd away from the zone of combat. Captain

America was at the pile of rubble, heaving chunks of it aside. Thor hurried over to help.

Cap had uncovered two men, one on top of the other. The one beneath stirred, slightly.

"Medic!" Cap shouted. "Some help here!"

He gently rolled the man on top over. Used to the vagaries of the battlefield, Thor recognized by his empty gaze that the man had drawn his last breath.

"Who was he?" Thor asked.

"I don't know," Cap said, his voice sounding strained. "A brave man." The Avenger had a tear trickling from the corner of his eye. He looked tired beyond measure.

"This shouldn't have happened," Steve said.

It wasn't a direct rebuke, but Thor felt it nonetheless. If he had followed the Captain's instructions—refused to let the fight spill into the street—this man would still be alive.

"In war—" he began.

"This isn't war," Captain America said, "and this isn't a war zone. People live here. These are their streets, their homes. Can you explain to his loved ones why he died? What we were fighting for?"

The greater good, Thor thought. If the Zodiac was truly the threat Strange made it out to be, wasn't it better for a few to die than for the entire world to suffer?

But he held his tongue. He had seen innocent casualties before. He believed he had felt their loss, but it had never been personal to him. Just a tally against an enemy to be reckoned with.

For Captain America it was personal. It might have been his own father lying there in the street. And Thor had done this. He'd let Taurus taunt him, as if he were a callow youth with less than a century of experience to his credit.

He had been haughty, and proud, and overconfident in the past. Odin had humbled him for that, and in swearing himself to protect the mortals of Earth, Thor had believed himself redeemed.

But he wasn't. Not until he could feel what the Captain felt. Not until he could truly put the needs of these fragile humans ahead of his own arrogance. He wasn't there yet.

"I am sorry, Captain," he said. "I did not think—"

"Stand aside, please."

The EMTs arrived, and he did as they asked. Thor watched as the all-too-mortal men and women attended to their own.

Captain America backed away, too. The younger man stirred again as an oxygen mask was placed over his nose and mouth. His eyes opened, and he saw his dead companion. He began to weep.

"Come on," Cap told him. "They've got this."

o⎯⎯⎯⎯⎯⎯⎯⎯⎯o

BACK inside the building, Strange was tending to his friend.

"Is he alright?" Steve asked.

"I'll live," the fallen man said. "Jericho Drumm, at your service." He had an accent. Steve thought it was some variety of Caribbean, possibly Haitian.

"A trusted ally known in supernatural circles as Doctor Voodoo," Strange said.

The man shrugged weakly. "I'm sorry I was of so little help. I knew they were coming but underestimated their power. Their connection to the Key is growing stronger."

"Hey, you held on against all four of them," Steve said. "That's pretty impressive. We should have done as well."

"You saved my life," Drumm said. "For that, I am grateful. I will not forget this."

"He needs rest," Strange said. He glanced at the gaping hole in his mansion and the curious crowd gathered outside. "And solitude." He gestured, and shards of wood and stone lifted from the rubble— swirling, settling, solidifying, patching the wall as if it had never been broken.

"We need to talk before I rest," Drumm insisted. "I failed my trust—they took what I brought to show you. They meant to end me before I could tell you what I know. It still might happen. There are eight more of them. We could be beset again in moments."

"If they do, they will find the defenses of this house are far greater when I am here," Strange said. "You are safe for the moment, Jericho. You have my word."

"Nevertheless," Drumm said, but then he coughed, violently, and his eyes drooped closed. He had blood on his lips. Steve started forward, but Strange wove a pattern with his hands.

Drumm lifted gently into the air.

"I'll take care of him," Strange said. He looked pale, and seemed a little unsteady on his feet, as if levitating Drumm took nearly everything he had left. "Then I'll be back."

"You don't look so good yourself, Doctor," Steve said.

"I'll mend."

Then the two sorcerers were gone.

Thor glanced at Cap.

"I acted rashly," he said. "You warned me against it, and I disregarded your order."

But Cap shook his head.

"I was upset a minute ago," he said. "You did what you thought was best. That's all any of us can do."

THE house wasn't quiet while Strange was away; it continued to heal itself. Steve never quite saw it happen; he would notice something from the corner of his eye, and when he turned he would find a stairway or door where none had been before. How much of the place was real and how much illusion, he couldn't say.

This was the fourth time the Avengers had come up against the Zodiac, and the fourth time they had been found wanting. If these guys were really getting more powerful with each passing moment, what chance would the Avengers have when they reached full power? When they had to deal with all twelve of them at once? Strange and Drumm lived in this supernatural world, and yet both of them had been battered in the last fight. He was a soldier—not a sorcerer, not a god. This wasn't his kind of battle.

Whoa there, Steve, he thought. No matter what he thought of it, no matter that he didn't completely understand what he was dealing with, he had a fight in front of him. If he failed to win it, more than one civilian would die.

He realized then someone was standing nearby, someone he didn't know. How had they crept up on him? He turned, slowly, every muscle tensed for a fight.

The man who stood there bowed slightly.

"Captain America," he said. "My name is Wong. I am a colleague of Doctor Stephen Strange. Regrettably, I was away when the Sanctum was attacked, but I've returned and enhanced our wards."

"So if the Zodiac attacks again?" Steve said.

"They already have," Wong said. "Twice. Unsuccessfully. May I offer you refreshment?"

"I… I do have a thirst," Thor said.

STRANGE summoned them to Drumm's bedside less than an hour later. Drumm looked weak, but his voice was firm, and his eyes clear.

"Some years ago," he said, "I came into possession of a scroll. It had been copied from an earlier scroll, and from a tablet before that. The script was a form of Demotic Egyptian, but the language was obscure. I did not know what it was or what it said, but I kept it as a curiosity. In my profession, you never know what will prove useful. It didn't occur to me, however, that it was of any real value until someone tried to steal it from me a few weeks ago."

"The Zodiac?" Thor asked.

"I believe so," he replied, "but not one of these we just fought. Another. I surprised the would-be thief and drove him away. Then it made me wonder what I had, so I bent my mind toward deciphering it. I consulted with some others, more expert than I, who were able to elucidate parts of it. What I learned concerned me, so I contacted Doctor Strange. He thought it fit into a pattern of similar thefts of which he had become aware—and that led us to this moment."

"What did this scroll say?" Steve asked.

"The translation was incomplete. It concerns something called a *mazkah*. It can mean both 'key' and 'gateway.' In the scroll it represents an item sacred to the Zodiac. It details a story about a man called Scorpio, who sought a hiding place for the Key. He went many places in search of something called a *kha*, or 'well,' a place where the Key would be safe, and he left clues at each location."

"So Scorpio did survive," Steve said.

"As my predecessor suspected," Strange said.

"And now the Zodiac knows where the Key is," Steve said.

Drumm shook his head. "Not exactly," he said. "The story in the scroll is a bit like a fairy tale. Whoever wrote it was retelling fragmentary stories they had heard—and speculating a good bit. Scorpio was supposed to be a trickster magician, chased by a murderous evil spirit. The locations are mostly fabulous, probably invented by the writer."

"Then it is as useless to them as it is to us," Thor said.

"I said *mostly*," Drumm replied. "Two locations I believe to be real. The first was an island known to the Mycenaeans as the Isle of Penthos. That's where the battle between the Zodiac and the ancient Sorcerer Supreme took place. The second is a place known as Kha Indara, in the kingdom of Baxol."

"Baxol?" Steve said. "You mentioned that, Strange."

"It hasn't existed for millennia," Strange said. "It was home to a civilization older than Sumeria and Babylon—and the birthplace of the Zodiac. Its location was in what is now Turkmenistan."

"Then after his defeat, Scorpio went back home," Steve said.

"So it would appear," Strange said.

"That's our starting place," Steve said. "You say you know where this Kha Indara is located?"

"I've never been there," Strange said, "but I've a general idea."

"They've got the jump on us," Steve said. "They can pop in and out like you. Are you feeling up to taking us there?"

"I am," Strange said.

"Thor?"

"As always," the Asgardian said.

"Okay," Steve said, "but I need to talk to Tony first."

"Don't you have a phone?" Strange asked.

"Not in this get-up," Steve said. He sighed. "I never remember it," he admitted.

"There's one in the next room," Strange said, "provided it wasn't destroyed in our latest unpleasantness."

TWELVE

TONY hired some contractors to begin the job of patching up holes in the walls of the AIM building. Once they had got started, he checked into his hotel room and grabbed a quick shower.

He tried to give Cap a call to see how things had gone on his end, but no one answered, and the locator showed that Cap's phone was back in the Quinjet.

Of course.

Tony was dressed and ready to head back to the Quinjet when someone rapped on the door. It was Natasha, who also looked as if she had cleaned up a bit.

"Bruce holding down the fort?" he asked.

"Yep," she said. "Although I'm not sure it's necessary. I figure the Zodiac got what they came for, but Bruce is determined to hang around. Rappaccini is with him, of course."

"What's your read on the two of them?" Tony asked.

"Oh," she said, "he's got it pretty bad, I think. I don't blame him. She's impressive."

"And her?"

Natasha shrugged. "I don't know her all that well, but she doesn't seem to be the sort to get swept away. Not the romantic type."

"So you think she has some other motive for getting cozy with him?"

"I've been wrong before," Natasha said. "Once, at least. Bruce isn't a kid. Let him figure it out."

His phone rang—a landline in Greenwich Village.

"Let me take this," he said.

It was Cap.

"There you are," Tony said. "Still alive, I assume."

"More or less," Cap replied. "Look, we have a situation."

"When don't we?" Tony asked. "But go ahead. I'm putting you on speaker."

He listened as Cap laid out all he knew.

"So the Zodiac is on the move," Tony said.

"Big time," Steve replied. "It feels to me as if we've lost the initiative."

"Initiative? What initiative? They've been a step ahead of us the whole time," Tony said. "Can Strange pop over here and pick us up? Take us with you to this 'Kha Indara' place?"

"The Zodiac didn't manage to kill Drumm, so they might figure we're coming after them."

"All the more reason to bring our A game."

"No," Nat said.

"Hi, Nat," Cap said. "What's your take?"

"Tony's right, we would just be playing along with them. I know where Capricorn is now. You guys follow the breadcrumbs. Tony and I can skip straight to the gingerbread house. They might not be expecting that."

"I'm not comfortable with analogies in which my name would be Hansel," Tony said.

"That's good," Cap said. "Maybe you can throw some sand in their gears. You're how far from Taiwan there?"

"Four hours by Quinjet."

"That's already too long," Steve said.

"Quicker than if we'd been in New York," Tony said, "but we'll get going. Let's keep in touch, shall we?"

"I don't have my—"

"I know," Tony said. "It's in the Quinjet. Hurts my feelings. I thought it was a great birthday present. Hoped you'd appreciate it."

"Sorry," Steve said. "I'll remember it next time. Which reminds me: Strange says his friend Wong sent you a file of some sort with current information about the Zodiac. The most important part is that this alignment thing is coming up pretty fast. A few days. So the clock is ticking."

Tony checked. "Got it."

"You and Nat be careful, okay?"

"Always," Tony replied.

ANOTHER moment of stomach-turning displace-ment, and they were no longer in the Sanctum Sanctorum. The air was thinner, hotter, drier, and smelled like salt. The sun was a distorted red globe approaching a jagged mountain peak. Steve's feet slipped, for they had appeared on a sandy, gravelly hill.

These were the slopes of a mountain range that stretched as far east and west as he could see. North was desert, all the way to the horizon, white sand dissected by darker stream beds where a few hardy plants clung to existence. The mountains were a little greener, with some slopes carpeted in short, tough grass. If there had ever been a great civilization here, as Strange claimed, Steve didn't see much sign of it.

"What are these mountains?" Thor asked.

"The Kopet Dag range," Strange said.

"And the Well of Indara? Where is that?"

"Not far," the sorcerer said. "At least according to the map I consulted. We might be a little off—it was two thousand years old." He nodded. "It should be this way."

"This way" was up a winding trail that looked too narrow to have been made by humans. Steve guessed it was probably an animal track. The sun continued to sink in the west, draping red shadows on everything.

"Indara," Thor said as they made their way along. "Indra, yes? That name is familiar. He is an immortal, like me."

"Much like you," Strange said. "And like you, he was worshipped in some places on Earth. Baxol may have been one of them, or the name may be coincidence."

"Perhaps I will ask, if I ever run into him," Thor said. He nodded toward the path they followed. "Captain, should I fly ahead?"

"I don't know," Steve said. "Strange, what are the odds the Zodiac has beaten us here?"

"I can't say," the sorcerer replied. "They know to go to the Well of Indara, just as we do. The question is whether they also know the location. The Zodiac has been around for a long time. They've been collecting information for millennia—and destroying it, as well."

"Destroying it?" Steve said.

"Yes. They have always garnered knowledge for themselves, while denying it to others. They looted the library at Alexandria and then burned it. The archives of Dejer Khun, the Temple of Thoth—their mark is on the ruins of those places as well. My knowledge of this place comes from the ancient books collected in Kamar-Taj, where I apprenticed. It is one of the few ancient libraries the Zodiac have never compromised, so they would not have access to the texts I've seen. But this place—these mountains, and the once-great cities of these plains—is where their cult and their power originated. If anyone else on Earth knows where Indara's Well is located, it is the Zodiac. Even if they have the information, however, it might take them some time to dig it up." He paused.

"Ah. I think this must be the place."

In front of them lay a valley sharp enough to almost be considered a crevasse. The dark of approaching night had already settled into it but Strange, with a turn of his wrist, called into being an ambient illumination that moved as they did.

They followed a stream trickling steeply downhill until they reached a shallow pool. There, the stone walls of the canyon were carved into figures and symbols so worn by wind and water it was hard to make out anything, at least at first. But as the weird light Strange had conjured played over it, Steve began to pick out details. A bull, a ram, a scorpion…

"This looks promising," he said.

"Indeed," the sorcerer responded. "I believe our goal is beyond that wall of stone."

"That's fine," Thor said, starting to whirl his hammer.

"Stay your hammer, god of thunder," Strange said. "Let me see what I can do first." He sat down and crossed his legs into a lotus position. "I'm going to enter using my astral form," he said. "If you gentlemen would be so kind as to protect my mortal body."

"Why don't we just—you know—pop in there together?" Steve asked.

"This was once a place of great power," Strange said. "Eldritch forces linger here. I cannot sense where the cave might be, or if there is indeed a cavern at all. It might have collapsed long ago. And I can assure you, teleporting into solid matter is hardly fun. Best I scout it out."

Steve nodded. "We're in your world now," he said. "Go ahead. We'll keep watch."

Strange nodded, then closed his eyes. He became very still.

Thor watched him for a moment, then began to pace restlessly.

"My brother Loki sometimes travels in astral form," he muttered. "Usually up to no good. Dangerous, too."

"Strange knows what he's doing," Steve said.

"Wizards are a shifty lot," Thor replied. "Not always trustworthy. How do you know this man?"

"He's right there," Steve said. "Don't you think he can hear us?"

"No, he's not in there." The thunder god thumped Strange's head. No reaction. "You see?"

"We've worked with him before," Steve said. "While you were gone. He's never given me reason to distrust him."

"Very well, then," Thor said. "I respect your word. Probably more than anyone I have ever known."

"Any human, you mean," Steve replied. "Surely, in all of your years—"

But Thor was shaking his head. "Gods demand respect, but it is often unearned. Humans tell many legends of the gods, but gods rarely tell of the exploits of humans. Hector, Beowulf, Horatius, Jim Bowie—very few. You are one of them. You are an exception. Before you vanished from human ken, you were noticed by some of our kind, and the story spread.

"What I heard, I doubted at first," he continued. "Gods are as given to exaggeration as men, perhaps more so. And the story of a mortal who can stand against great odds is often fashioned more of moonbeams than reality. But then I met you. Saw you melt from the ice. We doubted who you were, remember? We thought it was perhaps some sort of trick—and then you reminded us."

Thor rubbed his jaw. "I still remember the blow you struck me. It was indeed mighty, and not just for a mortal."

Steve laughed. "Is that how you remember it?" he said. "I was confused. The last thing I remember was my friend dying, and then the cold. I didn't have any idea who you guys were."

"Nor did you care," Thor said. "You gave us all notice that Captain America was not only real, but never to be trifled with. No, Captain. I have never lacked respect for you. It is *your* respect I hope to earn."

He was trying to think how to navigate an appropriate response when he heard an all-too-familiar sound. Nothing weird or magical.

Just a round being chambered in a rifle.

He let his gaze wander up the canyon walls, noting how many hiding places the dark crags provided. Strange's magic lantern continued to glow, even though he was absent. But it couldn't pierce all of the shadows.

"Thor..." he whispered.

"Yes," the Asgardian said. "I heard it too."

"Up there, eight o'clock..."

The gorge was suddenly filled with the roar of gunfire. Steve crouched behind his shield and moved to cover Strange, who still sat, unperturbed, with his legs crossed.

"Captain?" Thor asked.

"Go get 'em."

Thor looked positively gleeful as he let his hammer fly at the nearest muzzle flash. Mjolnir smote the mountainside, crushing tons of stone and sending it sliding down the slope. Steve winced, hoping that hadn't been a hunter with bad eyesight, but he knew better. At least two dozen gunmen were shooting at them. They knew very well that they were attempting murder.

The thunder god leapt upward, toward another of their assailants. Steve saw the streak of a shoulder-fired missile in time to utter exactly one syllable before Thor was engulfed in a ball of flame. The Asgardian flipped over backward and crashed hard into a hillside. Belatedly, his hammer came whirring back to him as the gunfire not only continued but increased in intensity.

"Strange," Steve said to the unmoving figure as bullets spacked off his shield like hail from an umbrella, "if you can hear me, you'd better pick up the pace."

○━━━━━━━━━━○

BULLETS stung Thor's flesh as he struggled back to his feet. In his mind's eye he saw the trail of the rocket that had hit him, and he let Mjolnir fly back along the way it had come. He felt satisfaction when the far arc of the weapon produced an explosion bright enough to light up most of the canyon.

When the hammer returned to his hand, he whirled it and flew up the mountainside to where the nearest gunman crouched, firing down at them.

Thor had to give the man some credit: he didn't flee. Instead he tried to shoot the Asgardian point-blank. Thor seized the weapon, cast it down to the floor of the canyon, and sent the mortal to temporary oblivion with the back of his hand. Then he whirled and leapt toward the next.

○━━━━━━━━━━○

THE fighters along the canyon's side found themselves defending their very lives against an angry god of thunder. Steve wondered again if this was some military faction or guerilla group whose territory they inadvertently had invaded.

But he didn't believe it. Given what Strange had said about the Zodiac and their goals, it was quite plausible that they should have followers or employ mercenaries who weren't super-powered, especially here on their home turf. No, this was an ambush, pure and simple—just not a very good one. Thor would clean out all of these guys in a matter of minutes.

Something bright flickered in his peripheral vision. Not above, but at the level of the valley floor. He spun and ducked behind his shield.

Something came *through* it. It looked like an arrowhead made of light, shining as brightly as a magnesium flare. Only an inch of it came through, but he felt the heat and it stung his arm—which should have been impossible. Having Libra phase through it was one thing, but no projectile should be able to punch through.

To his relief the arrow faded, and there was no hole in the Vibranium. Some sort of energy, then, like Leo's roar or Virgo's whip, but more concentrated. Peering over the edge he saw the culprit, a tall man with a glowing bow in his hand, setting another arrow made of light to the string.

"This is not meant for you," the man shouted.

Steve had already figured that out. It was Strange they were trying to kill.

As the flashing missile left the bow, he flung his shield and sprinted after it as best the rocky terrain would allow. The shield met the arrow obliquely and deflected it into the canyon wall, where it flared like lightning striking, then ricocheted from a rock formation and hit the Archer. Sagittarius, if he remembered his aunt's newspaper correctly. Except wasn't Sagittarius supposed to be half horse or something?

The Archer staggered under the impact but didn't go down. As the distance closed, Steve saw that his opponent was wearing a form-fitting outfit, white and orange, bordered at the cuffs and waist with arcane symbols. He wasn't wearing a quiver and didn't need one—the arrows appeared in his fingers as fast as he moved them. He got off three more shots. Steve dodged the first two, but the last came at close range—just as his shield slapped back onto his arm and deflected it.

Delivering his best uppercut, he followed up with several blows to the body. It felt like he was punching rubber, but it seemed to hurt the fellow. The Archer swung the bow at him, but Steve had had enough experience with his teammate Hawkeye to expect that. He ducked the glowing weapon and landed a kidney punch.

Then he understood.

The gunmen had been a distraction, and so was Sagittarius.

Steve had been forced to leave Strange to deal with the Archer, and the Sorcerer Supreme's inert body was alone and unguarded. Steve turned back and saw two figures descending the canyon wall. One was clothed head-to-toe in black, and flashed and flared as if he contained lightning, like a living thunderhead. The other, visible in the lantern light, was as white as a cloud, a wind-dervish surrounded by whirling leaves and dust.

He let fly his shield at the flashy one, who seemed the more dangerous of the two. He dealt Sagittarius a blow that sent him sprawling, then raced toward Strange.

The spinning shield turned in midair and came sailing back at him. He grabbed it, but lightning followed close behind, and he blocked the bolts with the Vibranium disk. Before he could continue his assault, however, he was engulfed in gale-force winds that threatened to blow him off of his feet.

Then an even more brilliant flash of lightning strobed the dark canyon as Thor descended, bringing his own storm. A ragged bolt of electricity arced past Steve. It struck Sagittarius, who had recovered consciousness and was readying an arrow. Then Thor was with the dark and light twins, whirling his hammer. First one, then both of them were sent flying across the canyon.

Sagittarius reached for the bracelet on his wrist and vanished with a sort of thumping sound. Across the canyon, their other two attackers also disappeared.

The winds died down, and everything was still.

Doctor Strange's hand lifted. His eyes opened.

He looked around.

"All quiet out here, I see," he said. "I hope you weren't bored." When they didn't answer, he added, "Ready to go inside?"

○————————○

STRANGE led them into a circle, and a moment later they were someplace utterly dark. The air was cool, stale, and smelled faintly of dry rot and sulfur.

A moment later, a nimbus of light appeared around the sorcerer's hand. It expanded until it was several yards wide, illuminating their surroundings in a lemony glow.

Unsurprisingly, they were in a cave. Some of it seemed natural, but a great deal of it had been carved. Unlike the bas-reliefs outside, which had suffered from thousands of years of wind and rain, the sculptures in the cave might have been carved the day before. Dozens of dragon-scaled men in short kilts stood in silent rows, staring vacantly through stone eyes. The statues held up the low, gently vaulted ceiling, where glowing gemstones picked out familiar constellations. Most were as Steve remembered them from the night sky, but a few seemed distorted, as if modeled on slightly different— earlier?—star formations.

The focal point of the underground chamber was a stele of translucent white stone engraved with some sort of flowing script, although it didn't look like anything he recognized. Toward the bottom, however, a chunk of the stone was missing. The shattered and blackened edge seemed recent.

"They beat us here," Strange said. "They destroyed Scorpio's message."

"Obviously," Thor said. "Then they laid a trap for us and waited for us to arrive."

"Was the Key here?" Steve asked. "Do they have it now? What is this place, exactly?"

"The Well of Indara," Strange said.

"I don't see a well."

"In this context, the word *kha*, or 'well,' doesn't mean a place from which to draw water. It refers to an extradimensional pocket, a bubble of isolated space-time sandwiched between two or more realities. Power may be drawn from a *kha*, so they often become holy places like this. Scorpio was looking for such a well in which to hide the Key. He began here, with one he knew of from legend, but the well here wasn't stable. It has dissipated—been absorbed by the dimensions around it. So no, I do not believe the Zodiac found the Key here. Scorpio moved on, looking for the next well, but he left a clue here to guide future followers."

"The clue was there, I guess," Steve said, pointing to the shattered edge of the stele. "Making sure we can't follow them."

"Of course."

"Then our quest ends here," Thor said.

"Not necessarily," Strange replied. "The destruction of the clue is quite recent. Judging from the damage, it likely happened moments before our arrival. If you two would step back a bit, I will see what I can do." As they complied, he settled back down into his cross-legged pose, resting his hands on his knees.

The amulet hanging from his neck began to glow. It was fashioned in the shape of an eye, and as Steve watched the metal lids opened, revealing a glowing orb that looked unsettlingly like a genuine human eye—but also, somehow, quite *alien*. As he watched, the orb drifted from the opening in the amulet up to Strange's forehead. There it sank into his flesh and deeper, into his skull, until the sorcerer had three eyes.

He closed his normal ones, and the one in his forehead blinked once, slowly, and then a cone of pale yellow light shone from it, playing on the broken edge of the stele.

For a moment, nothing changed. Then the light flickered—like in an old silent movie—and the stone was whole. The newly revealed part of the stone was figured in symbols—but these looked more familiar, the angular lines and triangles of cuneiform, the ancient writing of the Fertile Crescent. It looked out of place among the whirls and curlicues that otherwise adorned the standing stone.

Another source of light fell across the marks, and then shadows. A black, weirdly armored hand reached from the edge of the eye's illumination and stroked the incised characters with needle-like claws. A voice spoke from the empty air, intoning syllables in a language Steve didn't recognize. Whoever it was seemed to be reading the inscription out loud.

We're looking at the past, he realized. *If Strange can see the past, can he go there? And if he can go there...*

He tried not to let the thought distract him. But it was in his mind now, the moment of his own past he played over and over in his head, trying to see a way out, a different ending, or even the way it *did* end, after the blast took consciousness from him. To know for sure whether Bucky lived or died that day. Logic told him there was no way the young man could have survived, but logic said the same thing about Cap. If he could have been preserved in ice, maybe Bucky could have been, too.

To at least know for sure, to see the actual moment...

There was a flash of light and the sound of stone shattering. He fell into a fighting stance, and the stele was back to its present appearance. The light faded, and the uncanny eye detached from Strange's forehead. It floated back down to the amulet and slipped inside. The metal eyelids closed. A moment later, his less unnatural eyes flickered open.

"You can see the past," Thor said. "A useful skill."

Steve couldn't take his eyes from the amulet.

"How—how far back can it see?" he asked.

"Hours, usually," Strange said. "A day or so at most."

"But there must be a way to see back further."

The sorcerer frowned slightly. "There are ways," he said, "but they are not easy, and far from certain—otherwise I would try to follow Scorpio's trip through time and space." Strange's eyes narrowed. "What exactly are you asking me, Captain?"

Focus, soldier, Steve thought to himself. *Fight what's in front of you.*

"Never mind," he said. "We can talk about it later, when this is all done. The question is, did we learn anything?"

"We did," Strange said. "Scorpio—the ancient one—made that inscription, and he was dying when he made it. He felt he had only hours or days remaining before his body failed, but he was determined to leave a record for future allies, even though he knew the message might come to his enemies. When he arrived at this place, however, he was out of choices."

"And his message was?"

"As I inferred, the well here was not sufficient for his purposes. The message pointed toward a second choice—the nearest geographically."

"And where is that?"

"The inscription said to 'seek in the Heart of Hanlin,'" Strange replied.

"That's good, then," Thor said. "We know where to go next." His brow wrinkled. "You do know where that is, don't you?"

"I know where it *was*," Strange replied. "Hanlin was one of the chief cities of the Pyu Empire, which was located in the country we now know as Burma or Myanmar. But Hanlin came into existence a thousand years after Scorpio's defeat at Penthos. He was traveling not just in space, but in time."

"Does it make a difference," Steve asked, "if he put the Key in this Hanlin place a thousand years ago, instead of three?"

"Not to us," Strange said. "If he put it in the Well of Hanlin, it should still be there. Except…"

"Except what?" Steve said.

"Hanlin, and presumably everything in it—including the entrance to the Well—was destroyed by a flaming sandstorm more than a thousand years ago."

THIRTEEN

NATASHA was already aboard the Quinjet, checking her Widow's Bite gauntlets to make sure they were combat ready, when she got the signal. There was a call from Maria Hill coming in through the vessel's secure link.

"Maria," she said. "To what do I owe the pleasure?"

"A couple of things," the SHIELD commander said. "One is a confirmation that the location your friend gave us checks out. It's a mansion in the mountains outside of Taipei. I'm sending along satellite images and the coordinates."

"Understood," Natasha said. She hadn't had any doubt about Ivan's information, but it was always good to have confirmation. The satellite imagery would make it easier to set up their plan of attack. "What else do you have for me?"

"We ran background checks on everyone at Advanced Idea Mechanics," she said. "Standard procedure, especially when enhanced types are involved. Rappaccini and Tarleton check out. Both are eccentric in their own ways, but no red flags. Blonsky, on the other hand, comes with quite a history. Guerilla fighting, sabotage, espionage—he was on a couple of terrorism watchlists back in the day."

"That fits," Natasha said. "I ran my own checks. But he's been quiet for years, with no record since moving to the States. The way I read it, he's trying to make a fresh start. Did I miss something?"

"Nothing obvious," Hill said, "but it's interesting. I think he bears watching."

BLONSKY was in his office. He was in his uniform, but Nat could see the bandages bulging beneath it.

"What is it?" he asked.

"Let's take a walk," she said in Croatian.

He stared at her, and then sighed heavily.

"*U redu*," he said, slipping the phone into his pocket.

"Your Croatian is good," he said, continuing to speak in his native tongue as they walked along the way to the docks. Gulls squawked overhead and picked about on the quay for scraps. The sky was as clear as she had seen it since arriving here, although what little real sunlight shone through the clouds had a brittle feel to it.

"Thanks," she said. "I've had some practice. You know a little about me, I guess."

"Yes," he replied, nodding. "Where I'm from they tell stories about you. Mostly to scare children. There's Baba Roga—and there is you."

"How flattering," she said. "It's nice to know I'm remembered."

He didn't reply, and he didn't meet her gaze.

"How are you doing?" she asked.

"I've felt better," he said.

"I'm sure you have," she said. "You nearly died."

He shrugged. "Not the first time."

"Right," she replied.

"Why are you asking me this?" But the raw tone of his voice betrayed him.

That was the funny thing about empathy, she mused—so many ill-informed people talked about it as if it was such a wonderful thing. But empathy was just about being able to get into someone else's mind, to understand what they were feeling. Like anything, that ability could be used for good or evil or anything in between. All of the best interrogators were highly empathetic. So were torturers.

"You and I have some things in common," she said. "If I had your job, and someone came in and knocked me around the way you got knocked around—I'd have some feelings about it."

"Yes," he conceded. "I guess I do have some feelings about it. But begging your pardon, I don't see that it's your business."

"You're staying on here, I understand. That's admirable. But I think you've got something to prove, yes? To everyone. To yourself."

His features were neutral, as if he didn't feel anything at all. "I wasn't prepared," he said. It might have been a machine talking. "Next time I will be. But what do you care?"

Because Bruce is my friend, and he is here, with you. I would rather you not act foolishly."

Blonsky uttered a harsh laugh. "What does the Hulk have to fear from me?"

"I don't know," Natasha replied. "But it's the thing you don't know that often gets you in the end."

FOURTEEN

"HOW'S your homework coming?" Tony asked as the swells of the Pacific rolled by miles below them. The roar of the engines was a distant whine in the thin atmosphere. The radar showed that everything was clear, at least for the immediate future.

They wouldn't cross into anyone's sovereign airspace until very late in their flight, but it was impossible to know what was going to turn up in the stratosphere, and they could never be sure how some of the touchier countries along the Pacific Rim would react to unidentified aircraft moving at more than Mach 2. That included the U.S.

"I think I'll pass the test," Natasha said, looking up from her screen. She'd been going over the file Strange had sent—mostly a bunch of scans, some handwritten translations, and a few diagrams. Alongside that she had the information she'd been able to pry from various sources about Capricorn and his operation in Taiwan.

"What are *you* up to over there?" she asked. "Playing video games?"

"Yes," he said. "It's a game I like to call 'Let's not get blown out of the sky.'"

"How's it going?"

"I've got the high score so far," he said. "Of course, it's the *only* score. I've upgraded our radar invisibility, but I have it on good authority that the Chinese have better detection equipment than they did last time we were out this way. So this is sort of a test. They noticed something a little while ago, and we've been probed by sources I'm just going to call 'unknown,' but no one has fired on us, and I'm pretty sure no one knows for sure we exist. So, tell me about our friend Capricorn."

"There's not a lot to tell," Natasha said. "He's got his fingers in a lot of pots—SEACS, the Russian SB, and so on—but he's not directly involved, just does business with them. The KGB had files on him going all the way back to the thirties and forties, when he was supposed to be involved with Hydra."

"That can't be the same guy, right?"

She looked at him strangely. "That's a rhetorical question, isn't it? I mean, we've got a man that age on our team."

"Sure, but—"

"No, it probably isn't the same person," she said. "What I got from Strange is that these guys inherit their positions. The man we're after more likely is just the latest Capricorn."

"Do we know anything about his abilities?"

"Not really, but Capricorn is the Greek name," she said. "It means 'horned goat,' which seems a little redundant to me. The older, Sumerian name was Suhurmas, 'goat-fish.'"

"So, goaty, fishy powers. That's a tremendous help."

"I've been thinking about that," she said. "We know a little about six of the Zodiac members, right? Leo is pretty straightforward—looks like a lion, has claws and an… energy roar? Should we call it that? Libra, that's a little weirder. Her modern sign is scales, but her older associations are with Ishtar, the Queen of Heaven, and with Venus as the Morning Star. According to the *Tetrabiblos*—"

"I'm sorry," Tony said, "the *what?*"

"*Tetrabiblos*. It's a book."

"Okay, so there's a book now."

"Yep. Written by the Greek philosopher Ptolemy. It's the source for most of what we know about the Zodiac."

"So… science. Go on."

"Libra is an air sign," she obliged. "Changeable."

"So she can walk through walls."

"Yes," Natasha said. "Taurus, on the other hand, is associated with the Bull of Heaven. She's an Earth sign, fixed. Immovable."

"Because she manipulates gravity," Tony added. "At least that's what we can surmise from Cap's scrimmage with her."

Natasha nodded. "Virgo was known to the Sumerians as the Maiden, the daughter of the god Sin, and in the earliest depictions of her she has a star on her forehead and a whip in her right hand."

"Sounds like our girl," Tony said. "You said six."

"I'm assuming the two I met in New York were Zodiac. One of them was probably Scorpio, given how he both poisoned and dehydrated that guy. The other one attacked me with some sort of sonic and heat blast. I'm thinking that was Aries, a fire sign."

"So, Capricorn? What's his deal?"

"Earth sign, like Taurus," she said. "He's linked to the planet Saturn, which means illness, poverty, corruption of the air, decay, 'fearful cold.' In one Babylonian legend he has a talking mace."

"No kidding," Tony said. "A talking mace. Hear that, JARVIS? This guy may have a talking mace. I absolutely need one of those. Include it in the next armor design."

"*Noted, sir.*"

"Really?" Natasha said.

"Hey, if Thor can have a hammer, why not? It sounds fun." He sighed. "I know you're trying, Nat, but I don't see a pattern here. We have no idea what we're up against. Capricorn could be a goat-fish or a walking disease with a huge… mace. Or something else entirely."

"Yeah," she agreed. "It's all too obscured by history and myth. What little we know comes from Ptolemy, via the Sumerians and Egyptians who got it from an older, mostly lost source. It's gotten all bent from what the original Zodiac was exactly. If we're to believe Strange, their powers come from the constellations themselves, which in turn represent some sort of extradimensional powers. Maybe Strange knows more about Capricorn."

"But he's not here," Tony said. "If he has a phone, I don't have his number, and I'm fresh out of crystal balls."

"What about Cap?"

"His phone is right over there, on the charger."

"Oh," she said. "Typical." She leaned forward. "Here's the thing, Tony. Strange said these guys are getting stronger all of the time. The *Tetrabiblos* talks about how to make predictions according to the stars and all of that, but it also lays out some worst-case scenarios: hurricanes, chasms in the earth, flooding, civil war, pestilence, desertification—"

"This is an end-of-the-world scenario."

"Okay," Tony said. "That's a little alarmist. If this Greek guy—"

"Ptolemy? He may have been Egyptian."

"—if this *guy* knew so much, where is he now?"

"There's only one account of his death I can find," Natasha replied. "He was said to have died of venom, most likely the sting of a scorpion."

"You just made that up."

"Hey, I'm just the messenger," she said.

"Uh-huh," Tony said. "But there's something else bugging me."

"What's that?"

"Up until now, none of these guys has been alone. Aries and Scorpio. Leo and Libra. Virgo and Taurus—and then all of the last four in New York. Makes me think Capricorn probably isn't by himself either. Who else is in Taiwan?"

Natasha frowned. "I noticed that too," she said. "We should be prepared for at *least* two of them. Maybe more."

o———o

TONY detoured a little south to avoid crossing Japan proper. Radar invisibility was all well and good, but a kid on a bike with a cell phone could still blow your cover.

By the time the Quinjet began dropping fast to approach the island of Taiwan just above sea level, it was close to midnight. When they finally grounded in the mountains outside of Taipei, he was fairly certain they hadn't been tracked.

He and Natasha went back over the aerial photos of the mansion. "I've been thinking about this," Nat said. "SHIELD estimates at least forty guards down there. I don't know if we can get to Capricorn without starting a small war, and I'm not sure it would do any good. We know these Zodiac people can pass their roles—and probably their powers—to someone else. They've been doing it for thousands of years, so we can assume they've made the process more or less foolproof. Kill the current Capricorn, and there'll be another one to take his place a day later.

"If Strange is right, there's no long game to play here," she continued, "but we might not want to get too short-sighted either. Our goal is to prevent them from getting the Key and showing up for this cosmic alignment, or whatever it is. Learning more about their organization takes precedence over killing just one of them."

"That seems like sound logic," Tony said.

"Also, Cap wouldn't approve of a straight-up assassination."

"Very true."

"But to get the intel we want, we might need to capture Capricorn and question him," Nat reasoned, "and like I said, that could get nasty. Nastier than just an in-and-out deletion."

"JARVIS can provide some cover from the Quinjet," Tony said. "Between him and the suit, we can button things down outside, if it comes to that."

"I think I can slip in here," she said, indicating a section along one of the outer walls. "He's got his own computer servers, so once I get in, everything we need ought to be accessible through his system. Provided it has the intel we need, we might be able to pull this off without ever letting them know we were here."

"Yeah," Tony said. He pointed at the map. "These look like the generators, so I'll bet the servers are housed nearby. I can't tap in from this far away, but if I get close enough in the suit, I might be able to do so. They'll have an automated security system, though..."

"I can find that and disable it," Natasha said. "Plant a signal booster to let you download everything from a greater distance. So you wait well outside the walls, where they're less likely to spot you."

"Sounds like a plan," Tony said. "But if something goes wrong…"

"We fight a small war," she said.

Iron Man liked that about Natasha. She always assumed something would go wrong. It was why she was still alive.

○————————○

THEY suited up, Tony in his armor and Black Widow in her customary black bodysuit and gauntlets.

They were about a mile out, but in his armor that was next to nothing, even with Nat clinging to his back. They set down a respectable distance from the mansion and continued on foot, clambering up the often-steep, tree-covered slopes until the walls of the house came into sight, dim but clear enough in the darkness.

Natasha padded off to do her thing. Just to be safe Tony moved further back, found a comfortable spot, brought up his long-range sensors and the satellite feed, and made himself comfortable.

○————————○

THE walls around the house were only shoulder high, made of poured concrete designed to resemble marble or perhaps alabaster. They seemed strictly ornamental—which they were when it came to stopping intruders. Even a child could climb over them. That wasn't their purpose. They were for *noticing* invaders, and slowing them down just long enough for the guards to arrive. She couldn't come closer than a yard without tripping motion sensors.

The Black Widow stayed out of range of the sensors until she reached the southwest corner, where the aerial view had shown an elevation. Trees and other vegetation had been cut back from the wall, and for the most part the ground around the barrier sloped down and away, often at steep angles. In this spot, however, the terrain rose from the wall, though maybe not as sharply as it looked from above. Eyeballing it, she thought it was enough. Tony could have flown over it, of course, but the odds were good that he would have tripped some other sort of alarm.

She climbed the slope and found her footing. This was a perfect jump. She flipped twice and landed without a sound, passing well above the range of the motion sensors.

Moving around to the back, she found a small loading dock that marked the kitchen entrance. Servants' entrances were high-traffic, and tended not to have alarms that spent way too much time going off. If they did have them, they often disabled them unless there was an overt threat. They instead relied on the staff knowing one another and reporting strangers. This was far from ideal, as servants could be fooled, rendered unconscious, or killed.

There were two bored guards lounging on the dock itself, and she took them out with the Widow's Bite shots from her gauntlets. That got her into the kitchen, where she found a man and a woman cleaning up. After rendering them unconscious, she put them—along with the guards—in a walk-in pantry and locked it from the outside.

Proceeding toward where Tony guessed the servers would be, she found it easy going. Too easy, really. Like they knew she was coming. She began recalibrating her expectations. Coming to a set of doors she stood quietly for a moment, listening. A flickering light on her left gauntlet told her Tony still had track of her.

She pushed the door open slightly.

Then wider.

If the servers were there, they were someplace behind the tastefully appointed office, the massive desk, the bookshelves, the guards.

And Capricorn.

He was waiting for her, sitting behind the desk on the other side of the room. He was a big man with sallow skin and dark eyes. He wore an expensive-looking suit. So did the twelve armed men lined up around him, six on a side.

She sized it all up. Difficult, not impossible. She hadn't expected to find him sleeping, after all.

"Black Widow," he said. "I'm honored. May I introduce myself? They call me Capricorn."

"I met some of your men," she said. "In New York."

"The tablet," he said. "Yes, that was rightfully ours, so we took it back."

"And murdered a man."

"Surely that doesn't bother someone with your reputation," he said. "After all, standards must be kept. If I allow one thief to prosper at our expense, why would others hesitate? The logic cannot be lost on you."

"No, it makes perfect sense," she said, "but put yourself in my shoes, and apply the same reasoning. Your men attacked me and killed the man I intended to interrogate. How can I allow that to go unpunished?"

He smiled. "I remember in school there was a sort of 'logic' problem that went around. We loved to discuss it. 'What if the unstoppable force met the immovable object?'"

"I fear I did not attend that sort of school," Natasha replied. "Where I studied, we had no time for such abstractions."

"Well, everyone thought they had an answer," he said. "Some said the unstoppable force would keep bouncing off of the immovable object, others that they would cancel each other out. But no answer could satisfy the terms of the conjecture. Do you know why?"

"Yes," Natasha said. The man on the far right stood far too stiffly. He would be slowest. The guy at Capricorn's left hand was the one to watch out for. "It's a silly proposition," she continued. "If an unstoppable force exists, then by definition an immovable object cannot also exist, and vice versa. It's a situation you can hypothesize with language, but which can't exist in reality."

"Exactly," he replied, the smile growing larger. "So you can frame your dilemma as being the same as mine, but it's just as silly. I am what

I am, and so by definition, you cannot be what you imagine you are."

"If you say so," she said.

She sprinted, firing her pistol at the man to Capricorn's left. She'd been right about him; he was already taking aim at her. He even got a shot off, although it missed her by nearly a foot. She danced to the side, fired again, shot a wire from her gauntlets to fasten at the base of the chandelier above them, and was suddenly off the ground. She used her Widow's Bite to subdue the next three, and then she was close enough to settle the rest of them hand-to-hand. Capricorn spent his time stumbling back toward an exit, but before he had reached it, it was just the two of them.

"Now," she said. "Let's have another talk about the 'unstoppable force.'"

She saw his eyes cut and knew someone was behind her. She spun, bringing up both guns—just in time to see the pincers as they sank into her skull. She felt an immediate dislocation, and saw the pistols drop from her numb hands.

Then her thoughts came apart like paper tissue in the stream of a firehose.

FIFTEEN

GIVEN what the Sorcerer Supreme had told them about Hanlin, Thor had expected a wasteland or perhaps blasted ruins, the remains of a once-great kingdom. In his wanderings, he had seen many such places. There were far more dead empires than living ones.

But, when Strange's powers brought them to their destination, he had to quickly dodge a man on a two-wheeled motorized vehicle. The driver honked his horn, as did the woman in the small car that whizzed past an instant later.

They had materialized in the middle of a hard-packed road of red earth.

"Oops," Strange said, but that, fortunately, was the end of the traffic—Thor couldn't see any other vehicles in either direction.

"Morning rush hour, I guess," Cap said.

The road stretched off across a relatively flat landscape made up of fields and scrub punctuated by isolated trees. In the distance he saw the crowded, dirt-colored houses of a modest village. Further up the road stood some sort of building surrounded by a little more greenery.

The man on the two-wheeled conveyance pulled over, and aimed something at them. Thor lifted his hammer and began to whirl it. Strange quickly held up a hand.

"I think he's just taking a picture with his phone," the sorcerer said. "Why don't you hold off for just a second."

Thor cocked his head. The man on the scooter put the phone

away and continued down the road. Thor let his hammer slow, stop, and hang at his side.

"We were ambushed in the last location," the Asgardian pointed out.

"And may be again," Cap said. "Nevertheless, let's stay restrained until we're sure."

"Of course."

Cap studied their surroundings. "What are we looking for?" he asked Strange.

"We should be near what little remains of the ancient city," Strange said, "and the well Scorpio was seeking. If you'll give me a moment, I should be able to—"

"I think it's there," Thor said, pointing ahead.

"Why?" Cap asked. "Oh."

Down the road, a dark cloud of smoke rose toward the clear blue sky.

Thor looked at Cap.

"Shall I take a look?" he said.

"Go ahead," Cap said, "but if there are hostiles, report back instead of engaging. We don't want to walk into another ambush."

"Understood," Thor said. He whirled Mjolnir and let it pull him toward the fire. From the air he could see that they were in the broad bottomland of a river valley flanked by hills on either side. Besides the nearby village, a larger town lay in the distance. He came to earth near the column of black smoke, which emerged from a red-brick building—or what was left of it. Cautiously he searched the area for signs of the enemy.

About a dozen people were scattered around the building, watching from a respectable distance, but there was no obvious sign of whoever had set the fire. He waved his hammer to signal an all-clear, reckoning that Strange likely had some eldritch way of spying on him.

Then he heard a weak cry from within the burning building.

Thor hesitated only an instant, fearing a ruse then deciding it didn't matter. He rushed up to the flaming structure and, after a moment, chose what looked like the front door. It was on fire, but he hardly felt the heat as he knocked it in.

"Hello!" he cried. "Where are you?"

For a moment he heard nothing but the crackling of flames. Then he made out another faint cry. He charged down the flaming hall. Almost immediately his lungs began to sting from the smoke, which he thought to try and clear by whirling his hammer. The rush of wind, he realized, would only fan the flames to greater strength. He could call for rain, but the sky was empty and dry as bone, and it would take too long to summon clouds…

The building, he realized, was some sort of shrine. Many objects were venerated, placed in transparent cases and labeled in various scripts. Few looked valuable to his eye—clay pots, ornaments of metal and stone, assorted scraps—but he could never tell what people were going to worship.

Following the cries of distress Thor came to a stair which descended below the building and into the hard red earth. Here the fire was hottest, burning from the brick and earthen walls, with no wood or other fuel in sight. It was as if he was descending in a volcano.

He entered a larger gallery and saw the source of the cries—an older man on his hands and knees. Another man stood over him—or at least something man-shaped. His skin looked more like the armor of an insect and was dark, a sort of blue-black. His eyes shone like sparks of electricity. His fingers were overlong and ended in sharp points. A pale mist arced over his head from somewhere along his back, looking for all the world like the ghostly tail of a scorpion.

Behind him stood a woman holding a crackling whip of energy.

"Step away from him, Scorpio," Thor warned, "or face the wrath of the god of thunder."

The scorpion-man grinned.

His teeth were very white.

"In a very short time, you will see what it is to face the true gods, Asgardian," he said. "Gods more primordial, and far more powerful than your upstart clan."

"I've warned you," Thor said. With an underhand snap of his wrist he sent Mjolnir flying.

Virgo's whip flashed, wrapping instantly around the uru weapon. She could not stop it, of course, but the effort yanked it out of line, so it missed Scorpio by a hair's breadth and cratered into the wall. In the same heartbeat Scorpio stooped and sank his fingers in to the old man's neck. He stepped back with a mocking smile, touched his wrist, and vanished.

An instant later, Virgo did the same, leaving Thor alone with the old man. He was gasping, his skin already taking on a gray tone. Quickly Thor gathered him in his arms.

"Don't worry," he said. "I'll have you out of here in just a moment."

He looked back the way he'd come, saw the flames, and thought better of it. Instead he whirled Mjolnir and hurled it at the ceiling. The hammer smashed through it, and through the ceilings above, then came back to him. Holding the man to his chest, he leapt up through the hole. Wind rushed down to meet him as the fire greedily sucked at the outside air, but no mere wind could deter him.

Coming down as gently as he could outside of the building, he took several paces to make sure they were at a safe distance. Then he lay the man down.

The poor fellow still struggled for breath, and his flesh had turned an awful bluish hue. What could he do? He had no power over venom. He remembered Natasha's tale of her ruse gone wrong, how quickly that man had died from this same villain's touch. What use to have the power of the storm in his very hands while a man lay dying?

"Let me see him."

Thor looked up, startled, to see that Strange was there. Cap was at his side.

"He was in the building," Thor explained. "Scorpio—"

"I can see that," Strange said. He laid a hand on the man's forehead.

"Can you help him?" Thor asked.

"It's too late," he murmured. "Unless…" His face suddenly set in grim lines. He traced the air with the fingers of his other hand. Symbols glowed and faded. "By the Vishanti," Strange said. "Let the death that has entered into this man enter instead into me."

For an instant, nothing happened.

Then the old man coughed up black spittle. Strange uttered a terrible cry of despair, but he kept his hand pressed hard against the old man's brow. As Thor watched, the sorcerer's flesh took on a distinct bluish cast.

"Strange!" Cap shouted as the warlock slowly toppled onto his side. Thor watched as Cap placed a finger on their companion's neck.

"There's almost no pulse," Cap said. "He's dying!"

The old man, Thor noticed, already looked better. His flesh had returned to a more natural tone and he was breathing deeply, eyes rolling about beneath their lids as if he was experiencing a vivid dream.

"Strange cured this man," Thor said. "Somehow…"

"I don't know what to do for him. He needs help." Cap sounded more than frustrated. He sounded angry.

One of the bystanders came sprinting toward them, with others following at a slower pace. The frontrunner was young, not a child but not fully mature. She knelt by the old man, going on in a language Thor did not recognize. The elder coughed again, and this time he opened his eyes.

The girl's cries became more excited and joyful. Jumping up, she threw her arms around Thor's neck and gave him a hug.

"*Tor*," she said. "*Avengers. Kyeizu tin ba de?*"

"It's all right," Thor said. "I think."

The old man pushed up on one elbow and met Thor's gaze.

"She says thank you," the man said.

"You speak English," Thor said.

"Learned in school," the man said. "Also, I am a guide for tourists." He nodded toward the burning building. "Or was, anyway," he said.

"What happened?" Thor asked.

The man closed his eyes and grimaced in terror.

"*Kainn myee kout*," he said.

"I don't—"

"Scorpion," the man said. "He was a scorpion."

"Yes," Thor said. "I saw. And the woman with the whip—but what did they do?"

"Scorpio," Cap said. "The same guy Natasha ran into. His venom…" He shook his head, looking down at Strange, whose lips were as black as if he'd adorned himself with Egyptian kohl.

"Is he…?" Thor asked.

"Still alive," Cap said. "Barely, though." He looked up at the old man. "Is there a hospital nearby?" he asked him.

"The nearest is in Singu township," he said. "More than an hour by car. Better ones in Mandalay, but that is further. You can fly though, yes? Perhaps there is time."

"Which way?" Thor asked.

"To Singu? Northeast." He pointed. "Just across the Irrawaddy River. It's on the main street, not too hard to find. Some there will speak English. Look for older people. We had to learn in school."

Thor looked at Cap. "I'll take him there."

Cap nodded agreement. "It's better than not trying at all," he said, "but I'd say it's too late." Thor bent to collect Strange in his arms. He had begun to whirl his hammer when the sorcerer groaned and his eyes slitted open.

His eyes were entirely black.

"Just… wait," Strange croaked out. "Put me down. Heaven knows what they would do to me in a hospital."

"You're on the verge of death," Cap said. "We have no choice."

"Not my first time, Captain," Strange said. "I have survived stronger poisons than this. I will recover. I need water, and to be out of the sun."

"My house is not far," the old man said. "He is welcome. You all are."

THE old man's name was Suta, and the girl—his granddaughter—was named Thawda. They lived in a modest brick house a few hundred yards down the road. Once inside, Suta spoke a few words to Thawda, who quickly brought tea and a platter of shriveled leaves that Thor gathered were snacks. Everyone, Cap included, took off their shoes or boots at the door, so he did also, albeit reluctantly.

Suta insisted that Strange be given the only chair in the house, so they propped him in it and helped him drink some water. After a short time, they gave him a little of the tea. The snack leaves were pleasantly sour, accompanied by ground nuts and chilies that would be far too spicy for most Asgardian tastes.

Cap asked Suta about the building that had just burned, which it turned out wasn't a shrine but a museum documenting the history of the region and especially the Pyu Empire which had once ruled the area.

"I grew up near here," Suta said. "My father told me the stories of our past. Archaeologists came when I was a little boy, and I volunteered to help them dig. Mostly I removed dirt for them, but it was very interesting to me. When they built the museum, I studied to get a job there. I hoped one day they would expand it, but... now it's ruined."

"Will your country rebuild?" Cap asked.

"I hope so," Suta said, "but the government has many concerns." He fidgeted a little. "Can you tell me why?" he asked, finally. "Why my museum was destroyed?"

"They didn't care about your museum," Cap said. "They were looking for something."

"I know," Suta said. "They questioned me, but I did not know what they were talking about. They laughed at me and said I knew nothing."

"Did they find anything?" Thor asked. "Did they take anything from the—?"

Abruptly Strange began coughing. Suta signed for Thawda to bring him more tea.

"No," Strange murmured. "I'm fine, thank you. Thank you for your hospitality."

"Thawda told me you took the poison from me," Suta said. "If I had a million times what I have, I could not repay you."

The sorcerer did look better, Thor thought. His color had improved —he was no longer blue—and his eyes had returned to normal.

"SHIELD analyzed that toxin after the New York incident," Cap said. "It's supposed to be pretty nasty stuff."

"I am... acquainted with many poisons," Strange said. "Over the years I have been exposed to more than my share. Even so, this was more virulent than I expected. Not entirely of this Earth, or any of the realms I ordinarily frequent. I miscalculated my ability to adapt."

"You seem to be doing okay," Cap said.

"Fortunately," Strange said. "But I was expecting, you might say, an ant bite. It was more like being dropped into a pit of cobras." He took a deep breath. "That's an analogy," he said. "I've actually *been* in a pit of cobras, and it wasn't nearly as bad."

"You saved this man from certain death," Thor said.

Strange shot him a sidewise look. "That's the minimal definition of my job," he said. "You don't get extra credit for doing what you're supposed to do. And you did your part, god of thunder. Another few seconds and there would have been no help for him." He paused. "You saw them? Scorpio and Virgo?"

"Yes," Thor said. "They fled, using their bracelets before I could deal with them."

"Did they have the Key?"

"I don't know," Thor said. "I was just asking Suta, but... what does it look like?"

"Oh," Strange said. "Did I neglect that part? It *would* be helpful, I suppose." He lifted his right hand and stretched out his index finger. He traced a design in the air, leaving a faint golden line to mark its passage. The line formed a cross with a loop at the top. The short line of the cross was bent slightly upward.

"This reminds me of an Egyptian symbol," Thor said. "I once met this god named Horus—"

"The Egyptian ankh is similar," Strange said, "and I would love to hear this story about Horus. Someday. But for now—did you see anything like that?"

"I did not," Thor said, "though our encounter was brief."

"I have seen it," Suta said.

All eyes turned to him. Thawda said something, low and fast, but the old man shushed her with a motion of his hands.

"Where?" Strange demanded.

"In the museum," Suta said. "I saw it in the new section, down below. Not an object, but a carving. A symbol. I noticed it because it was so different from other Pyu inscriptions."

"This symbol," Strange said, "down below. Was it in a… cave, or a basement? A shrine of some sort?"

Suta nodded. "Only discovered recently, beneath the building. It was quite strange. Not just the symbol, but everything—altogether different from other things of that period. The archaeologists say it was a shrine dedicated to star formations."

"Was there anything else—unusual about it?"

Suta hesitated. "I've been a museum keeper for many years," he said. "I used to go down there, sometimes at night. There was—a sort of presence. Not of a person. More like a place I thought I could see sometimes, from the corner of my eye. Like a thing seen in the desert that isn't really there."

"A mirage," Cap said.

"And that's where Scorpio went?" Strange pursued.

"He made me take him, and the other. The woman with the whip."

"Yeah," Cap said. "I've made her acquaintance."

"Did they find anything?" Strange asked. "In the weird place?"

"The scorpion-man went in," Suta said. "He became like smoke, but I could still see him. When he came out, he was angry. He shouted at me."

Strange closed his eyes and breathed out a long, slow breath.

"So they didn't find it there," he said. He looked back at their host. "Yet you say you have seen it? The symbol I showed you."

"A carving of it," Suta said. "A depiction. There was a stone slab, like a grave marker, but with no grave underneath. It was inscribed with Pyu writing on the front. Normal things—but on the other side, something else."

"What do you mean?" Cap asked.

"Symbols," he said. "Strange. Lines and sketches. Stars, I think, and your symbol."

"What became of this slab?" Strange asked.

"They destroyed it," Suta said. "First the scorpion-man read it. Then he touched it and it crumbled into dust. I tried to stop him, but he was strong. He knocked me down. That was when Thor arrived."

"Like the stele in the mountains," Thor said. "They attempt to cover their tracks, to keep us from following them."

"Can you pull your trick again?" Cap asked Strange. "With the amulet? See it before they destroyed it?"

"I fear too much time has passed," Strange said, "and I'm too weak. If I push further into the past there will be problems. It's not impossible, but I will need to recover more fully, and I doubt we have time for that."

"Were there any photographs of the slab?" Cap asked.

"In the museum," the old man said. "They will have burned. Perhaps the government office in Naypyidaw has copies. The archaeologists, too."

"Do any of the archaeologists live nearby?" Cap asked.

"No," Suta said, shaking his head.

"We don't have time to track down photographs that may not exist," Strange said. "Each second that passes, the Zodiac draws farther ahead of us and nearer their goal. Did they say anything about where they were going?"

"Not that I understood," Suta said, and he looked strangely pleased.

"But—I have something. It could be of use." He stood and left the
room, returning a few moments later with a large sheet of paper that
had been rubbed over with some sort of dark gray material, like ash or
charcoal. Thor was puzzled at first, but then realized he could make out
strange runes on the paper.

"I was curious," the old man said. "I wasn't supposed to, but I made
a rubbing of the stone, as a keepsake."

Strange closed his eyes, exhaled, and drew a deep breath.

"I could kiss you, *U Suta*."

The man took a step back, eyes widening.

"No," the sorcerer said. "It's an expression. I won't touch your
head." He pointed toward the rubbing. "May I see that?"

Now that he looked closer, Thor saw that there were figures, as
well. Some were familiar—the scorpion, the lion, the crab, and so
forth. And the image of the Key, in not one but several places. He
thought it looked familiar, but in a general way.

"Is it a map?" Thor asked. "A star map?"

"Yes," Strange said. "I believe so. But it is also a map of the world,
in a sense."

"Really?" Cap said. "I'm trying, but I can't make head nor tail of it."

"It's not like a modern map," Strange said. "The exact shape of the
continents isn't important. It's more like a conceptualization, or a flow
chart. It shows the relationship between places sacred to the Zodiac.
The wells in particular."

He pointed. "You see this in the center of the map. That's where
we were before, the Well of Indara in the Kopet Dag mountains. It's
where this cult originated, so Scorpio placed it in the center of the
world, both in time and space. It's the beginning." He moved his hand
up. "And here we are in Hanlin," he said. "Further away in space, but
also in time."

Strange kept moving his finger along the map.

"This shows the stars aligning in different ways," he said. "Just
as different days come under influence of the different Zodiac signs,

so do various parts of the Earth. We were attacked by Gemini and Sagittarius at the crypt of Indara because their signs are strongest there right now. This place favors Scorpio and Virgo, but there is a progression. The next place to look is here." His finger traced to the very edge of the rubbing.

"Where is that?" Thor asked.

"It's an island in the Pacific," Strange said. "If my guess is correct, it's the capital of the Saudeleur Kingdom—Nan Madol."

"Saudeleur," the old man said. "They said this word. I did not know it meant anything."

"Pohnpei," Strange said. "That's the name of the island."

"So, we have a destination," Cap said. "Strange, are you well enough to take us there?"

"I'll have to be."

"If you are too weak, I could summon the Bifrost," Thor said.

Strange seemed to think that over for a moment.

"I can manage," he said at last. "I fear the Bifrost might be too blunt a weapon for our purposes. You can call it to yourself, I assume, but having it take us somewhere else—we would have to travel to Asgard first, wouldn't we?"

"Normally," Thor replied, "but there are mysteries of the Rainbow Bridge only its guardian, Heimdall, knows. He might be able to move us directly there."

"I'm weak," Strange said, "but teleportation from spot to spot on Earth isn't too taxing. We may need a favor from Heimdall later. Let's leave him out of it for now."

"He's probably watching us right now, you know."

"Then he knows I would rather do this my way."

"Wait," Cap said. He was still looking at Suta's rubbing of the map. "Here—this is the Key again, right?"

"Yes," Strange said. "That's probably their next destination after Pohnpei. In case that, like the last two wells, didn't work out. Scorpio must have known he was only hours from death when he reached

Hanlin. His next destination would have been Nan Madol—the map gives it more prominence—but if he came up empty there, he wouldn't have time to leave a hint. He had to hedge his bets."

"So where is *that*?" Cap asked.

Strange frowned at the map for a moment. "In Alaska," he said.

"Why not go straight there?" Cap asked.

"Well, because if the Key is at Nan Madol, we will miss stopping them," Strange replied.

"But they can split up, yes?" Thor said. "There are twelve of them."

"That's true," Strange acknowledged.

"So they probably sent teams to both places," Thor said. "Perhaps we should also split up. Because if it's at this other place, we'll be wasting our time on the island." He looked over to Cap for approval.

"He's got a point," Cap said, "but these guys seem to be getting tougher, like Strange said they would. There's only three of us as there is."

"We could contact Stark and Natasha. Banner might be persuaded to join us."

"Iron Man and Black Widow have their hands full right now," Strange said. "They can't help us."

"Are they in trouble?" Thor asked.

"I'm not certain," Strange said. "They are in a blind spot, so to speak. I can't see them. We must trust they can take care of themselves." He leaned forward, gathered his feet under him, and stood. "We shouldn't split up," he said. "We're having trouble as it is. We should go to Nan Madol. We'll quickly know if the Zodiac has been there already." After a moment he added, "We don't have to seek clues this time—if the Saudeleur Kingdom is a false lead, we can go straight on to Alaska."

"And if they already have the Key?" Cap asked.

"Then our mission becomes all the more difficult. Perhaps impossible," Strange said. "They will be an order of magnitude more powerful than they have been up until now—but until the constellations reach full alignment, we still have some time to prepare. They had the Key once before, and were beaten. We can do it again."

"I hope you're right," Cap said. "You have to be. As I recall, you said that battle caused a dark age that lasted for centuries."

"I know more than Shaushka did," Strange replied. "Our world will not suffer the same fate as hers, not if I have anything to say about it."

"Okay, Doc," Cap said. "You're the authority here. Whenever you're ready."

Strange took a step. He wobbled a bit, looking as if he might fall down. When they moved to help him, he held up a hand to stop them.

"I'm ready," he said. "U Suta, thank you again for your hospitality."

The old man nodded. "Peace, happiness and well-being to all of you."

"I don't know about the peace part," Thor said, "but I appreciate the well wishes."

"Step near," Strange said.

"Before we go," Cap said. "You said that different Zodiac members have greater power in certain parts of the world. Our next stop—which of these people are we likely to meet there?"

"Nan Madol is under the signs of Pisces and Aquarius," the sorcerer said.

"And what can we expect from them?"

"Aquarius is the lord of water, associated with Ea, god of the depths. Pisces is also a water sign, master of magic, transformation, illusion, empathy. How these qualities will manifest in their powers, I cannot say. There is little about them in my texts."

"I guess we'll find out," Cap said.

And then they were elsewhere.

SIXTEEN

THROUGH Natasha's feed, Tony saw the door open, the man in the suit and his guards, and the brief fight that followed. Then the feed blinked out, along with every other indicator that Nat was still alive—
She had turned around first—had those been *claws* he'd seen? Like the pincers of a lobster?

Was she dead already? He couldn't let himself think that.

"Crap," he said, grabbing his helmet and snapping it on. "JARVIS," he said, "as soon as I'm out, take the Quinjet to the position we discussed and follow the Force Ten protocol."

"*Yes, sir.*"

"Crap, *crap*," he repeated, as he jetted through the night toward the building. Capricorn's people must have activated some sort of jamming field; that would explain Nat going silent.

But it all seemed a little... out of step. The ones who had attacked Bruce and Cap hadn't come equipped with henchmen. Why was this guy so well supplied? Maybe because the bracelet teleporters were expensive to build, or hard to come by. In the other two confrontations, the Avengers hadn't been invading—you know—lairs. Maybe Leo had a house full of thugs someplace, too. He just didn't take them on out-of-town jobs.

Anyway, it looked as if he was about to find out what Capricorn's chops were, along with whatever else was in there. The image of the claws still haunted him. There was a crab in the Zodiac, he remembered, along with a scorpion.

He was just in sight of the house when the first missile came screaming at him. He dodged and tapped it with a repulsor beam for good measure. The missile gouged a trench of fire in the mountainside.

"You're going to ruin your landscaping," he said. His transmitter was on, but there was no way to know if anyone was listening.

Muzzle flashes lit up the darkness, and a hard rain of bullets spanged against his nifty new suit. He answered with micro-missiles and repulsor beams. Since any chance of surprise was gone, he figured he would just blast his way in through the front door. He wasn't picking up any anomalous readings, like a hidden ion cannon or the like...

Off to his left, the Quinjet arrived and set up a firing pattern, targeting anything shooting at *him*. The rain of bullets ceased abruptly as the guards looked to their own well-being.

In we go, he thought, then an explosion flared near the Quinjet. It was so bright that his lenses had trouble compensating in time, going almost opaque. So he didn't see what was coming at him, although radar showed a warning blip. Something slower and bigger than the missiles.

Whatever it was hit him and grabbed on, pulling him from the sky.

As he slammed to earth on his hand and knees, he realized that the something was a *someone*, who was on his back and had gained a chokehold on him. His armor prevented any choking, though, so he wasn't sure what the point was...

Then he understood. The guy was trying to twist his helmet off. That shouldn't even be possible, but he felt the strain. This guy was *strong*.

Tony fired repulsors, throwing them both up into the air. There he pivoted and hurtled back to the ground, this time back first. He felt the impact even through the armor and inertial dampeners, which meant whoever was on his back must have taken a real kick in the behind—but whoever it was still managed to keep their grip. In his rear view he now saw a face with glowing, curly goat horns.

Capricorn?

"No fair," he grunted.

Spinning again, he tried to get his attacker to shift enough so he could punch him, but Capricorn just held on. Worse still, Tony felt… weaker, as if his armor wasn't powered all the way up. A quick glance at his heads-up showed him he was right. Battery levels were dropping rapidly.

Why?

"*External temperature dropping rapidly,*" JARVIS announced.

That would do it.

He jetted along the ground, grinding his attacker against the earth until they slammed into the wall around the house. Capricorn took the brunt of the impact with his head, and he finally let go. Tony scrambled to his feet, but everything about his armor seemed—slow. He heard and felt something crack on his joints.

He was iced up!

"JARVIS?"

"*The exterior of your armor has dropped to negative fifty degrees Fahrenheit,*" his computer said. "*Power has been diverted to the internal heating system.*" Before he could say anything else, Capricorn tackled Tony again, and another wave of sub-zero temperature surged through his circuits.

"Ahhh!" Tony shouted. He moved with the tackle, flipped over, and sent Capricorn flying, but the guy landed on his feet and lunged, punching Tony in the face. He staggered back, powering up repulsors, but when he fired them the temperature in his suit dropped another thirty degrees. He was chilled to the bone.

The blast knocked Capricorn back a few steps, but he recovered quickly, grabbing Tony by the arms. Suddenly it was even *colder*. Once more he took flight, smashing his opponent with the weird glowing horns against the building. But he was starting to shiver uncontrollably as the temperature inside his armor continued to plummet. Minor subsystems began shutting down everywhere. All of his hazard lights blinked at once.

Tearing one arm free, he sent shards of ice scattering in the air, then punched Capricorn with everything his systems had left to give. His jets sputtered out, and they fell. Tony's breath was starting to come in quick, shallows gulps, and the cold wasn't letting up.

"CO_2 *levels in your air supply are exceeding safe limits*," JARVIS notified him.

"Pipe in outside air," he said.

"*I'm already doing that, sir*," JARVIS said. "*The atmospheric CO_2 in your vicinity is likewise far above normal.*"

"Emergency cells."

"*Internally compromised, sir.*"

That didn't make sense, he knew, but it was becoming hard to hold a steady thought. He couldn't feel his fingers or his toes, and black spots were dancing before his eyes. He sort of remembered Natasha talking about Capricorn being associated with "corruption of the air" or something, but it all seemed distant, a conversation from a dream.

He fired his repulsors again, but they flared only weakly. Capricorn hit him, hard, and he was down on his knees again. His ears were ringing, and he couldn't breathe. Darkness swallowed his vision until he could only see straight ahead, and all he could think about was getting out of the freezing armor, of taking a breath of real, clean air.

Then, once he had power again...

"JARVIS..." he began.

"*Oh dear*," JARVIS said. "*Mr. Stark—*"

He turned in time to see the Quinjet explode and rain liquid fire all over the compound.

"Unlock armor," he gasped. "On my voice authority."

"*Voice command accepted*," his suit said, but it wasn't JARVIS anymore—just the suit's emergency AI. The uplink relay to JARVIS had been in the Quinjet. He took a deep breath, but it didn't help.

He saw Capricorn gazing down at him, smiling.

Then nothing.

o———o

THE scent of smoke and dry earth was instantly replaced by the taste of the ocean. It wasn't the bright tang of iodine and seaweed of the northern seas Thor had frequented in his youth, but the flavor of a deeper, warmer sea, redolent of life and decay. The late-day air was thick and hot, and a steady rain fell, like a shower of diamonds and liquid gold in the light of the westering sun. Tall palm trees shot up above lush, climbing undergrowth. Standing up from the vegetation was what appeared to be an ancient city of black stone. From his vantage on the mounded remnants of an old stone wall, Thor could see that a system of swampy canals radiated out from the central buildings, and beyond that the ocean stretched off, broken by a few smaller islands and shoals.

"Nan Madol," Strange said, "seat of the Saudeleur Empire. Founded by two brothers who came from afar, who stood taller than the average islander. Magicians, who commanded strange powers and knowledge. It was said they used a dragon of some sort to move the stones to build this city."

"Let me guess," Captain America said, looking around. "Ancient Zodiac members?"

"Doubtful." Strange shook his head. "It generally wasn't the Zodiac's style to set themselves up as rulers. They preferred to play the roles of advisors, court mystics, and astrologers, that sort of thing. That way if things went wrong, they could scuttle off while their 'masters' were beheaded or what have you. You're right, however, to see their influence in this place."

"If the Key is here, where would it be?" the Captain asked.

"There is a dimensional anomaly in the tombs," Strange said. "Over there." Through the fading light he indicated the central part of the ancient stone settlement, but Thor hardly heard him. He was staring at the canal beside which they stood, at the massive thing moving beneath its surface.

"You mentioned a dragon?" he said as the water raised up. In truth it looked more like an eel, but dragons came in many forms, and often the word was loosely thrown around to include anything big and snakelike.

Spinning, Strange spouted off a string of alien syllables; Thor couldn't tell if they were obscenities or spells, but whichever they were, they didn't stop the thing from striking at them. Steve reacted with his usual agility, but Strange, in his weakened state, hesitated. Captain America grabbed him and hauled him aside, yet they were both clipped by the watery foe.

Thor struck with Mjolnir, but it was like hitting a sea wave. It raised a considerable splash, but there was no bone to break or armor to crunch—only water. The liquid worm took notice of him, though, rearing its head high above, gaping a toothless maw and striking down. He stood his ground, smashing the creature with his hammer—to no better effect than before.

Then the watery head gulped him down, pulling him into its gut with the strength of a whirlpool. He fought, kicking at the water with his legs.

His feet found the stony bottom of the canal, and he leapt up with all of his might. He broke through the watery hide of the beast, but it wrapped him in coils and dragged him again beneath the surface, crawling seaward. Through the furiously bubbling water he saw Strange and Captain America, also trapped within the monster's coils, but protected by a scintillating bubble that appeared to contain air. Strange was glowing, and as Thor watched a beam of light lanced from the sorcerer toward him.

The watery bands loosened, and once more he squirmed free. He burst into the rain-drenched air and called lightning. This was no desert as before—these clouds were ripe, full, and more than willing. Guided by his will, a jagged arc of electricity snaked through the tropical air and into the crown of the water-dragon. The monster fluoresced a bright orange and its head exploded into a cloud of steam. Heartened, Thor struck again, but the headless trunk dodged aside. The vapor rising up suddenly condensed and fell upon him, and the rain struck him not just from above, but from all directions. He gasped and water stung his lungs as the sphere of water surrounding him rose above the ancient city, taking him along for the ride.

Rays of sun gleamed through his watery prison, shattering into rainbow colors. The horizon looked strange. Very near, and very high, and then he saw the breakers forming on the crest and knew this was no horizon, but an immense tidal wave churning toward the island.

He brought lightning from the clouds to strike his uru hammer, turning his watery restraints into scalding steam. He heard a strangely human gasp and saw what appeared to be a person falling toward the water below. Was this Pisces, transmuted back to human form, defeated by his sky-born powers?

But if Pisces was defeated, why was the wave still there?

Strange had described Pisces as a master of transformation and illusion, but Aquarius as master of the depths. The sort of being who might summon a destroying wave...

The names and details didn't matter at the moment. What was important was stopping the tsunami. He spun his hammer desperately. The wave would arrive in less than a minute. There was still time to grab Strange and have him teleport them away, but how many people lived on this island? How many would perish because they had come here?

Cap would try to save all of the inhabitants, even against impossible odds. Thor knew he could do no less. If he could fly fast enough, bring the storm with him, he might be able to part the mighty wave so it went around the island.

But looking at the size of the tsunami, he knew it would never work.

Perhaps there was another way. It had never been tried, but...

"Heimdall!" he cried. "Heed me!"

Crackling with lightning, he flew toward the rushing wall of water. As he plunged into it, he summoned the Bifrost.

The full might of the rainbow bridge struck down, through Thor and all around him as he unleashed every iota of the storm at his command. The twilight colors all went strange, as if broken by an underworld prism into a dark rainbow, and then scattered around him. Everything seemed suspended. Then, with a tremendous rush, he was falling *upward* in a column of boiling water, gaining speed by the heartbeat.

He wondered if Heimdall would be prepared for the sudden torrent. At least the farseeing god, the Son of Nine Mothers, would have notice.

No doubt there would be apologies later, to be made over a tankard of Kvaserian mead.

Spinning his hammer in the maelstrom, he flung himself free of the bridge. Light flashed so brightly he could hardly see, and then he was in the storm again, battered by wind and lightning. Far below he saw the pillar of the rainbow bridge still thrust into the depths of the water, but in the next instant it jerked upward, flashed past him, and was gone.

As the energy of his tempest faded, Thor saw the tidal wave was slumped in the middle, split in half, while the rest of its unbroken length rushed past either side of the island.

Everything went pale, then white, then nothing.

○———————○

HE woke to someone with a firm grip pulling him through the breakers. He struggled to help, but his limbs were weak. Through sea-grimed eyes he made out the familiar blue and white uniform.

A moment later he lay on rough shingle.

Cap sat beside him.

"You're heavy," Cap said. "They must feed you boys pretty well in Asgard."

"Lots of meat and ale," Thor said, blowing water from his nose. His hair lay lank and salt-stiffened on his shoulders. "Where is Strange?" he asked. "Is he… Did the wave—"

"He's checking around the island," Cap said. "Looking for anyone in trouble."

"I failed, then," Thor said.

"Are you kidding?" Cap said. "You took on the ocean itself, buddy—and you won. The wave that hit the island was a little less than a yard tall. You should be proud. You saved a lot of lives today. Probably all of them. *I'm* proud of you."

Thor had been praised by gods, demigods, and creatures that defied easy description, but never had he felt any approval as deeply, and never had he felt he deserved it less. He remembered the man who died back in New York, and was ashamed.

"I am—trying," he said.

Cap clapped him on the shoulder. "You're doing better than that," he said.

The thunder god watched silently for a moment as the storm of his making continued to break up, and the last ruddy light of the sun peeked through from the horizon. The tall palms of the island swayed gently, no longer bent by furious wind. The sea itself was as calm as it had been murderous.

"The Key," Thor said. "Was it here?"

"If so, then they took it," Cap said. "Strange found no sign of it."

"Then we must go to Alaska," Thor said. "If one of them has the power to raise the sea like that now, imagine what they will be like at full strength."

"You've got that right," Cap said. Then he looked up. Thor followed his gaze, and together they watched Doctor Strange return, his cloak billowing as he descended toward them.

"How fare the islanders?" Thor asked.

"Shaken up," Strange said. "Confused. Grateful. So far as I can ascertain, there were no fatal casualties."

"That's good news," Thor said.

"Agreed," Strange replied. "Unfortunately, we cannot remain to accept their hospitality. Are you both ready?"

Thor glanced at Cap. The Avenger looked tired, but he nodded.

"Yes," Thor said. "Let's end this."

SEVENTEEN

THE first thing that Tony noticed when he came back to consciousness was that he was no longer in his armor. A quick look around showed it nowhere in sight. He tried to think back to his last clear moments, with all of the systems failing. He had unlocked it, hadn't he?

He'd made it easy for them.

But he hadn't been able to *breathe…*

Anyway. That was his starting point, and not a good one. He figured he was someplace inside of Capricorn's mansion. It was a nice room, actually, the walls done in expensive tropical woods, a roomy meeting table—sort of like a board room. And maybe it was, because despite being cuffed to the chair he sat in, it looked as if he was in the middle of the meeting, right along with Natasha, who in addition to being fastened to her chair and having her gauntlets removed was also festooned with a whole slew of other restraint devices.

He found it a little insulting that she was so much more tied up than he was.

"How's it going over there, Nat?" he asked.

"Really good," she said sarcastically. "I got a little turned around, is all."

"How about you?" Tony asked the man at the head of the table. "How's your day going? Capricorn, isn't it?"

"My day is developing admirably well," Capricorn said. His "horns" had faded to small, glowing bumps on his forehead. Aside from the woman who sat next to him, he was the only other person in the room.

The woman Tony hadn't seen before. She had mostly silver hair bound up in a bun. Her black, whiteless eyes were about twice the size they ought to be, and little wiggly protrusions like feelers or antennae projected from her cheekbones. Her mouth, on the other hand, was small, and closed in what looked like a permanent grin.

"Glad to hear it," Tony said. "I've got to thank you, actually. I thought the design of my armor was pretty decent, but now it's clear that I have to take it up a notch, especially in the life-support department. I've been thinking about developing a suit for deep space—I think you've given me just the nudge I need."

"Tony," Natasha said. "Watch what you say. The woman, she has some sort of—she can get in your head."

"Is that so?" Tony said, looking at her. "I'm in here already. I don't recommend it, frankly. Not to anyone."

"There's no reason we shouldn't be civilized," Capricorn said. "I welcome a discussion, if there's any chance of it producing useful information."

"Okay," Tony said. "Untying us would be an excellent start to that sort of dialogue."

Capricorn smiled. "You invaded my home and damaged my property. You did harm to many of my employees. I think it's incumbent on you to show good faith before I'm expected to." He leaned toward them. "Why are the two of you here? How have I offended you?"

"You already know that," Natasha said. "The theft in New York. The tablet, the fellow your man Scorpio murdered. I take things like that personally. Tony agreed to help me ferret you out."

"The Black Widow taking things personally?" Capricorn said. "Maybe. But you should know, I'm aware that you've spoken with the Sorcerer Supreme. I expect he told you something about us, albeit a distorted version of things. Even now your friends are attempting to interfere with our affairs elsewhere. So if you could drop the pretense that this is all some sort of vendetta, Natasha Romanoff, we can move on to more productive topics."

"Such as?" Tony asked.

"You Avengers," Capricorn said. "You fight for what? Law? Order? To protect the planet?"

"Something like that," Tony said. "Maybe not in that order."

"What if I told you we are doing the same? That we merely seek to fulfill the cosmic destiny humanity has long been denied?"

"That sounds great," Tony said. "Do you intend to take that to a referendum? Lay out your plan and have everyone vote on it?"

"Now, Mr. Stark, don't be a hypocrite," Capricorn said. "You're a man of vision. How often have you consulted with the masses before making a momentous decision? Do you ask the human race for permission before engaging with what you see as enemies of Earth? No. You take that on yourself, because you think you know better than most." He sat back again. "And you're right, so far as it goes. As are we."

"Yeah, we're exactly the same," Tony said. "You might as well untie me."

"I see," Capricorn said. "Well, if nothing else, can we at least consent to an exchange of information?"

Tony glanced down at his bonds. "Why do I think this will be an unequal exchange?" he said.

"What would you like to know?" Capricorn asked.

"What time is it?"

"What?"

"You took my phone, my watch, all of that. I'm just wondering what time it is. Makes me antsy not to know."

Capricorn laughed softly. "It's 6:34 PM," he said. "Does that relieve your anxiety?"

"Sure," Tony replied. "Okay. Your turn."

"What do you know about the Zodiac?" Capricorn said. "In as much detail as you can."

"Well—it seems like you're the boss."

Capricorn shook his head. "Nice try. Not that it matters, but we each become the 'boss' when our sign is ascendant, in accord with the cosmic order. One person's ego can never dominate the Zodiac. Now. What do you know about us?"

"This morning's paper said your day would start with high hopes, but not to set too much stock in them," Tony said. "Pride cometh before a fall. Also, you should stay away from caffeine and strangers with candy."

Capricorn finally looked a little annoyed.

"Childish," he said. "Although I understand. Humor is a defense mechanism, and you're obviously feeling defensive."

"Let me," the bug-eyed woman said.

Capricorn nodded.

"Ms. Romanoff," he said, "you were briefly acquainted with my colleague, but I fear I failed to make the proper introductions. I'll remedy that now. Mr. Stark, Ms. Romanoff, I present to you Karka of the Shining Herd, known to the Sumerians as Allul. Or as you may know her, Cancer."

The woman rose and approached Tony with her hands clasped behind her back. Her eyes seemed to grow larger as she grew nearer. He tried to tear his gaze away, but couldn't do it for long.

"Relax, Mr. Stark," she said. "This won't be difficult."

As she spoke, something horrifying happened. Her temples began to glow, and something pushed out of them—ghostly appendages, blurry at first, but quickly appearing to become more solid. Jointed limbs like those of an arthropod, terminating in pincers.

Pincers that began extending toward his face.

"I don't mean to doubt you," he said, "but from here it looks like it's going to be *very* difficult."

EIGHTEEN

EMIL watched Monica on the security camera. Besides him, she was the only one in the building, and she was hard at work on—something.

He sighed and eased back in his chair. Everything still hurt, but he couldn't stand the idea of not working; it only emphasized his uselessness in a position he desperately needed.

He suddenly realized that Monica was looking at him, staring directly into the camera. Like she knew he was watching her. He quickly switched the monitor to Tarleton's lab.

A few minutes later, he heard the door to Monica's lab open.

"Mr. Blonsky," she said. "I wonder if I can have a word with you."

Great, he thought. He didn't know how she knew he had been watching her, but she probably had the wrong idea about it. She was an attractive woman, but that wasn't why he'd been keeping tabs. He'd overheard her talking with Banner about possible cures for his condition, and it had gotten him thinking about her work. Science had made the Hulk, hadn't it?

It was only a half-formed idea, but he knew he couldn't share it with her. It was better to let her think he was obsessed with her, although that would also probably get him fired.

He followed her glumly back to her lab, where, surprisingly, she offered him a seat.

"I haven't asked you how you've been," she said. "Since the attack."

"Oh," he said, put a little off-balance. Maybe this wasn't going where he thought it had been headed at all. "I've been fine. The doctors say there is nothing wrong with me a little time won't heal."

She smiled, slightly. "Is that true?" she asked.

"If the doctors say so," he said.

"Your body will heal," she said. "I'm worried about the rest of you."

"I don't understand."

She sighed. "I know this is difficult for you," she said. "I know about your past, or at least some of it. When I met you, you had a certain... confidence. I don't see that now."

His heart sank. So this was going exactly where he'd thought it was going.

"I have asked for more resources," he said. "I proposed more aggressive defenses—"

"Of course you did," Monica said. "Because you are excellent at your job. You had the foresight to understand something like what happened was perhaps inevitable. We... I... didn't listen as well as I could have. That was my mistake. But I've been thinking about your request. About the need for more—uncompromising—security measures. And I think I might have at least one option that might interest you."

"I should like to hear that," he said.

She nodded. "Look here," she said, pointing to a piece of equipment.

He had seen it before. It reminded him a bit of some sort of fancy aquarium, a big steel rectangular box with a transparent face. It had various ports for long plastic gloves and robotic arms to operate within it without exposing its contents to the air.

"This is called a barrier isolator," she said. "I use it to cultivate various cells and tissues. As you may know, I'm keenly interested in curing illness, and the like."

"Yes," he said. "That's very good."

She nodded, reaching her arms into a pair of the long gloves. She opened a metal box and took out an opaque black tube. She opened it and, using a dropper, put a tiny bit of liquid on a slide underneath a digital microscope. Then she pointed to a screen overhead. It showed various globs, brightly lit. All were a faint green color.

"These are stem cells," she said. "Do you know what stem cells are?"

"No," he replied. "Not entirely."

"They are undifferentiated cells. Each of these could become a skin cell, or a neuron, or a part of your bone marrow. Any cell in your body."

"I'll take your word for it," Emil said.

"But these are special, even for stem cells," she said. "Do you want to know how?"

For a moment, he feared to say anything. But then he decided, what the hell.

"They're green," he said. "Are they from Banner—ah, the Hulk?"

"That's a good guess," she said. "And not far off, but no. I made these myself, combining gamma radiation with... something else. It took me a long time to get the results I wanted. In the end, it was the Terrigen Crystals that unlocked the puzzle." She withdrew her arms from the machine.

"But you don't care about that," she added. "You care about results."

The skin of his scalp was tingling. Was she getting at what he thought she was?

"What results?" he asked.

"The Hulk was created through an uncontrolled exposure to gamma rays," she said. "The result was, as you know, similarly uncontrolled. With these stem cells, I believe I can achieve similar results—but controlled. Better."

"Like the Hulk?"

"Better, I said. Stronger. And without the unfortunate side effects—the diminishment of the intellect. Imagine what you could do if you had all of the knowledge you've acquired over the years—all of the skills—but also the strength, the speed, the invulnerability of the Hulk."

"Are you—are you offering me that?" he asked.

"Perhaps," she said. "In time. I only meant this as a preliminary conversation about the future. To go to human trials at this stage—"

"But you think it will work?" he demanded.

"I'm certain of it," she said. "But at this stage, others might object. Bruce, George—they wouldn't understand."

"They don't have to know," Emil said. "If it works, you are vindicated, yes? And if it doesn't, there is no one to know."

She frowned. "That's true," she said.

"Then please, I'm willing to try it," he said. "I've nothing to lose."

"If I'm wrong, you could lose your life," she said.

"Like I said," Emil replied. "I have nothing to lose."

She was silent for a long time, gazing over at the barrier isolator. "You are sure about this?" she said.

"As certain as I've ever been about anything," he replied.

She closed her eyes. He could see the conflict.

Then she sighed. "We can begin," she said. "Slowly. But if there are any contraindications, I must insist on stopping immediately."

"Yes, of course," Blonsky said.

Her gaze met his. "You can tell no one," she said. "This must be our secret."

"I can keep a secret," he said.

NINETEEN

THE sand and spray, the blue sea and supple palms were replaced by the scent of evergreen needles and towering forest, moss-covered logs and stones, cerulean sky studded with clouds. All seemed very still, as if the group had been transported not just through space but back in time, to some primordial forest in which no human had ever set foot.

Steve resisted the illusion. Each time Strange teleported them to a new place, an ambush had been waiting for them. There was no reason to think this time would be any different. The lack of birdsong might be because their unnatural arrival had frightened the nearby animals to quiet, but it was just as likely they were silent because others had already come this way.

"Which direction?" he asked.

Strange stood still for a moment, eyes closed.

"That way," he said, pointing.

The air was cool, almost cold, as they made their way through the hushed woodland. The land rose up steadily until they reached a steep fern-covered incline sloping down from a high hill. It looked as if it had been formed by a mudslide, but given the size of some of the trees on it, that must have been some time ago.

The base of the hill had been excavated, recently and violently, revealing a dark tunnel leading in. Steam drifted up from the edges of the opening.

"Always ahead of us, aren't they?" Thor said.

"Maybe not too far ahead," Strange replied.

The tunnel went no more than a few yards, and they entered what must have once been a large wooden structure. Sand and mud had washed into it over the years, and in some places the ancient cedar planks had split, but it had clearly once been an impressive building, several times longer than it had been wide. Elaborate wooden masks combining human and animal features stared down at them from the walls.

"It reminds me of a Northman mead hall," Thor said.

"Tlingit, I believe," Strange said.

"Were they into the Zodiac, too?" Steve asked.

"Not that I know of," Strange replied, "but in times gone by, they were sensitive to the powers of this land. They may have built in this place because the well was here. They may have abandoned it for the same reason."

"This one is the real deal?" Steve asked.

"Unlike those we've encountered thus far, this one feels— vigorous," Strange said.

"I don't see anything," Thor said. "Although there is something weird about this place. As if a spirit haunts it."

Strange didn't answer, but his amulet opened, and once again the Eye floated out and attached itself to his forehead.

"Let what is hidden be seen," the sorcerer intoned.

Light flooded the chamber, pushing all of the shadows into the corners of the longhouse. Right in the middle something persisted, like smoke, or a film upon water. It formed a slight curve in all directions, seeming to be a sphere, although most of it extended through the walls of the structure and into the earth outside. It vibrated slightly, like the strand of a spider's web with a fly caught in it. The "sphere" was largely featureless—except just in front of them, where it appeared to have a seam in it, as if it had been sliced open and glued back together.

"That's the portal?" Thor asked.

"Not exactly a portal," Strange said. "As I said earlier, it is more like a pocket dimension, with no real entrance or exit. When they are old, and unstable, they sometimes rift open, but the resulting doorway doesn't take you anywhere except inside the well. It's not a hall connecting two rooms, but more like a closet with only one way in and out. This one is rather young, and highly stable, so it is essentially a closet into which no one built a door at all. To enter, the wall must be sliced open or smashed in—and even so, it quickly repairs itself."

"So this line here?" Steve asked.

"That's where they went in," Strange replied. "They used an extraordinary amount of energy to do so. Released it all at once, almost like a bomb. I can still feel the aftereffects of it. Energy not of Earthly origin."

"Tarleton's crystals."

"Yes," Strange replied.

"So how do we get in?" Steve said. "I don't think we can get the crystals delivered that fast."

"No," Strange said, "but we have something similar." He looked pointedly at Thor. "We need a powerful surge of force, channeled properly. I can provide the channel. The energy itself must come from elsewhere. Like, for instance, from a weapon forged in the heart of a dying star."

"Mjolnir and I are at your disposal." He glanced at the ceiling, the fine roots pushing through the rafters and hanging down like hair. "I'd best go outside, though," he said. "If I'm to catch some proper lightning."

A few moments later Steve heard the wind pick up, and the creak of the tall trees bending in winds to which they were not accustomed. Meanwhile, Doctor Strange did his own hocus-pocus, painting glowing symbols with his fingers and tracing a circle around the seams on the well.

"Any time now," Strange said, finally. "Captain, you should step aside."

He took the sorcerer's advice, pressing against the nearest wall.

A moment later a bolt of lightning flashed through the tunnel, into the buried longhouse, twisting itself into the air next to Strange, sputtering against the curved edge of the well. Unlike the usual lightning bolt, this one continued to flare for several long heartbeats, strobing the chamber so shadows danced like ancient spectres.

Then, slowly, seemingly reluctantly, seams in the air split open. As the crackle of electricity faded, a new, stranger light seeped through those widening cracks, glowing with a color on which Steve found it hard to focus. As he watched, it grew to fill the circle Strange had sketched.

"Quickly," the sorcerer said. "It will not stay open long."

Steve didn't see any point in hesitating. He took a couple of steps, and then jumped through.

It wasn't like Strange's teleportation. It was more like he'd run through a giant cobweb, and some of it was still sticking to him, cloying at his face and sucking into his nostrils. When he brought his hands up to brush the sticky strands away, there was nothing really there. Even so, he couldn't see very well, so he stood still, waiting for the others. As he did, his vision cleared.

The sky was that weird color he'd just seen—maybe gray, maybe green, not really either.

The landscape was equally outlandish. The curve of the horizon was very near in every direction, as if they were at the top of a steeply rounded hill. The ground was relatively smooth and covered in some sort of very flat moss or perhaps lichen. All around them peculiar rock formations thrust up. They tended to be thick at the base, narrowing as they rose, but then often expanding outward as they went higher. They looked precarious, and seemed to defy gravity. A bit higher than the highest of the formations, what he at first took for clouds drifted by, but then he realized they were actually big rocks sailing along. They looked like the tops of some of the rock formations that might have broken off and gone into orbit.

They were "orbiting" maybe forty feet above the surface.

Steve felt a little weird, too. Dizzy, and like something was sort of pulling him—as if his head was lighter than his feet. It reminded him of lying on a playground merry-go-round when he was a kid, with his feet out at the rim and his head near the center.

"The Key is here," Doctor Strange said from behind. Thor followed. "I can feel its presence, but cannot determine exactly where it is."

"Do you think they have it already?" Steve asked. "The Zodiac?"

"I don't know," Strange said, "but I suspect..." He trailed off, looking around. "They're here."

"Where?"

Steve's question answered itself, at least partially, as the flash of a familiar-looking arrow appeared, streaking down from one of the tallest rock formations. Before he could move a muscle, Strange summoned a glowing blue disk of energy and deflected the deadly missile. Then Steve saw Sagittarius perched up there, loading another of his energy darts.

The Archer wasn't alone. Virgo stepped out from behind another stone column, snapping her whip toward Thor, while Leo and Taurus charged across the curved ground toward them.

"Captain," Strange shouted. "They haven't found the Key yet. There must be at least one more of them here, searching for it."

"While these four keep us occupied," Steve said. "Strange, can you find it?"

"I can better serve here," Strange said. "Scorpio intended for the Zodiac to find the Key once they reached this place. It should be in an obvious location, with some sort of sign. This universe isn't large. You have as much chance of finding it as I would. Go!"

"What, wait—" But then he felt a sense of dislocation, and suddenly he was looking at Strange and Thor from a distance, watching the three Zodiac members close in on them. Before he could take a step back in their direction, a hazy orange dome appeared above everyone else.

Strange and Thor were sealed in with the Zodiac, to give Steve the space to find the Key.

Only he and Sagittarius remained outside of the dome. The Archer drifted across the sky in a slow arc, firing arrows at him. At this range they were easy enough to dodge or deflect, but it meant he had to keep one eye on the fellow.

He ducked behind a rock formation, eyeballing the distance, thinking about throwing his shield—but something held him back. Sagittarius hadn't shown any ability to fly before, and Steve didn't think he was flying now. He wasn't in control of the motion, either; he just kept moving in the same direction. Gravity was funny here, but it wasn't clear *how* funny. If he threw his shield at Sagittarius, would he be able to get it back, or would it just keep going?

Not willing to take the chance, he decided just to get out of the Archer's line of sight. That proved easier to do than he might have expected; he just ran at right angles to the bowman's arc across the sky. Within a matter of moments, Sagittarius was behind the horizon.

Then Steve realized that they weren't at the top of a hill. They were on a very small planet. Or an asteroid.

Scientists had known about asteroids when he went into the ice, but no telescope back then had been powerful enough to show what they looked like. Most everyone had assumed they were spherical, like planets. Later, as he lay in hibernation, space probes went out and found out that most asteroids were irregular lumps. This asteroid—if that's what it was—was more like those early ideas. Round as a marble. Weirder still, it seemed as if the gravity on the surface was as strong as Earth's—but once you left the surface it weakened very quickly.

Yet they weren't in outer space. They were in what Strange called a pocket dimension. It seemed likely the rules that governed his universe just didn't apply here. It bore thinking about, but maybe not too much.

What was important was finding the Key.

So he ran around the little planet, searching the near horizon for clues.

○————————○

"HA!" Thor said. "You've caged them in with us!"

"And us in with them," Strange cautioned.

"We'll see who likes that least," Thor said, hurling his hammer at Leo, who was only a few yards away. The fellow tried to dodge, but Mjolnir hit him square, lifting him off the ground and hurling him back. He saw Strange summoning shields and turning to confront Virgo and her whip. That left him Taurus.

The bull-woman stamped, but this time Thor was ready, leaping high to avoid the crushing gravity of her attack. That worked, but he got more than he bargained for; his leap carried him far higher than expected, so that he slammed into Strange's magical barrier. There was no pain aside from that of the impact, as if he'd hit a solid wall, but the rebound sent him drifting in an arc, not plummeting back toward the ground.

As he looked around, he saw why. The planetoid below was small, probably less than a league in diameter, and its natural gravitational pull tapered off quickly. A belt of large rocks floated around the small world. In the distance, he could see the Captain, running, and Sagittarius, floating across the sky, shooting at him.

Holding out his hand, he waited for Mjolnir to return as he watched Taurus leap toward him.

He twisted to grapple her, but when their hands met he suddenly *did* fall—not with the weight of one Earth's gravity, but with that of several. As he plummeted he caught Mjolnir, but he didn't have time to whirl the weapon before he struck the surface of the planetoid, hard. The packed stone didn't yield to his body, and the impact very nearly left him senseless. Then the lion was back in the battle, arcing toward him, burning claws bared. Thor managed to get up and hurl his hammer again, but this time Leo twisted aside and kept coming.

Thor didn't bother to block Leo's punch—he just threw one of his own. That usually worked against strong opponents, like the Hulk. Leo had proven to be strong, but nothing special.

At least not the last time they'd met. This time the lion-man's blow felt as if it came from a greater rock troll. It sent him back four uneven steps. Fortunately, his own punch had had the same effect on his opponent.

Except that Leo wasn't bleeding from a chest wound, and Thor was. The cat-man's claws hadn't cut deep, but they had cut through his hauberk and into the skin.

Leo came back at him, feinting a high punch and then dropping low, going for his legs—trying to hamstring him—but Thor ducked along with him, putting his opponent's head in Mjolnir's return path. The hammer struck Leo's skull with an almost metallic sound, and the fellow dropped with a grunt. He was still alive, but he didn't get up right away. Mjolnir should have split his skull like a walnut.

Strange had Virgo bound in some sort of sorcerous bands. Taurus was standing, and looked like she was charging the Sorcerer Supreme, but a moment's observation showed that she wasn't actually moving, instead frozen like a statue. The sorcerer had not been idle.

"I've got these," Strange said. "I'm dropping the barrier—you go help Captain America."

"Are you sure?" Thor asked. "You seem weary."

As he spoke, the orange glow above them faded.

"I'm still the Sorcerer Supreme," Strange said, "and they are still mortal, albeit barely so. If their companion finds the Key…"

"I understand."

Leo began to stir where he'd fallen, trying to get up.

"One thing first," Thor said.

Picking Leo up, Thor heaved him onto his shoulders, spun a few times, and threw him off toward the horizon. He laughed as the lion-man flew up, and then kept on going, curving above the tiny planet's surface, dwindling until he was just a speck.

He began to whirl his hammer.

"Thor!" Strange shouted. "Take a lesson from what you just did. The escape velocity of this planetoid is negligible."

"Oh," Thor said, letting his hammer slow. "Yes, of course." He'd been in outer space before, without the benefit of gravity or within the pull of very faint gravity. It wasn't impossible to navigate a flight path in such conditions, but it could be complicated. He might lose time.

So instead he began trotting, then sprinting in the direction he'd last seen Captain America.

TWENTY

STRANGE had said the sign probably wouldn't be subtle, and it wasn't.

Captain America had first seen it rising like a moon on the horizon—which he supposed it was, since it seemed to be orbiting the planet. Although it at first appeared to be a sphere, it wasn't—rather, it was a disk. It had been extensively carved, divided like a pie into twelve sections, and in each section was a symbol. Some, like the horned sign that looked like a bull's head, were familiar to him. Others were not, but there could be little doubt that they represented the Zodiac, albeit an older version of it than the one his aunt used to look at in the papers.

The problem was, the disk wasn't attached to the ground, but was instead in a low orbit around the planet, spinning on its axis and gradually flipping like a tossed coin.

Standing a few dozen yards in front of him, back turned to him and also staring at the weird moon, was Scorpio.

That was an assumption, but Steve felt it was a pretty safe one. The scale of the planet made everything difficult to judge, but the man looked big—head taller than Steve, maybe more. He wore a sort of kilt-like affair and a wrapped shirt that left his shoulders and arms exposed. His skin was blue-black, and even from this distance Steve could see that it wasn't so much skin as chitinous plates. A segmented tail curved up from a slit in his garment and arced above his hairless head.

Steve took a step toward him.

Scorpio turned and looked over his shoulder. Then he began to run toward a sharply sloping ridge of stone that lay ahead.

Steve ran, too, hurling his shield without even pausing. It struck Scorpio below the knees, sending him stumbling to the ground. He was nearly back on his feet when Steve reached him, but by then he'd figured out what Scorpio was up to, so he didn't stop to fight. Instead he kept running, bending down slightly to collect his shield.

"No!" Scorpio shouted behind him. He felt a strong, hot wind strike his back, but he ignored it, running up the slope of the ridge until he reached the top. From there, he jumped.

On Earth, he would have flown forward a bit and then come back down. Here, his speed carried him toward the orbiting disk, because his brisk run and his vault from the ridge had achieved escape velocity. He'd timed it right, too, so his path would enable him to reach the coin-shaped moon.

Out of the corner of his eye he saw a flash of light, and realized that Sagittarius was back in sight, still drifting along above the planet's surface. Steve awkwardly tried to turn, managing to get his shield between him and the energy bolt. Everything went white as it struck, and agony went up his left arm.

Sagittarius's arrows were getting stronger.

He blinked, fighting for consciousness, and saw that despite the force of the projectile he was almost upon the disk. He tucked and curled and hit it feet first, which proved to be a mistake. If the "moon" possessed gravity it was negligible, so the impact bounced him back away from it.

He deflected the next arrow rather than blocking it directly. That still stung, but it didn't threaten to knock him out. Flailing, he tried to fight his way back to the Zodiac disk. That didn't work, but fortunately it was flipping toward him a little faster than he had bounced away from it, and in a few seconds it caught up with him. He curled under his shield as the giant coin continued to turn. Sagittarius got off a few more shots before the disk blocked his line of sight.

Grabbing onto the carved surface, Steve pulled himself toward the axis. He was held on by a very slight simulacrum of gravity caused by the end-over-end motion. While it shielded him from his opponent, the disk's spin on its axis pushed him toward the rim. Even so, as long as he held tight to the carved surface, he could "climb" to the center, where he hoped the Key was.

So intent was he on his purpose that he didn't see Scorpio drifting toward him until he was nearly there.

Steve somersaulted toward the center, keeping a grip on the carvings with one hand. The scorpion sting sank into the stone with a hissing sound. Bracing his foot in a groove in the disk, he launched himself back, snapping a punch into his attacker's face. It felt like hitting a football helmet, but it had the desired effect of sending Scorpio flying away from the moon. The reaction sent Steve skidding back toward the center, still in contact with the stone.

He hurled his shield, but Scorpio twisted wildly and managed to avoid it. The moon kept turning, and soon the Zodiac chief would be back in contact with it—Steve had a few seconds at best. He was only yards away from the axis when he felt a sudden heat pressing on him from every direction. His mouth became dry, and he couldn't swallow; every breath burned his lungs like flame. He remembered Natasha's encounter back in New York, how the man she'd been trying to interrogate had been both envenomed and dehydrated.

"You needn't die, Captain," Scorpio said, still floating, reaching toward the stone once more. "But you will, if you don't stop. The Key is mine, by any conceivable measure."

Steve's abdomen started to cramp, and he was light-headed. He recognized the symptoms—he was dehydrating, fast. In moments he would be too weak to move.

But he didn't need moments. He was almost there. The center of the disk had a hole bored through it, a few feet in diameter. He couldn't see inside, but was close enough to push his hand in. He did so, feeling his lips begin to split. Gripping the hole, he pulled himself closer.

Glancing behind, he saw Scorpio inches from the stone.

Managing to pull himself into the shaft, Steve found himself staring into the empty eyes of a skull. The rest of the skeleton was there, too, pulled apart and fused like a fossil into the substance of the disk, so that the ribcage outlined the shaft.

"Scorpio senior, I presume," Cap grunted as his vision began to fail. He reached for the golden object that was clutched in one half-melted, calcified hand.

The Key.

It felt cold to the touch. He closed his fist on it.

Behind him, he heard Scorpio gasp.

"No!"

Just the touch of it made him feel better, like taking a long, cool drink. His thirst eased, the heat backed off, and his head began to clear as he pulled the Key from the frozen fingers.

It was bigger than he'd expected, almost a yard long. The depictions of it had been pretty accurate; it did look like an ankh, a cross with a loop on top, with crosspieces bending. He withdrew from the tunnel, brandishing it at Scorpio.

"This what you're looking for?"

Scorpio snarled and leapt at him, his tail arching down toward Steve's head. He covered with his shield and batted the tail away with the Key, but the collision sent both of them tumbling away from the coin-shaped moon. No longer worried about trying to stay on the disk, Steve slammed Scorpio's head with the shield and kicked with both feet, shooting away from him...

...and right back into Sagittarius's line of sight. A string of the actinic arrows flashed toward him. The Key throbbed in his fist, and he heard what sounded like distant voices in another language, shouting at him, telling him to *do* something. He could feel the almost limitless potential in his hands, but he had no idea how to command it.

The first of the Archer's arrows struck his shield, detonating into an energy discharge. He didn't feel anything, though. The Key seemed to be protecting him. With each second he held it he felt more powerful. If he could just figure out how to control it actively instead of passively…

His push had sent him directly toward one of the orbiting chunks of rock. He turned, hit it with his feet, and kicked toward the planetoid's surface. He needed to find Thor and Strange; then they could decide what to do next.

In his hand the Key throbbed, glowing brighter and brighter.

Suddenly he heard another voice in his mind; this one he understood, and even recognized.

You must hurry, Strange said. *Now that the Key is free of its confinement, they are all growing stronger. Much stronger. I am having trouble detaining them.*

He felt weird just *thinking* a reply, and spoke aloud.

"It's okay," he said. "I'm on my way back."

You aren't attuned to it, Strange replied. *Scorpio is. He might be able to use it, even if he isn't touching it. Hurry.*

"Use it h—?" Steve asked.

He got his answer before the words were even out of his mouth. One of the big rocks—no, *several* of them—came flying toward him. Not moving in orbit as before, but propelled under power. Sagittarius stood on one of them, Leo on another.

Coming at him faster than either was a third boulder, this one carrying Scorpio.

Looking around, he saw nothing to push against to alter his course. He seemed to be falling toward the planetoid, but not rapidly. He reached toward it and felt a pull on his arm. His arc downward grew shorter, but he still wasn't falling fast enough. He was about to get caught between three rocks and a hard place.

Then, ahead, he saw one of the taller rock formations. He wasn't quite going to hit it, but if he could change course just a little, he could manage it. There was only one way he could figure how to do that.

Every action had an equal and opposite reaction. Newton's third law, the principle upon which rockets flew. He wasn't a rocket, but could get the same effect by throwing something in the direction opposite of where he wanted to go.

Steve had only two things to throw.

He let his shield loose at Leo; he was closest, and the angle was right. That changed Steve's course just enough that he would come very close to the rock formation. If he could get hold of that, he could return to the surface, where the gravity was strong enough to actually allow him to *fight*.

Leo roared. A column of stellar energy shot from his mouth and struck the shield, deflecting it and sending it off into a higher orbit. That was bad, but there was no use dwelling on it, since Steve was about to miss the rock. It was still just out of reach of his hand.

But not of the Key. He swung the artifact, so the curved crosspiece scratched and then caught in a crevice in the stone. He yanked hard, and swung around so he was standing on solid rock. From there he dove toward the surface.

It was a weird fall, because at first he went slowly. Only in the last fifteen feet did he start to pick up speed. He landed almost softly, as if he'd jumped from the roof of a single-story building.

Using the Key he batted aside several more energy arrows, but all three of the Zodiac thugs were converging on him. The stones they were riding came falling from the sky like slow-motion meteors. He scrambled to outrun them, but one of Leo's blasts caught the ground near his feet. The eruption sent him tumbling, and before he could get his footing to dodge, Scorpio's stony mount hit him with the force of a car going at city speed, knocking him up and over. He managed a flip and landed on his feet, but Leo and his asteroid were right there...

Until the stone was suddenly blasted into bits.

Leo went tumbling into the sand.

A hammer came whistling by over Steve's head.

Thor had arrived. He hurled Mjolnir again, but Sagittarius leapt from his rock and sent three arrows flashing at the thunder god. The first two missed, but the third hit him squarely in the chest, exploding and sending Thor sprawling on the lichen-covered stone.

In Steve's grip the Key began quivering, pulling his hand, pointing toward the fallen god of thunder. Before Thor could get up the stone beneath suddenly became viscous, engulfing him like pudding, and then hardened again, leaving the thunder god with only his head and one of his feet visible.

"What?" Steve muttered. He hadn't done that.

Then his own feet began sinking. He leapt up; it was like jumping from a tub full of taffy, but he made it—or thought he had, until, in mid-flight, the air itself seemed to jerk him forward. Toward Scorpio.

Strange was right. He might be holding the Key, but Scorpio was its master.

Steve tumbled in the air as the scorpion's wicked sting flashed at him. His feet hit ground again and he lashed out with an uppercut that popped Scorpio's head back. A glimpse from his peripheral vision warned him to turn, just as Leo's claws slashed through the standing stone behind him. Off-balance, he lashed out with the Key.

And Scorpio caught it, by the loop end. Steve yanked back, but the Zodiac chief was terribly strong. Leo was turning for another run at him, and Sagittarius was taking aim.

He planted his feet and swung Scorpio into the line of the oncoming arrow, shielding himself from the flare of light and heat. Scorpio rasped out a rough cry, but *still* he kept hold of the Key. It pulsed, growing brighter. Scorpio's grip was fiercer than ever, and the Key felt slippery in Steve's grasp, as if it were made of wet soap.

Suddenly, it wasn't there at all.

It was as if it had become liquid in his hand, then vapor, then nothing. He felt a deep, powerful vibration, as if a bell the size of the planetoid had been struck, and for a few heartbeats a rainbow's worth of color obscured his vision. When he could see again, Scorpio stood over him, looking two feet taller, grasping the object of his desire. His toothless smile did not look human at all. He stooped forward, his tail arching over. Then he looked up and beyond Steve.

Just before Thor crashed into him.

The Asgardian was like a whirlwind, lashing out everywhere at once, sending Leo hurling back into the weird sky, striking lightning through Sagittarius and landing blow after staggering blow on Scorpio, who fell back. Steve scrambled up, ready to dive in. Clearly, it wasn't too late. Scorpio had the Key, but Strange had said that wasn't the end, that the "alignment" had yet to happen.

Before he could reach the fight, however, Scorpio struck back, hammering Thor on the side of the head, using the Key like a club. As the thunder god stumbled, a pulse of light strobed out from the golden object, engulfing him. His limbs seemed to twist in its light; his cape unraveled, became thread, drifting in the wind.

Howling, Thor staggered one step toward Scorpio, and then another, even though it looked almost as if he, too, was evaporating.

The light faded. Scorpio shot up into the air.

"Not yet, Asgardian," he said, "but your time will come." He raised his arms wide, lifting the Key—and then was gone. Leo winked out of existence behind him. A quick look around showed no sign of Sagittarius.

Gripping his hammer, Thor stared at where Scorpio had vanished. Then he looked at Steve.

"Strange!" he said. "We must find him!"

They found the sorcerer where they had left him, floating a foot or so off the ground with his legs crossed, that weird third eye of his blinking curiously from his forehead. When they drew near, his other two eyes opened.

"They have the Key," he said.

Steve nodded. "I had it. I had it in my hands."

"I underestimated them." Strange sighed. "Even knowing what I knew."

"We shouldn't have split up," Steve said. "If we'd had Tony and Natasha—"

"And Banner," Thor said.

"Yeah," Steve nodded, "but that's all hindsight now. We fix that mistake. We get the others, figure out where they're going to do this thing of theirs, and put an end to all of this."

"Yes," Thor agreed. "They are stronger than they were, but no match for all of the Avengers. Of that I am certain."

"It's an excellent plan," Strange said, "but there is one modest problem."

"What's that?" Steve asked.

"I'm afraid we're trapped here."

TWENTY-ONE

NATASHA knew exactly what was happening to Tony Stark, and she didn't envy him at all. Cancer's claws dug deep, and when she wanted to know something, it was impossible not to speak. She knew that firsthand.

The only upside was that if Cancer didn't know exactly which questions to ask, she couldn't get the answers—not if you had been conditioned like Natasha, anyway.

Tony's training hadn't been quite so extensive. He answered every question Cancer posed, and then some. Oddly, only a few of those questions were about the Zodiac, the AIM labs, what the other Avengers were up to, or Tarleton's power source.

They were nearly all about Bruce Banner.

When they were done, Tony was in the same near comatose state from which Natasha was still emerging.

Cancer nodded toward her.

"Shall I question her again?" she asked. "Now that we know more?"

Capricorn leveled his gaze at her. "I don't know," he replied. "Ms. Romanoff, do you have anything to add?"

"Not yet," she said. "Check back with me later."

"Of course," he replied.

"But I do have a question," she said.

"Ask it, by all means."

"I don't understand your curiosity about the Hulk," she said. "A couple of your guys tangled with him, I know, but he's out of this. He's no danger to you."

"No, we're aware of that," Capricorn said. "This has to do with things which are, I'm afraid, far over your head. Ancient prophecies and all that."

"Horoscopes, you mean?"

"Your interrogation skills are legendary, Ms. Romanoff. You seek to provoke me into revealing something you could use, should you escape this place. Now I must tell you, I have every confidence you will not escape, but I am not so foolish as to believe it impossible, especially knowing what I do of you. So I leave you with your curiosity on the subject."

"Yet you've already told me something," she said. "You guys screwed up last time. Back in the Bronze Age, wasn't it? Screwed it up so bad you're three thousand years overdue for a second try. I wonder what happened? As I understand it, the woman who was Sorcerer Supreme stopped you from carrying out your by-the-stars plan. Last time I checked, we still have a Sorcerer Supreme—so even if you get this Key thing, you're still playing a game you've already lost once, and there's a better-than-even chance you'll lose again.

"So you've been checking the stars for a few thousand years," she continued, "tossing your knucklebones, opening fortune cookies, all of that. And from all that, you figured you needed something different this time—an ace in the hole, yes? But you didn't know what it *was*. You weren't expecting the Hulk to be at the AIM labs, but when you ran into him, all of your stargazing made sense.

"You need him to make this work."

Cancer stepped closer, her claws stretching out.

"How did she—"

"Quiet!" Capricorn thundered. "She's playing you."

Natasha made a point of looking crestfallen. In fact she was, a bit. She had hoped to get a little more out of them—but now she knew her guess was right.

○———————————○

AROUND two in the morning, Emil checked all of the cameras, and brought up the video feed from Rappaccini's lab. He cut the live feed and set up a loop with a false time stamp. Then he got up from his station and made his way into Monica's lab. Everything was quiet. The day had been a noisy one, full of workmen he didn't know, the growling of machines, the screech of saws cutting wood and pipe.

The major repairs were done, including the walls the Hulk had smashed. They had only been primed, not painted, so there remained a huge white blotch signifying Emil's failure. The surveillance system still had some bugs in it, as well. One of the nexus boxes had been damaged, and a power surge they hadn't noticed before had led, over the course of two days, to a cascade of failures that resulted in a partial collapse of their computing systems.

In other words, security was in a shambles. A new computer system had already arrived from Stark Industries, one with five times the computing power of the old one, but it was still in boxes. Until it was up and running they were stuck with security roughly equivalent to that of a shopping mall in the 1980s.

Monica was in the lab, waiting for him.

"None of this will be recorded," he said. "I've scrubbed the record of our last conversation, too."

"Good," she replied. "I'm glad you understand. Have a seat," she said, motioning.

He sat down in the chair. Banner's chair.

"I should warn you that the process will likely be painful," she said, gently. "You will experience disorientation, nausea, vomiting. It's not going to be fun."

"I understand that. Just so long as it works."

"As we discussed earlier, I can't promise that either," Rappaccini warned. "This is an experiment. You must see it in that light. It might not work out at all. I need to know you understand that."

"I do. How will it—what will happen?"

"We'll start with eight injections," she said. "The most painful will be in your spinal column. I have some local anesthetic, but nothing to put you under."

"That's okay," he said. "Pain and I are old friends. Do you perhaps have a mouthguard? I do not care to bite off my tongue."

"Yes," she said. "I have one."

"And will I be like him? Green?"

"I can't say for certain," she said. "This first round of injections should improve you—make you stronger, more durable, that sort of thing. But I do not believe it will alter your appearance. Later treatments might, but we can discuss that again when we reach that point."

He nodded.

"You still want to try this?" she said.

"I do," Emil replied.

TWENTY-TWO

UNDERSTANDING gradually came back to Tony. He'd not really been unconscious—Cancer's depredations weren't that merciful. She had literally picked his mind to pieces, making his throat and voice box produce noises without his permission.

He remembered the questions—about Strange, what he'd told them, what he knew about the Zodiac, what the Avengers' plans were. But there had been more, hadn't there? Something about Bruce, and Tarleton's energy source?

Tony tried not to answer at first, but as it went on it was as if he had ten different brains, all detached from one another. As if each question created a new Tony Stark, a smaller one, with just the knowledge of the particular thing he was being asked. Ten voices talking at once, not listening to one another, all of them him.

And none of them him.

Eventually he lost all understanding of—everything. Nothing remained but lights, shapes, textures, pain…

Now it was coming back. As if his operating system had been wiped and was now reloading itself. He was still in the conference room, and Natasha was still with him. Capricorn and Cancer were nowhere to be seen, although there were abundant guards. He located his tongue and tried to use it, but it was like an alien organism had camped out in his throat.

"Just wait," Natasha said. "It'll get easier. It'll wear off. You'll be yourself again."

That was hard to believe, he thought—but Nat should know, shouldn't she?

Okay, he tried to say, although it came out more like "*Awghhh.*"

"Heads up," Natasha murmured.

His neck was shaking but he managed to follow her gaze.

Capricorn and Cancer returned.

"Mr. Stark, Ms. Romanoff," Capricorn said. "I'm happy to inform you that no further conversation is needed between us. Between what you told us and the good news we've just received, I'm certain anything you might have managed to hold back will be superfluous. Our business is therefore concluded."

"So nice of you to say goodbye," Natasha said.

"I wouldn't think of leaving without seeing you off first," Capricorn said. "It would be irresponsible of me. Mr. Shen and Mr. Wells will now shoot each of you in the head several times. I'm sorry if that seems blunt, but I've learned over the years it's best to be honest when possible."

Two of his men started toward them. Tony heaved in a breath, struggling against vocal cords that didn't want to work.

"In wone worg," he grunted. "Key is uzlez."

Capricorn signed to his men.

"I'm sorry, Mr. Stark?"

"The... Key..." he said, speaking slowly, trying to get each syllable out. "I found... frequency. Rig... rigged phase interrupter. On satellite. When you try... to use it for your big number... kablooie. Overload. Like before."

"He's lying," Cancer said. "There was nothing like that in his mind."

"You... asked the wrong questions," Tony said.

Capricorn cocked his head, and looked from Tony to Natasha.

"I'm sure he is lying," Capricorn said. "I would too, if I were him. To extend my life. But let's consider the situation. The other Avengers aren't coming to their rescue. Scorpio is in possession of the Key. The conjunction has not yet begun." He paused, then added, "We can afford to keep them here for a bit longer. I will inform Scorpio of this new intelligence, and he can look into it. If there is indeed some sort of device designed to affect the Key, he can probably detect it, and you can go back into Mr. Stark with much more specific questions. Yes?"

"I could do it now," Cancer said.

"He might die before we learn enough," Capricorn said. "Better to let his mind recover a bit. In the meantime, I will report to Scorpio."

Cancer stared at him for a few heartbeats.

"He hid something from me," she said. "Nothing important, I'm sure, but there was something to which I couldn't quite turn his mind." She leaned forward, staring at her prisoner. "Next time it will be easier," she told Tony. "You will not survive, but I will get what I need. And it is a very unpleasant way to die. I've been there, firsthand, feeling what you will feel."

"I have to tell you," Tony said, "you're an excellent conversationalist. Really."

Capricorn shrugged and left the room. Cancer hung back, eying him, and then took a seat.

A few minutes passed, and Tony began to feel better. Not in great shape, by any means—but better. He turned to look at Natasha.

"Do you know what time it is?" he asked.

"You keep asking that," she said. "No."

"Right," he said. "But if I've called this right, it's probably about time."

"For what?"

He looked up at the ceiling.

"Well, maybe not," he said. "I might be off—wait, hang on—"

The ceiling exploded.

Imploded?

Something blew a hole in it. It came down right in the middle of the conference table, blasting wooden shrapnel in every direction. For the first few seconds there was so much dust Tony couldn't make much out, but he didn't have to.

"Get down," he told Natasha. Then he kicked back so his chair flipped over.

One of the gunmen yelled something in Mandarin. That was followed by gunfire, deafeningly loud in the enclosed space.

"Targets Stark and Romanoff null," Tony yelled. "Everyone else is fair game."

"*Understood, sir,*" JARVIS said.

The whine and blast of repulsors joined the gunfire.

As the air cleared, Tony saw the missile had buried itself head-down in the floor, and the sides had opened like the petals of a metal flower. Autoguns mounted at the base swept the room, but the real beauty stood revealed in the center.

A suit.

Capricorn's gunmen saw it, too. Bullets spanged from it as its metal arms lifted and repulsor blasts began firing.

"JARVIS," Tony said. "We're a bit tied up over here."

"*Understood, sir.*" Two small drones popped up out of the rocket casing. One hovered next to Tony, the other approached Natasha. "*Don't move please, either of you.*"

A bullet dug into the floor a foot from Tony's head.

"Fine," he said. "But hurry."

The drones needled his bonds with tiny pulsar beams, and in the space of a few breaths he was free. It took a few seconds longer to disable Natasha's more extensive bonds. Meanwhile, more of the gunmen poured into the room.

"I'm going for the suit."

Natasha nodded. "I'll see what I can do to give you cover."

"JARVIS," Tony said. "Tailor mode."

The suit opened up. Tony jumped up and sprinted. Natasha was already in motion, a black whirlwind. Before he'd even reached the armor, she'd liberated a gun from one of their antagonists and was dropping gunmen left and right.

He'd just stepped into the armor when Cancer appeared, reaching toward him with her ethereal claws. Only they looked more solid now, and she looked—bigger.

"JARVIS!" he shouted.

One of the suit's arms lifted and blasted Cancer in the face, hurling her back. Then the armor began closing and locking around him. His heads-up appeared, and then he had control of his repulsors. He hit Cancer again, and began taking out the gunmen as they entered the room.

Something blinked on his right arm's weapons deployment. He frowned.

"JARVIS, what is that?"

As an answer, one of the panels on his arm opened. Something slid out and locked in place—a metal rod with a heavy ball on the end.

"*The talking mace you requested, sir,*" the weapon said.

"Oh," he responded. "JARVIS, we need to have a little talk about jokes—"

But then he didn't have time for that. Another dozen men rushed into the room, one with a rocket launcher. Tony leapt up and took flight, diving into the mass of Zodiac thugs. The mace was still in his hand, so he figured he might as well use it.

A rocket launcher lined up with his head, and he fired his repulsor down the barrel. The resulting explosion knocked him back, along with everyone else. By the time he stood back up, the gunfire had stopped. Natasha clambered to her feet across the room, a gun in each hand, ready for the next wave, but none was coming. She located her Widow's Bite gauntlets and scooped them up.

Of Cancer, Tony saw no sign.

"IT'S a standing order," Tony explained, as they made their way out of the room and up the hall. "If my suit goes dark, JARVIS sends me another one. How he does that depends on where I am."

"So in this case, ballistic missile," she said.

"*Intercontinental* ballistic missile," he corrected. Up ahead, someone leaned around the corner and fired a few rounds. Tony splashed him with a repulsor beam.

Cancer seemed to have skedaddled, no doubt to join Capricorn, and the last of their thugs were in the room with the server, doing their best to destroy it. They didn't seem to have been at it that long, but a couple of well-placed grenades had done a fair amount of damage. Natasha stood guard while Tony did his best to tap into what was left.

"Just out of curiosity," she asked, "how are we getting back? Riding you piggy-back across the Pacific isn't my idea of a good time."

"You'd be surprised how often I hear that," Tony replied. "But don't worry, I've made other arrangements."

"Good," she said. "Anything yet?"

"Yeah, maybe," he said. The core memory was shot, but he'd managed to find backups in a variety of temporary files. They'd been poorly wiped and were at least partly recoverable using his built-in hardware. It was a little like going through a bunch of books shredded up and dropped in a pile on the floor. He could put them back together, but it would help a lot if he knew what he was looking for.

JARVIS could look for things a lot faster than he could. He told the computer to scan for addresses, locations, maps, things of that sort.

"*Sir?*" JARVIS said, after a few moments. "*Could this be of use?*"

Tony frowned at the image that came up. It looked sort of like a map, but of what? He recognized the symbols scattered on it—Taurus, Aries, the other Zodiac symbols—but not much else.

"Might be some kind of chart," he said. "Maybe the locations of the other Zodiac members. JARVIS, copy that and anything like it."

"*Yes, sir,*" JARVIS said. "*Sir, I've detected anomalous energy signatures appearing outside of the house.*"

"Have you?" Tony asked. "How many of them?"

"Twelve, sir."

Natasha looked over at him.

"Tony?"

"Yeah," he said. "It's time to go. JARVIS, keep copying files as long as we're in range."

"*Of course, sir.*"

They beat a retreat back the way Natasha had come in, until they reached the loading dock behind the kitchen. Virgo and her whip were waiting for them, along with a couple of others he assumed by their appearance were Taurus and Aries.

"*The rest surround the house and are converging, sir.*"

"Remember what you said about riding piggy-back?" he asked Natasha.

"I remember you said I wouldn't have to."

"I lied."

"You said you made other plans!"

"Well, the best laid plans, and all that," he said.

Virgo's whip lashed toward them, stretching unreasonably long as more of the Zodiac came into sight. One of them was Capricorn.

"You've overstayed your welcome, Mr. Stark," he said. His voice was strangely amplified. The horns on his head were bigger, looking more solid, and something weird was going on with his legs. They seemed to be fusing together.

Natasha clasped her arms around Tony's neck and wrapped her legs around him.

"Hold on," he said.

Riding up, he lifted to avoid Virgo's whip, and headed toward the lush forest. It was light now, so they'd need to find some cover.

Nat was strong, but he couldn't take the suit to full speed with her hanging on it, nor could he maneuver too abruptly for fear of throwing her off. As he twisted again to avoid the whip, his perimeter alarm alerted him to incoming missiles. He wasn't sure what they were, but he couldn't outrun them. A turn to the left proved that they weren't heat-seeking, though, so that was a bit of a break.

They streaked past and set some trees on fire.

Suddenly servos whined as if his weight had tripled—which it probably had, given what he remembered about Cap's fight with Taurus. It wasn't more than he could deal with, but he felt Natasha's grip weakening, so he paused long enough to blast the bull-horned woman, hoping it was the right call. It was. His speed kicked up several notches, and he had to rein it in.

Could any of these guys fly? If not…

He saw her at the last instant, a misty shape shooting in from his three o'clock. No telling what she would do to his circuits if she got inside, so he did a hard roll. Natasha's arms came loose and she nearly slung off of him, but the wrestling hold she had with her legs held as he dodged a blast of energy from yet another direction. Ahead, he saw two more of them in the air—they looked like twins, one dark and one light. The dark one had a storm building around him, and Tony could already feel the force of the winds.

Turning, he pointed straight up and *pushed*.

Natasha gasped, but she had her arms back around his neck. Glancing down, he saw at least four figures in pursuit. More of the energy bolts lanced past. Lightning flashed from below, coming perilously close. His suit could probably handle a thunderbolt or two, but Natasha couldn't.

Something caught hold of him, and his speed dropped alarmingly. It was nothing he could see, so he figured it must be Taurus again, wielding her control of gravity. And yet the range was way more than what Cap had described.

There was no doubt about it. These guys were getting stronger.

"JARVIS!" he shouted. "Where are we?"

"*Just arriving, sir*," the computer said.

"Fire some missiles at the targets below, maximum spread, as soon as you're in range."

"*In range now, sir.*"

A quick glance at his six o'clock showed it was true. His new Quinjet prototype was cutting a nice silhouette toward them. Half a dozen contrails left the craft, following the missiles as they jetted toward the ground below. An instant later explosions blossomed in the house and the yard around it. The tug on him vanished.

"Pick us up, JARVIS," Tony commanded. "Fast."

The agile craft flew up beneath them and the cockpit canopy popped open. Tony came to a near stop and dropped in. Natasha, breathless and wild-eyed, rolled off of him and into the pilot's seat.

"Are we staying to tussle?" she asked.

"No," he said. "Get us the hell out of here."

She nodded, and a second later multiple Gs crushed them back in their seats. Several shocks rocked the craft as something or other struck them, but the engines weren't affected, and a few moments later Taiwan was miles behind them.

"We've got to get in touch with Cap," Tony said.

"First you need to get in touch with Bruce," Natasha said. "Immediately."

He looked at her, puzzled.

"Why?"

"You don't remember? All of the questions about Tarleton's labs, the repairs, all of that? They're planning another attack there."

"Why? Didn't they get what they came for the first time?"

"Yes," she said. "Or they thought they did—but something's changed. They may need more power, more than they originally thought, but most of their questions weren't about Tarleton's power source. They were mostly about Bruce."

"Crap. They can teleport, so they'll go immediately, while we're still hours away," he said. "JARVIS, call Bruce. Now."

TWENTY-THREE

BRUCE woke up alone again, but the impression in the bed next to him was still warm. He heard the shower going and smiled, just a little. Another good morning.

He heard a humming sound and realized it was his phone. He'd put it on silent the night before. Sighing, he picked it up, dreading to see who it was. Not that many people had this number, but those who did he didn't particularly look forward to hearing from.

The number came up as Tony Stark. Of course. He'd been briefed on their mission, and they hadn't been gone long enough to worry about. Most probably they'd found something out and were trying to drag him back into it.

Then he noticed that Tony had tried to call six times, starting about an hour ago.

"Oh, crap," he said, and he played the first message. Then the second.

"Monica!" he shouted, as he dialed the lab.

"In the shower!" she said.

"I know," he said, feeling his pulse quicken, willing it to stay down. Nobody at the lab was picking up. "Do you have Tarleton's private line? Or Blonsky's?"

"What's going on?" she asked.

"Tony thinks there may be another attack on the lab," he said. "You try to call them. I'm going down there."

"Bruce—"

"I know," he said, "but Tony and Natasha are hours away, and I don't even know where Cap and Thor are. Don't worry. I don't plan to… change."

○————————○

WHEN he got the call from Monica, Emil was on a cot in the storage room, running a fever of a hundred and five. His assistant, Colin, was on duty in the front and transferred the call back to him.

After he was done talking to Stark, he put down the phone and pushed himself to a sitting position. His gut clenched and white spots threatened to overwhelm his vision, but he managed to climb to his feet. He gulped down some of the electrolyte solution Monica had given him, chambered a round in his pistol, and went up front.

"Boss, you look terrible," Colin said.

"I'm fine," Emil said. "I'm taking over. You can call it a day."

"But, boss—"

"I'm serious. Get out of here now."

"Should I call the police?"

Emil shook his head. As Colin left, he went to the intercom and buzzed for Tarleton. The scientist's image appeared on screen.

"What is it?"

"Stark called," Emil replied. "He thinks there is going to be another attack on the lab."

"What? Why?"

Emil closed his eyes as a wave of vertigo swept through him.

"He didn't say."

Tarleton frowned. He didn't say anything, but the screen went dark.

So. He'd been warned.

Emil settled down to wait. He felt even hotter than before, and a profound ache that went all the way to his bones, but he hadn't turned even slightly green. His pains and fever could easily be a sign that his immune system was fighting the change. So maybe it wasn't working. If it was, it wasn't happening quickly enough. When the Zodiac showed up, he was barely going to be able to stand up again, much less exact revenge.

With a grunt he fought back to his feet and stumbled into Monica's lab. He found another hypodermic in the drawer. Blinking sweat from his eyes he brought out the black tube, stuck the needle through the port barrier isolator, filled it, and brought it back out. Hesitating only an instant, he plunged it into his carotid artery.

The pain was far worse than any of the earlier injections. Blinking, he realized his face was pressed against something hard and cool. He was on the floor but didn't remember falling.

How long had he been down?

He checked his phone, but he didn't remember what time he had taken the injection, so it didn't help. Rising unsteadily, he returned to the security desk.

The hurt was still there, and now his pulse was pounding in his ears. It felt as if his blood pressure was way up, and he thought how ironic it would be if he died of a stroke before the Zodiac even arrived.

The door behind him opened. He swung around, but it was only Tarleton, carrying a heavy metal briefcase. He glared briefly at Emil and then hurried out the door.

Emil returned his gaze to the surveillance feed, feeling exposed.

Something moved on the outside monitors.

They didn't send the eerie woman in this time. They knocked the door down. He squeezed off three rounds before a flash of light hit him in the shoulder and sent him screaming to the floor. His whole body contorted, trying to escape the agony, but there was nowhere to go—it was all inside of him. He lifted his gun to try and shoot again, but fingers as hard as steel closed on his wrists and lifted him up, bringing him face-to-face with bulging black eyes and a visage that seemed more arachnid than human.

"Banner," the man hissed.

Emil shook his head. "Not here."

Behind the thing that was holding him, he saw others. Among them was the lion.

"You," he said. "I'm going to kill you."

The lion smiled. "Who are you?" he asked. "Have we met?"

"Banner," the first man said. As he spoke, the others came pouring in, shattering the doors to the labs. "Find him."

Emil's head was throbbing more than ever. The light from outside was incredibly bright, and he couldn't see anything. He was only faintly aware that he'd been thrown, of his head hitting the corner of the desk, of the taste of blood in his mouth, and again, the cold, hard floor pressed against his cheek.

Then every muscle in his body cramped all at once. The sound of his own screams was strange to his ears, as if it was someone else, a different voice pitched lower. His flesh felt as if it was burning, splitting like the skin of a sausage cooked over an open flame. But that was all on the surface, the stuff floating on the ocean. There was something else coming up from beneath, a Leviathan rising.

The Leviathan was angry.

The pain dropped away as the Leviathan rose, as he stretched the surface, the merely human flesh, forced it into a new form, a form of power, a shape molded from rage, a mind grown for vengeance.

He opened his eyes and perceived a different world.

The lion saw him an instant too late, his eyes widening. Then Emil struck him a blow that would have shattered the bones of an ordinary man. The feel of the impact on his knuckles was sheer joy, and he roared as the golden-tressed monster flew across the room. He ripped the security desk from the floor and hurled it at the scorpion-man, but it split in half, glowing, turned to liquid and then a spray of droplets.

With a howl of frustration, he dove at the man. Didn't see the sting until it was too late, until it had dug into him between the shoulder blades and into his spine and put fire there. It didn't matter. Neither that nor anything else could stop him now. His muscles felt like steel, and he had grown. He wasn't as big as the Hulk, but his skin had taken on an olive-green hue.

It was working. Rappaccini's treatments were working.

He was becoming something more.

The scorpion-man danced away from him, waving a weird golden cross in his hand. The floor grabbed Emil's feet like tar. At the same moment, arrows of light cut into his chest. He felt the heat, his skin parting like wax before a red-hot knife...

He also felt his skin seal back again.

"I will kill you all!" he shouted, tearing his feet loose from the floor. He turned as a man with curled horns crashed into him. It felt as if lava had been poured on him—his eardrums hummed and his muscles, strong as they were, rebelled, but he was used to mastering pain. He grabbed the man by his head and hurled him through a wall, took hold of the next nearest attacker and threw him up through the ceiling. He felt stronger with each second, and realized he was still growing.

He felt another sting in his back, and whirled. The scorpion-man was there again, and Emil surged toward him, but the air was suddenly very thick, like molten glass. Another horned man, this one with eyes like those of a goat, seized hold of him. His lungs stung as if wasps were nesting in them.

"It's not Banner," he heard someone say.

"It doesn't matter," the scorpion-man said. "He'll do as well, if not better."

Emil lunged forward, batting aside the goat-man, swinging for the scorpion's head. The lion was back, leaping onto his back and slashing him with claws of flame. He leapt, blasting through the ceiling, shucking his antagonist off him and coming to ground in the street beneath a lowering thunderhead. He still couldn't breathe and the fire in his veins was starting to work up the back of his skull. There was something like pins and needles reaching deep into his brain. A bull-woman loomed in front of him, and he was suddenly too heavy to move, sinking through the earth.

"Take him," someone said. He thought it was the scorpion-man. He felt strong hands grab him at ankles, wrist and neck.

Then nothing.

TWENTY-FOUR

"TRAPPED," Cap said. "We got here, didn't we? Why can't we leave the same way?"

"We used Thor's power to enter the well," Strange said. "He harnessed the might of Earth's very atmosphere. There is nothing of the sort here."

Thor held up his hammer, reached out with his senses, but he felt no stir of air that might be magnified—no vapor, no spark between hot and cold that could be fanned into flame.

"It's true," he conceded. "I am god of thunder, but this place has no thunder. There aren't even any clouds. Neither, strange as it is to say, is this place under the watchful eye of Heimdall. The Bifrost cannot reach us here. I fear I can be of little help."

"It looked like the Zodiac used their teleportation bracelets," Cap said. "Why can't you just—pop us out?"

"It might have looked like that," Strange said, "but that isn't what happened. Their bracelets couldn't have worked in here. Scorpio used the Key to get them out. In doing so he not only returned the Zodiac back to Earth, but he repaired the well itself, erasing the weak point through which we entered. This place is not a normal part of the multiverse; as I said before, it is self-contained—now more so than ever."

"There must be a way out," Thor said. "Captain, by your leave, I would at least look."

"Knock yourself out," Cap said.

Thor blinked. "If you think ill of the suggestion—"

"No," Cap said. "It's an expression. It means give it your best try."

"That's a peculiar expression," Thor said, "and prone to misinterpretation."

"I see that now," Cap said. "Believe me, you're not the only one having trouble with vernacular. I tend to forget that half of what I grew up saying sounds nonsensical." He turned to the sorcerer. "Strange, is there anything in particular he should keep an eye out for?"

"Anything that seems peculiar," Strange said. "The more knowledge we have, the better. I will also reconnoiter in astral form."

"I'm not sure what would stand out as peculiar in this place," Cap said, "but see what you can find, Thor. While you're at it, if you see my shield, I'd sure like it back."

"Of course," Thor replied. "I shall return anon." He gazed up at the sky, featureless save for the stones scudding along in orbit. Then he whirled his hammer and flew up.

The planetoid shrank quickly behind him, its pull dwindling to nothing. He passed the larger rugged moons and then a few smaller ones, until all was below him, and the sphere was the size of a small jewel.

After that, it got no smaller, although his every sense told him he was still traveling at terrific speed away from it. He had encountered no barrier; the air still blew against his face with the wind of his own velocity.

Altering his course, he flung his hammer along what he perceived to be the axis of the planetoid, but still the object below showed no outstanding features, and no change. Frustrated, he returned to the belt of debris that orbited the small sphere, searching for Cap's shield. It would have been like searching for a teardrop in an ocean, except that in this case the "teardrop" was the only thing that had any color to it. So he found the red-white-and-blue disk, snatched it from its orbit, then returned to the surface.

"You found it," Cap said. "I'm much obliged."

"That was the easy part," Thor told him. "I found no escape for us. My quest was fruitless."

"Perhaps not," Strange said. "Each of these bubbles of reality is unique; some say they are a product of the Big Bang. I'm beginning to understand this one. Perhaps by factoring in what you've learned, we might find a solution."

Thor explained as best he could what he'd encountered.

Strange considered it for a moment.

"You've heard the old conundrum, I take it? Zeno's Dichotomy Paradox. If you take a step toward a door, and then a step half that distance, with each following step half the distance of the last, how long would it take you to reach the door?"

"You never would," Cap said. "You would always have half a step to go, although the steps would eventually be microscopic."

"Yes," Strange said. "That's how space behaves here. The farther you get from the planetoid, the more compressed space-time becomes—but it's still infinite. You can travel as fast as you want, and never get further away."

"So that leaves us with nothing," Steve said. "If we can't teleport, fly out, or open a portal—we're stuck here."

"Not necessarily," Strange said. "Thor's obser-vations are quite valuable. Space-time in this pocket dimension is organized entirely around the planetoid. It came first, and its properties generated the universe around it."

"Very well," Thor said, "but I still don't understand what that means."

"For gravity to behave as it does here, the core of this sphere must be incredibly dense, possibly as compressed as the matter of a neutron star. Yet if that were the case, the planet itself should have long ago shrunk to infinitesimal size. So the core of this planet must answer to different laws of physics.

"Therefore, if moving away from the center leads only to infinity, perhaps moving *toward* it will take us—well, out. Or at least someplace different," he said. "Of course…"

"Of course what?" Cap asked.

"If I'm wrong, the atoms of which we are composed may collapse." He shrugged. "We might simply be crushed to death."

"Is there any way to anticipate which will happen?" Thor asked.

"Since Thor was exploring outward, I thought I should explore the inner," Strange said. "I've been to the core, in my astral form, and found nothing peculiar. There were no ill effects. Our material bodies, however—of those I cannot be certain. Nor is there any indication of what lies beyond. So even if we do pass safely through, it might be into the core of a star or a plane farther removed even than this one. The only way to know for certain is to try."

"How? By digging a hole to the center of the planet?"

"No," Strange said, "but it can be done, if we're agreed on the risk."

"I don't see any point in sticking around here," Cap said. "Thor, what are your feelings?"

"I'm beginning to feel imprisoned," he said. "I dislike the sensation."

"We're agreed, then?" Strange said.

"Yes," Cap replied.

"Join hands with me, then," Strange said. "Thor, if you would be so kind as to lay your hammer in the middle of the circle we form."

Thor placed Mjolnir on the rocky surface, and they linked hands. The hammer quivered. It shook back and forth.

Then it vanished, sucked into the ground, leaving a black hole behind it—and yanking them along with it. The hole should have been far too small to accommodate them, and yet somehow, they fit. Thor had the peculiar sensation of being stretched out, as if his legs were infinitely long and falling at astonishing speeds while his upper body remained where it was.

Then everything seemed to catch up. All went white, and he felt that instead of being pulled, he was being *thrown*. Blood rushed to his head, colors flashed all around him, and then the light faded. Still he gripped Strange's hand, and Cap's.

But where were they?

They were surrounded by darkness, aside from great glowing clouds in shades ranging from magenta to reds almost too dark to see. Behind them something like a star showed itself, but quickly dwindled with distance. Other stars of assorted colors appeared, but far fewer than in the skies of Asgard or Earth.

As his eyes adjusted, he made out faintly glowing bodies nearby. They looked as if they were formed of glass or some other transparent medium, illuminated gently with light from within. Many had geometrical shapes, while others were more amorphous. All seemed to be moving under their own power, some traveling in groups and others independently. They reminded him a bit of fish in how they moved, if not in how they looked.

He noticed a glowing bubble around them, too.

"Well, we weren't crushed," Captain America said. "And it sure looks like we're someplace else."

"Indeed," Strange said, "and we are fortunate—there are an infinite number of realms. This, at least, is one I know, and not so far from home."

"That's lucky," Cap said.

"Yes," Strange said. "If we survive long enough to reach our own plane, we will be luckier still." He nodded into the distance, where Thor saw something—large. Like the smaller bodies nearby, it was mostly translucent, but there was enough light inside of it to make out that it was roughly cone-shaped, with a gaping maw that looked hungry.

It turned toward them.

Farther out, similar behemoths appeared, and began moving in their direction—like sharks, scenting blood in the water. Only these sharks appeared large enough to swallow moons.

"Hang on," Strange said, as spheres of eldritch force appeared around his fists. "This ride may get bumpy."

TWENTY-FIVE

BRUCE stepped cautiously from the driver's side of Monica's car, searching the streets, the sky, the rooftops, before returning his gaze to the fresh ruin of the AIM labs. All of the repairs they and the contractors had done had been erased, and plenty more damage added.

This time, Monica's lab had been trashed. Only one wall was still standing. Everything else—her computers and other equipment, the incubator and its pulsing green cells—all had been pulverized or scattered by what appeared to be one or several explosions. Fires licked at the periphery of the structure. In the distance, Bruce could hear fire and police sirens, indicating that this had all gone down only moments before.

Yet there was no one to be seen.

He plunged into the ruins, searching for Blonsky, his assistant, Tarleton—anyone who might have been present—but he found the place mercifully free of bodies. As the police arrived, it occurred to him he should probably get out. This looked exactly like something the Hulk might have done. There would be questions.

No.

He wouldn't run from something he hadn't done. The police needed answers, and so did Bruce. Tony had warned the Zodiac would return to rob the place. This didn't look like a robbery. It looked as if they'd come to destroy the labs. It didn't make any sense.

WITHIN the hour, Tarleton and most of the security and maintenance personnel had been accounted for. The only person missing was Blonsky. Despite Bruce's protests, Monica arrived by cab. He watched her pick her way through the ruined lab, feeling helpless, but also feeling… something else. Like he was missing something.

"I'm sorry," he told her.

She looked genuinely surprised.

"Why?" she asked. "You didn't do this. You didn't do *any* of this."

"Yes," he said, "but I should have been able to—" He broke off.

"What? Protect my lab? Bruce, surely you don't think I expected that. If you had been here, maybe you could have helped, but it also might have been worse."

"I don't know," he said. "They did a pretty good job of wrecking the place."

"That's not what I meant," she said softly. "You might be dead."

"Oh."

She came over and took his hand. "It's okay," she said. "Not the lab, of course—and Blonsky. I hope he's alright."

"Me too," Bruce said.

"He…" She stopped, seeming to think better of whatever she was going to say.

"What?" he pressed gently.

"I caught Blonsky the other night," she said. "After hours, looking at my gamma experiments. He was evasive when I asked what he was doing. Or so I thought at first—but it must be boring, at times, doing his job. I thought maybe he was just curious."

"Maybe he was," Bruce said.

"There's a lot we don't know about him," Monica said. "He was secretive about his past. What if—what if he is one of them? The Zodiac?"

"I doubt that," Bruce said. "They nearly killed him."

Monica nodded. "Of course. I'm not thinking straight. He's

probably been hurt or worse, trying to protect our labs."

"We'll find him," Bruce said. "But now that you mention the gamma experiments—what happened to them?"

"The incubator was destroyed," she said. "What's left of it is over there in the corner."

"But what if the Zodiac took some of the cells first? What if that's what they came back for?"

"It shouldn't matter," she said. "Without proper culture they would die within hours. Besides—I wasn't making any progress." Her eyes dropped. "I had hoped to help you," she said. "And others. But the gamma mutations were too unpredictable. Any traits I managed to isolate just mutated again. I'm sorry."

"It's okay," he said. "I've been working on the same problem for years. There might not be an answer."

He looked over at the wreckage of the barrier isolator. Maybe the Zodiac had thought they could find something there—to harness the same radiation that made the Hulk possible. If they had, they were in for a disappointment.

"Your friends are here," Monica said.

o————————o

"NEW jet," Bruce observed as he came on board.

Natasha looked up from the satellite images she was reviewing. Bruce was dressed in slacks and a button-up shirt. His hair was combed. If he'd been the green guy since she saw him last, it had been a while.

"Yeah," Tony replied. "The last one kind of got blown up, back in Taiwan."

Bruce glanced back and forth between the two of them. "That's rough," he said. "I'm sorry to hear that. I'm glad the two of you made it back in one piece."

"Thanks," Tony said. "Your concern is touching."

"Look, Tony—"

Stark waved him off. "Don't mind me," he said. "I'm a little cranky from the lack of sleep and the torture. But like you said, here we are, safe and sound. Meanwhile, it looks as if things here got a little out of hand again."

"Yeah," Bruce said. "I wasn't involved this time, though."

"No, you were too busy dodging my calls," Tony said. "Cap I understand. He was frozen for a few years. He missed handheld calculators, table-top video games in pizza joints, message boards, chat rooms—everything on which our current civilization is founded. But I figured *you* would check your messages once in a while."

"I do," Bruce said. "Once in a while. Not usually when I'm asleep."

"Tony," Natasha said, "lay off. Bruce, listen to me. Do you have any idea what happened here? Did you see anything?"

At first, it looked like he wouldn't answer. Finally he turned to her.

"No," he said in a quieter voice. "I didn't make it in time. I came as soon as I saw the message, but—no, nothing."

"And since we've been gone? Has anything happened?"

"No," he said, shaking his head. "I don't think so. Look, when Cap gets back—"

"What the hell makes you think Cap is coming back?" Tony shouted. At that moment, Natasha saw that he wasn't just pissed off. Stark was on the verge of tears.

Bruce saw it, too, and his face crumpled in dismay.

"Wait," he said. "Why? What happened? Where's Cap and Thor?"

Tony looked away. Natasha waited, but when it became clear he wasn't going to say anything, she turned to Bruce.

"Tony and I went to Taiwan to check in on this Capricorn guy. As you might have guessed, things didn't go so well. Cap and Thor went off with Doctor Strange to try and find the Key before the Zodiac got to it. You were paying attention to all of this when Strange laid it out, right?"

"Yes."

"Before we escaped from Capricorn's place," she continued, "all twelve of them showed up. The whole Zodiac. They had the Key with them, which means Cap and Thor failed to stop them from getting it. Not only that, but we haven't heard anything from any of them. I don't know what that suggests to you, but for me that reads... pretty bad."

"You think they're dead?"

"Something like that," she said. "Capricorn suggested they were no longer a factor."

"God," he muttered. "That's... No, there are other explanations. They could have been captured, or they may be hurt. We have to try to find them."

"We don't even know where to start," Tony said. "Strange can teleport. They could be anywhere. They might not even be on Earth. The only place I know to look is in some stretch of mountains in Turkmenistan. That's almost five hours from here at top speed, and then we would have to *find* them."

"It's worth a shot."

"No, it isn't," Tony said. "Because we have an appointment in Seattle this afternoon, with or without them."

Natasha watched Bruce absorb that. He looked dazed.

"So this conjunction thing is happening today?"

"Yeah. It's actually one of the last pieces of information I got from Strange."

"And it's happening in Seattle?"

"Near there," Natasha said. "An island in the Salish Sea. We got that from Capricorn's files in Taiwan. Unfortunately it's just a spot on a map, and not to scale. No coordinates. It could be anyplace within an eighty-mile radius."

"How do you know it's on the island, and not someplace else on the map?"

"It's labeled as New Penthos," she said. "And also as 'Scorpio's Island.' Penthos was an island in the Aegean Sea—the last place they tried this, back in the Bronze Age. I could be wrong, but it's a place to start."

"Couldn't they relocate?" Bruce asked. "If they suspect you might know where they're doing this thing, why not just do it someplace else?"

"Apparently the location is non-negotiable—they have to do it there. The good news is, they don't know we know the location."

"Because we don't," Tony said, "and Capricorn didn't seem like the sort of person to leave anything to chance. He'll plan for the worst-case scenario. They'll be ready."

"Maybe," Natasha conceded.

Bruce looked out through the windscreen at the wrecked facility.

"And they came back here why?" he said. "To steal more of Tarleton's power source?" At that Tony moved to a computer terminal, stood in front of it, and tapped the keys with rapid-fire precision.

"There's no trace of Tarleton's power source," he said.

"So did he take it out himself, or did the Zodiac get it?" Bruce asked.

"That's the question, isn't it?" Tony said. "But it may not be the most *important* question."

"What do you mean?" Bruce asked.

"I don't think they came back for Tarleton's power source," Natasha said.

"What then?" Bruce asked. "Why did they do this?"

"I think they came for you."

"For me?"

"For the Hulk," she said. "When they came here originally, they were looking for a power source. They found it, and they took what they needed—but they also found you. That fits into some sort of prophecy of theirs. Something the stars told them, I guess, if we're to believe Capricorn. They needed you for some element of their plan."

"But I wasn't here," Bruce said. "They didn't find me... or the Hulk."

"They were in a hurry," Tony said. "Natasha and I had escaped. They knew we would warn you, and the conjunction is tonight. They had to act before they were ready."

"So you think they wrecked the lab out of spite?"

Tony shrugged. Then he tapped a few keys and a new screen came up. The wrecked lab, as seen from the air.

"The thing is," Tony said, "there is a trace energy signature, but it's not Terrigen. It's gamma radiation."

Bruce sighed. "In Monica's lab," he said. "She was—experimenting. Trying to isolate the regenerative properties of gamma-altered cells. And maybe..." He didn't finish.

"Find a cure for you?" Natasha said.

He nodded.

"Well," Tony said, "I see what you're talking about, in her lab—or what's left of it, but that's a minimal profile. A cell culture, maybe?"

"Yes."

"Right, but the residue I'm talking about is something... bigger. Here, mostly." He indicated the area which had once been the foyer and the security desk. The computer had painted it with a green overlay of splotches, like a monochrome Jackson Pollock.

"I suspect if we do the forensics," Natasha said, "we'll find blood and tissue."

"Couldn't that be from me?" Bruce said. "After all, that's where the fight started last time."

"Sure," Tony said. "If we hadn't scrubbed the whole thing, and if any of this had showed up on my last scan. But we did, and it didn't. This is recent."

"But I didn't become the Hulk," Bruce said. "I mean, I forget things, but not like this. I woke up at Monica's, got your message, came here. I'm still dressed in what I was wearing when I left her apartment."

"I don't doubt any of that," Natasha said. "But—"

"Blonsky," Bruce said.

"What?"

"Monica caught him looking at her experiment. My cells—"

"If I'm up to date, Blonsky is missing, right?" Tony said.

Bruce nodded.

"So maybe there's a new Hulk in town," Natasha said.

"No," Bruce said. "That doesn't make any sense. Monica said the cells were useless, that the mutations were too random..." He trailed off. Random didn't mean *harmless*. It could mean quite the opposite. Monica might have underestimated the mutative power of the cells. She wouldn't be the first. Or maybe the Zodiac *was* involved. With the powers they had, they might have been able to multiply the power in the low-dose cells by factors of ten.

"I think it's safe to say he didn't go willingly," Natasha said, "but at least we have a decent idea of where they took him. The question is why?"

"I don't know," Bruce said. "If they wanted a Hulk—if Blonsky has somehow become like me—I don't know. They need to break something?"

"No way to tell," Tony said. "I guess we're going to find out, though. I'm going to make a few repairs and a few calls, and then we're out."

"And Cap and Thor?" Bruce said. "We really think they might be dead?"

"Capricorn didn't say so," Tony said. "He said they were out of the picture, but he didn't say dead. It seems like the kind of thing he might brag about." He shrugged. "That's the only hope I have."

"Nat?"

"They're out of play," she said softly. "And like Tony said, we don't have time to go hunting for them."

"If they're dead, that's that," Tony snapped. "If they aren't, well—they can take care of themselves. It's us we have to worry about now. The guys you fought a few days ago? Those were baby versions of what they are now, and there are twelve of them. Not two. So not to step on your emotional languishing and all, but I sure hope you can finally see your way clear to get back in the freaking fight. Because even with you, I don't like our odds."

Bruce met Tony's outburst with lowered eyebrows, and when the inventor fell silent, he didn't say anything for the space of a few heartbeats.

"*What?*" Tony said.

"Just waiting to be sure you were finished," Bruce replied. "That you'd got it out of your system."

Tony opened his mouth, then sighed, slumping back in his seat.

"Yeah," he said. "No, I think that's about it."

"Fine," Bruce said. "Just let me know when you're ready to go."

○———————○

MARIA Hill sat still for most of the conversation, only occasionally interjecting a question. When Stark was done, she went directly to the point.

"What do you want from SHIELD?"

"Short term?" he said. "Support. We're down to three, here. In my opinion that's not enough."

"That must have hurt to say," she replied.

"Don't be a jerk about it," he said. "What can you give me?"

"What do you need?"

"Honestly, I don't know. The kitchen sink."

"In just a few hours?" she said. "I can provide some air support, maybe a strike force. A lot of our assets are currently committed."

"Why? Something else up?"

"There's always something up," she said. "Given time, I can organize more resources, but you've caught us flat-footed."

"I didn't expect to lose Cap and Thor," Stark said. "Sometimes we have to improvise. But I do have some long-term requests."

"Sure," she said. "As long as you're rubbing the lamp."

"We discussed a West Coast headquarters," he said. "Let's take that out of the hypothetical and make it happen."

"I'll take it upstairs," Hill said. "We'll get back to you. Meantime, I'm sending you some command codes. Your air support will be on the way in an hour. But bear in mind—this isn't some out-of-the-way location. Until you have a target you're absolutely certain of, we're not going to intervene. Even then, our response is going to be measured by the threat as we see it. So stay in touch and give us something actionable."

"I'll do my best," Stark said.

TWENTY-SIX

THE new Quinjet was a quieter ride than the old one, Bruce thought. Or maybe it was just that everyone on board was quieter than usual. Tony was making last-minute adjustments to his suit. Natasha was poring over the telemetry arriving from the SHIELD satellites.

And he was—well, not *bored*, but uncomfortable being stuck in his own head. He couldn't help Tony with anything, but maybe he could make himself useful with the satellite data.

"Any luck?" he asked Natasha.

"I've pulled up every available image of every island in a hundred-mile radius," she said. "We don't have energy sigs on any of them, just plain old photographs. A lot of them are just rocks. Others are residential, and have been for years. I've been focusing in on the ones that stand out in some way. This one here, for instance, has been used as a military base on and off over the years, but it's vacant now. This little one here was where a serial killer operated out of, back in the 1970s. A guy built a cold fusion plant here, although since cold fusion doesn't work, he went broke, so now there's a bed-and-breakfast.

"I've been trying to run them down with other databases. So if you see something—anything at all—let me know."

Bruce scanned through the images.

"I don't suppose any of them are registered as being owned by a guy named Scorpio?" he said.

"No. But believe it or not, I checked that."

"How long before we get there?" he asked.

"We're twenty minutes out."

The problem was, he thought, they didn't know what they were looking for. What would a Zodiac island of death look like?

"That other island," he said. "Three thousand years ago. Penthos. What do we know about it?"

"It was vaporized when the Key was overloaded," she said. "So we don't have a lot to go on, but there's a sketch of it in the stuff Strange sent." She tapped through a menu, then pulled up an image. It was an ink-on-paper drawing, with a reference saying it had been copied from a clay tablet, the original of which was destroyed in a museum in Dresden when the city was firebombed.

"That's not very good," he said. "I can't read anything on it."

"It's what we've got," she said.

He studied it a little closer. There was a sort of swirl in the middle, and then nine other locations marked as little ovals ranged out around it. The closest was very near to the swirl, the next about twice as far away, the next twice again. It reminded him of something—something nagging right at the edge of his consciousness.

He turned his attention back to the aerial photographs, trying to decipher the two-dimensional images and unpack them in three. What was he looking at? Usually something obvious. Houses, storage structures, docks. The nearby waters were traced by the foamy trails of boats.

He moved from one to the next. Then back. Something caught his eye.

The island was squarish. It looked like it was probably pretty hilly, and he wasn't absolutely sure what he'd noticed at first, besides the gleam of gold that was probably the gilt dome of a building. Then he noticed another dome farther out. Smaller, but probably still pretty big.

He zoomed in and saw several cupolas. And the spacing...

What if they weren't domes? What if they were spheres; after all, he could only look straight down on them.

"Tell me about this one," he said. "This island."

Natasha checked the reference and vanished into her screen for a few minutes.

"It's expensive property," she said after a moment. "Privately owned. In fact, it's been owned under the same trust for almost a hundred and fifty years. There's some interesting stuff here. The FBI put together a case back in prohibition. They had good evidence someone was warehousing liquor there. The bust never happened, but the agents on the case retired in style a few years later. So did the judges who might have granted search warrants. There are a lot of little whiffs like that over the years—possible ties to organized crime that were never fully investigated."

"You said it's been private for a long time. Who owns it?"

"Well, the trust seems pretty straightforward—the current trustee is Cornelius Van Lunt, a direct descendant of the Titus Van Lunt who bought the property in 1872. The family is in real estate, based in New York, but the island has been leased out over the years. There was a hotel there in the twenties, and a sort of a theme park."

"Theme park?"

"Believe it or not. Cosmopolis, it was called. It had an extremely brief heyday. A year or so."

Bruce pointed to the odd arrangement of spheres or domes.

"So was this some sort of roller coaster?"

"It wasn't that kind of theme park," she said. "There was a planetarium. I think what you're looking at is probably the orrery. Supposed to be the biggest one ever built. It *was* a ride, sort of, now that you mention it. You could rent a planet and sit inside of it sipping champagne while it turned very slowly. Very elegant, from what I can tell."

"So it's a giant mechanical representation of the solar system," Bruce said. "That does sort of sound like our guys. It must have been expensive."

"Yeah," she said, then her expression changed. Her eyes went wider. "Yes! Let me look at that."

He waited impatiently as she scrolled.

"It *was* expensive," she said. "The company that built it went broke."

"Are you sure about that?" Bruce asked.

Natasha glanced at him, frowned, and then went to work on the computer. He looked out the window, but there wasn't much to see but clouds.

"Nice," she said. "You're on a roll today, Bruce. The company that built it was a shell. It went broke, but it was probably designed to. Cosmopolis was never meant to make money."

"Which begs the question," Bruce said, "What was it meant for?" He pulled up the sketch of the ancient Isle of Penthos. "I'll bet you that swirl in the middle is supposed to be the sun. The spacing of these other things—standing stones, maybe? That's the relative distance between the planets. Compressed, but relative." He pointed to the aerial photo. "They've just done it bigger and better this time. The different Zodiac signs are associated with planets, right?"

She nodded. "It's complicated, but yes."

"Do you have any specs on that thing?" he asked. "Blueprints? Any idea how it was powered?"

"Nothing online," she said.

"Maybe SHIELD can do some kind of composite scan of it, using different portions of the spectrum," he said. "Infrared, ultraviolet—gamma."

"What are you thinking?"

"I'm not sure," he said, "but this place seems key to their plans. There's only three of us; maybe there's an approach to this that doesn't start with a frontal assault."

"Why not have our air support bomb it?" Natasha said. "If it's important to their ritual, we could just take it out."

"It's been there for more than ninety years," Bruce said. "They've had plenty of time to build defenses for it. If we call in an airstrike and it doesn't work, they'll know we're onto them."

She nodded. "Let's talk to Tony. I think we have the makings of a plan."

○━━━━━━━━━━━━━━━○

THE lights of Seattle glowing through the foggy skies faded behind them as the Quinjet moved over the tangle of bays, sounds, and straits that made up the Salish Sea. The sun was down, and beneath the overcast sky the calm waters were like obsidian, illumined at the lines of the coasts and by the occasional ferry or boat.

They moved well below supersonic speeds, with every stealth device engaged. The island, like the sea, was dark, but on their screens it showed as a complex of colors revealing elevation, radar density, heat absorption, and radiation. When they were about half a mile from the island, Tony put the craft in hover mode.

"What is it?" Natasha asked.

"There's some kind of field," Tony said. "I'm pretty sure if we go any farther, they're going to see us."

"Some sort of surveillance?" she asked.

"I'm not sure what it is. The energy signature isn't quite like anything I've seen before, but it's got to be there for a reason. Until we're fully committed, we'd better stick here for a bit."

"Anything else?"

"There's something under the sun," Tony said. "Or this big ball that's supposed to be the sun. Which of our Zodiac friends is that? Which sign?"

"The sun represents Leo, most generally," Natasha replied. "But you said 'below'?"

"Uh-huh. Near as I can tell, this is just a really big clockwork mechanism. Each of the 'planets' is perched on an armature. They're offset vertically so they don't bump into each other. All of the armatures come from underneath the sun, so there must be some sort of engine down there."

"It should be the Earth in the center," Natasha said.

"Come again?"

"In the *Tetrabiblos*, Ptolemy put the Earth in the center of the solar system."

"Imagine that," Tony said. "A book about fortune-telling got something wrong."

"But if this whole thing has to do with the Zodiac, why would the orrery be heliocentric?"

"I see what you mean," Tony said. "Their alignment would be based on the geocentric universe—but it's the same universe, isn't it?"

"Right," Bruce said. "You can use either an Earth-centered or a sun-centered model to predict the movements of the planets. You just use a different set of assumptions and different math to get there. The movements remain the same. Besides, whichever explanation you use, it looks the same when you're standing on the ground, looking up at the stars."

He shrugged.

"They built this thing for their own purposes," he added, "but it had to pass as part of an amusement park. Maybe they thought it would raise too many eyebrows if they built an Earth-centered model in the twentieth century. No sense in attracting attention."

Tony didn't reply, but keyed in a series of commands. The sensors focused on the central structure.

"Whatever it is, there's gamma radiation beneath it," he said. "So let's find out what that is, and why it's there. Who's up for a swim?"

"I could use a dip," Nat said.

o—————o

THE Salish Sea was cold. An unprepared swimmer—say, someone who fell off of a ferry—might drown in under a minute due to cold water shock. A strong person with some body fat might survive for ten.

Natasha wasn't unprepared. Her body suit was insulated well enough, but she still felt the chill.

Suit or not, it was a long swim, made the more so by her uncertainty over whether or not the field around the island had spotted her. Tony's best guess was that it was designed to detect aircraft and boats, and that if it saw her as anything at all it would write her off as some sort of aquatic animal.

But that's all it was—a guess. So she had to remain alert to a possible attack.

As she neared the island, she switched her goggles to infrared, and was quickly rewarded with a glowing outflow of warmer water from a conduit several feet below the waterline. Whatever powered the orrery—probably diesel or electricity—the mechanism required cooling, and the easiest way to do that was to sink the heat into the sea.

She surfaced for breath.

The clouds were breaking above. The island lay in the so-called "Olympic rain shadow," an area where the mountains fended off the precipitation that so often blanketed the region. The stars would normally be a welcome sight, but this night they just unsettled her. They seemed brighter than they ought to be, especially in the thick air at sea level. She felt exposed, as if the shining points were eyes, or the lights of security cameras.

Taking her breath, she dove, following the warm water up the pipe, away from the sea, until she finally emerged in a rather large pool girdling a brightly lit concrete platform. What had once been a natural tide cave had been enlarged and filled with machinery. Most of it was old—giant shafts and gears of oiled iron or steel, undoubtedly the "clockwork" that drove the sun and planets of the orrery. But in the heart of it was something that looked much more modern.

A sphere of glass or crystal.

Floating inside of it, as if it were filled with liquid or lacked contact with gravity, was a human body.

She had emerged in the far shadows of the cave, and the distance made it difficult to discern much more than that it was a man—a rather large one. What showed of his skin was green, a paler, more olive shade than that of the Hulk. He was festooned with tubes and wires, some of which contained green fluid. Every few heartbeats the man pulsed like an LED, emitting viridian light.

Outside of the sphere she counted six armed guards and four surveillance cameras, although she was sure there were more. Most likely she was safe where she was, but the minute she started moving, she was likely to be detected. Out on the sea, Tony and Bruce were waiting for her to get here, assess the situation, and figure out their next move.

She couldn't call them for fear of being detected.

So what *was* her next move?

Natasha adjusted the magnification on her goggles. It was difficult to make out the green man's features, but she thought it was probably Blonsky. That made the most sense. Whoever it was, his energy readings were enough like the Hulk's to assume that someone had been messing around with Rappaccini's gamma-infused stem cells. It was also pretty clear that he was a prisoner, not a volunteer.

But why was he *here*?

Strange had said the "descent" of the Zodiac would be powered by the Key, the golden ankh she'd seen back in Taiwan. Above the sphere, plugged into the mass of archaic clockwork, was something that looked like an electric engine and banks of fuel cells. It still didn't add up. She was missing something, and didn't have much time to figure it out. She had to decide what to sabotage first.

Because she might not get a second pick.

A loud humming began, followed by the complaint of metal pressed into service after years of neglect, clattering and groaning as the gears began to move.

○━━━━━━━━━━○

AFTER Natasha went in the water, Tony backed the Quinjet off a bit and made another call to Hill. Bruce listened in.

"I've been monitoring your satellite requests," she said.

"So how about softening them up for us?" Tony said. "Say with an airstrike."

"Can't do it," she said. "For all we know it's just an old amusement park."

"With a gamma signature beneath it?"

"Even if it *is* the Zodiac, there could be civilians on the island. Stir the pot, Stark. If we don't like what comes up, we'll pitch in. Until then, we're on standby."

"Great," he said. Cutting the connection, he glanced over.

"Any sign Natasha's in there yet?"

"I lost her heat signature the instant she swam under the island," Bruce said. "Let's give her a few more minutes, and then get this party started."

"You seem awfully eager for someone who wanted to sit this one out."

"Yeah," he said. "That was before..."

Tony looked at him with an expression of concern. "Bruce," he said, "we need the Hulk, and we need him on our side. Can you guarantee me that?"

Bruce surprised himself by laughing.

It wasn't exactly a cheerful laugh.

"You know better than that," he said. "There are no guarantees when it comes to the green guy, but this is a rematch. He's pissed off at these guys, and so am I."

"Yep," Tony said. "Just remember, these guys will be stronger than last time. Probably bigger, too."

"And I'll be madder, so it should balance out."

Tony nodded, then glanced at his screen. "What do you think?"

"The agreement was fifteen minutes after she went in, unless we see some kind of sign."

"Yeah." Tony heaved another breath. "It's just—with Cap and Thor missing..."

"I know," Bruce said. "I don't want to lose Nat either."

They sat in silence for a moment, watching the outline of the island and the faint starlight on the sea. Bruce thought back to his fight with Leo and Libra, what he could remember of it.

"There was one funny thing about the last time I fought these guys," he said. "I was the green guy, so I almost forgot."

"What's that?"

"The lion guy. Leo. He hit me with this energy beam. It had a hell of a kick, and it hurt plenty, but—it kind of felt like it made me... stronger."

"Well, the angrier Hulk gets, the stronger Hulk gets," Tony said. "We're all aware of that by now."

"Yeah," Bruce said, "but I know what that's like, and this wasn't that. It was almost like Hulk... *absorbed* some of the energy. Like it charged him up."

"That's—interesting," Tony said. "I wonder if that has anything to do with why they were looking for you?"

"It seems backward, though," Bruce said. "I was thinking maybe they wanted to use me as some kind of battery to power this operation of theirs. But if I actually can *absorb* the energy..."

"Maybe it goes both ways," Tony said. "Like a capacitor. You take it, store it, and they pull it out." He frowned. "I wish you'd remembered this earlier, that we had a little more time to think it through."

"Me, too," Bruce said. He glanced at the clock. "But it looks like our time is up."

On the island, lights suddenly came on. The spheres of the orrery glowed from the center, and began to slowly creak into motion. Above, every star in the sky suddenly shone a little brighter.

Bruce started unbuttoning his shirt. It was a nice shirt—there was no point in ruining it.

Glowing figures appeared, each hovering above a planet of the clockwork.

Twelve of them.

"Yeah," Tony said. "That's our cue."

TWENTY-SEVEN

NATASHA came out of the water three yards from the nearest guard. Using her Widow's Bite, she dropped him so fast he never even knew she was there, but the alarms were tripped, and the others turned to face her.

As their fingers closed on their triggers, she shot a thin cable from her left gauntlet up into the machinery above and jerked herself into the air. Bullets whined through the space she had just occupied. The gunmen tried to follow the arc of her swing, but she had already detached, kicking one man in the head as she descended, dropping to sweep the next off his feet, somersaulting over the third, and planting a kick to his back as she landed.

The margins of her vision warned her of a sentry she hadn't seen earlier, hidden by the crystal globe. His first shot almost hit her, but the recoil from the weapon bounced his next few rounds high and to her left. Dropping him with her sting, she spun back to the others, making sure they stayed down.

The machine above her was now moving in earnest. Peering inside the globe, she had a much clearer view of the green man. His body and face were distorted by his transformation, but it was definitely Blonsky, roughly the same size as the Hulk, maybe a little smaller. He was also unconscious. She could see his ribs moving in and out, so he wasn't dead.

Making a quick sweep to be certain there were no more guards, Natasha turned her attention to the machinery powering the orrery. It looked pretty straightforward, so if she sabotaged the fuel cells, it ought to stop moving. Then she could figure out what to do about Blonsky.

She felt more than heard something behind her, spun around, and dodged, again firing her Bite. What she saw was mostly shadow, although his eyes were clearly visible, large and glowing in the mist. If her Bite affected him, he didn't show it, and he didn't strike back.

"There's no point in this," he whispered.

The voice was both in her ears and in her head, and for a moment she thought it was Cancer again. There were no claws, however, and the thoughts didn't feel invasive. It was as if the voice revealed what she was already thinking.

Because really, it was pointless.

Cap and Thor were dead.

They had to be. Nothing else would stop them from being here. The power they faced was incomprehensible—she, Tony, and Bruce were like fleas trying to take down an elephant. And why should they both try? What were they even fighting for?

Liberty?

Free will?

Her every instinct, every bit of her training, told her that free will was the last thing humanity needed. Most squandered it when they had it, and those few who realized its potential did so in the worst possible way. *Control* was what humanity needed. Boundaries, certainty, safety. Surety. Clockwork, not chaos. Why should she fight against that?

Why would anyone?

She took a step back.

"Stop it," she muttered. "Get out of my mind."

The shadow contracted and vanished, revealing a young man with large, searching eyes. He didn't look dangerous at all—on the contrary, he seemed vulnerable.

"That's right," he said. "You could kill me. Easily. But why? How have I wronged you? How have I wronged anyone?"

Simmah, she thought. *The Great Swallow. Pisces.*

Yet she trusted him. He was telling the truth. This thing that Cap and Tony and even Bruce fought for—what did it bring but misery and discontent? She had been a good soldier once, done what she was told without questioning why. It had been easier then, hadn't it? The "why" question was such a troubling one. To be free of it, to go back to being clockwork herself, a machine just doing its job…

Pisces took a step closer.

"Join us, Natasha Romanoff. The Shining Herd will fill all of the heavens and the Earth. There is room for you. *Especially* you. One day you could succeed to one of the Houses, rule with us."

She wanted that. *Really* wanted that. She wanted it so much that she knew—

It couldn't be real.

Natasha acted before committing to thought, lashing out and striking Pisces on his beautiful chin. He staggered back, looking puzzled.

"Why?" he asked.

"You think you know me," she said. "You don't."

The boy shrugged. "That's too bad," he said. "The offer was genuine. The others could never have joined us. But you—you could have."

As he spoke, he grew. He changed.

○────────────○

TONY came in low and flat, skimming so close to the surface that the thrust from his repulsors plowed a furrow in the otherwise still waters of the sea. He'd punched through the energy field a few seconds before, but so far, the defenses hadn't responded.

At least not to him. They *were* responding, though. Across the island, quite a fireworks display was in evidence as the Quinjet launched missiles at the now turning orrery. None of the projectiles made it very far, though. The field wasn't a shield, but it did demark a no-fly zone. As the missiles passed through, bolts of white light flashed from the various planets of the orrery, meeting the incoming rockets, smelting them into slag and expanding gas.

He figured the only reason he hadn't been targeted was because he was below the line of sight of the device, but that would change as soon as he went for the Key—which was still where he'd last seen it. Gripped by the floating man who called himself Scorpio.

He had to admit, the name seemed more fitting with each passing second. In addition to his tail, several extra chitinous limbs had sprung from Scorpio's ribs. One of his hands was an immense claw, crackling with energy. The other still retained some semblance of its human form, although it was hard to be sure, since it was a fist around the Key.

The other Zodiac members were bigger and mutated, too, but they were all peripheral. Scorpio was his target.

Reaching the island he had to cut up sharply, aiming himself like a missile at the Key, punching his speed to maximum. If he could snatch the golden ankh and just keep going, they might avoid the all-out brawl he personally didn't think they were likely to win.

"*Sir—*" JARVIS began.

"See it," he said, cutting hard to the right as a ray of blistering white light flashed past him. Each orb had to warm up a split second before it fired. If not for that he would have been—at the very least —severely inconvenienced.

Correcting course, he had to dodge a second discharge. By that time, Scorpio had turned in the air. The Key briefly glowed brighter, and then Tony struck something. It was like hitting a concrete wall, but there was nothing visible. He flailed for a minute, regaining his bearings, his head spinning, managing to fire a repulsor beam at the eight-legged freak.

An egg-shaped shell of light flared around his target.

"*He seems to have some sort of energy-dissipating shield around him,*" JARVIS said.

"You think?" Tony asked, dodging another blast of energy and cutting a semicircle around the Zodiac chief. He fired repulsors again, with the same effect.

Scorpio waved the Key...

...and Tony was somewhere else.

Not far. The orrery was still there, but in the distance. His gyros cut in and straightened him, just in time for him to see Taurus streaking toward him. He had a glimpse of a massive bovine head and horns and eyes like pulsars, before—

The impact jolted through him. His heads-up display went black; the slight *whoosh* of circulating air ceased, and his limbs were suddenly dead, or at least too heavy to move. Through his eye slits he watched Taurus dwindle below him, but then his body turned in a slow flip so in one moment he saw the blazing stars, then the distant, fog-diffused lights of the mainland, then the black waters of the sea.

"Reboot!" he yelled. "Reboot!"

This is really going to sting...

o————o

WHEN Bruce dropped out of the Quinjet, his muscles were already knotting against bone, stretching, expanding, covering Banner's puny skin with emerald armor. As the jet sped off on its own mission, he watched the ground come up.

Light flared in the distance, and then a brilliant beam hit him, like when the lion had yelled at him. He was still in the air, so it knocked him back. He smelled blood, and something burned in his throat, but he also felt a surge of strength.

He hit the water, skipped like a pebble tossed by a titan, and then sank. Before long his feet hit bottom and he pushed, jetting upward and landing on the island. The lion was there to meet him—a lot bigger this time, even bigger than Hulk—and his flashing claws were the size of carving knives.

"You!" Hulk shouted. "I don't like you, Lion!"

He ducked the slashing claws and struck with an uppercut that barely budged the big cat-man. Then he set his feet, jumped up and slammed down, feeling his fist crunch into the lion's skull. He followed up with a haymaker which sent his now-giant opponent sprawling. He roared and charged forward, his rage building. He leapt, fists churning, pounding the lion into the stone of the island.

Something cold and wet closed all around him. It yanked him off of his foe, jerked him through the air, and plunged him back into the sea, dragging him against the shallow bottom. He clutched at whatever held him, but his hand just went right through it, like it was nothing but water come to life. He pushed against the sea floor, trying to leap back out again, but the watery fist didn't let go. It squeezed him even harder.

Hulk opened his mouth to shout his rage, but it filled with water. More furious than ever, he pushed his arms against the force gripping him, spreading them wider and wider. Nothing happened, but then his anger toppled over and he flexed them as wide as they would go. Then, with every ounce of strength he possessed, he clapped them back together.

The water exploded, racing away from him in all directions and briefly opening a hole in the sea itself. Quickly planting his feet, he leapt.

Shaking water out of his ears, he remembered what he was supposed to do. *Smash.* He was supposed to smash the funny machine with its big glowing balls.

Lion was back, standing in his way.

Hulk roared and charged him.

Then he remembered again. As much as he wanted to fight, instead he leapt straight over the lion's head, arcing up toward someone who looked like a bug—the one holding the funny-looking thing in his hand.

Hulk reached him, and something sort of sputtered. It felt as if he'd torn through a curtain. Then he landed a punch on the hard black armor the thing had for skin, and laughed at the look of surprise on the insect-man's face.

He snorted, grabbing his opponent with one gigantic hand. The nasty-looking tail darted down toward him, and he caught that with his other hand. They were locked like that for a second, but then Hulk started pulling the tail down. He would break it off, and then—

"No!" the bug-man hissed. "Desert winds take you, beast!"

Suddenly Hulk was thirsty. And dry. His throat burned and every breath hurt.

"Stop it!" he roared. He shook the bug-man, hard.

Then the bug-man hit him with the Key.

First it hurt, then Hulk felt better. Instantly. He grinned, pulling the tail down, feeling the armor on it start to crack.

Without warning the mist-woman was there. She jumped *into* him, and he suddenly felt really light. His hands gripped into fists, going right through the bug-man's tail and arm. It was like Hulk had been turned into smoke. He began to drift up, like a balloon. Twisted this way and that, trying to get her out from inside him—but no matter what he did, he couldn't make her leave.

He just kept floating upward.

The stars looked really funny. Big, and they weren't twinkling. They were just sort of shining, like flashlights or floodlights. Like when the army was hunting him.

Furious, he tried to punch himself, to find some way to hurt her, but she didn't seem to notice.

○———————○

PISCES stretched open a mouth large enough to take Natasha in whole, and lunged at her. She could still feel the press of his mind on hers.

The fight still seemed pointless. Her spirits continued dropping with no bottom in sight—but hitting him felt good. That he had transformed into a monstrous eel-thing seemed beside the point. She kicked him in the throat and blasted him in the eye with her Widow's Bite. He struck back, grasping after her with slimy, semi-human hands, but she whirled past him, snatching up a rifle from one of the fallen guards, and opened up on him, aiming for his eyes and mouth.

His needle-teeth shattered as the rounds raked across him, and one of his eyes imploded into black goo. His tail flipped around, swiping at her from behind, but she vaulted over it, firing the grappling line from her gauntlets and wrapping him up, pinning his fin-arms to his body. Then she ran up his back and kicked him in his head.

Continuing up, she vaulted toward the fuel cells.

A flash of light uncoiled toward her and she twisted from its path. Virgo descended, her whip rippling through the air and returning for another blow. Natasha only knew her from Cap's description, but she could tell Virgo was... changed. She no longer held her whip—it had become an extension of her arm. She stood at least eight feet tall, and her eyes were empty, as if they had been plucked out. The star on her chest was blindingly bright.

Natasha didn't give her time to send her lash out again. She landed on the catwalk, ran four quick steps and jumped, launching a flying kick at Virgo's head. She connected, then crashed full into the other woman, so they both plunged into the water. The whip hissed and boiled. Natasha swam rapidly back.

Pisces, free of his bonds, was waiting. He grabbed her arms and pulled them behind her back. Without hesitation she kicked up and did a backflip over his head, twisting free of his grip as Virgo's lash missed her and wrapped around the sea-monster Pisces had become. Natasha had the satisfaction of hearing him shriek as the whip cut into him, before a silent concussion of pain swept through her.

She landed on her feet, but her knees felt weak all of a sudden. Stumbling, closing her eyes against the pain and despair, she ran toward one of the ladders that led up into the machinery. A glance over her shoulder revealed Virgo, still clutching Pisces and swaying in the water, her eyeless face crumpled with despair.

Go, she told herself. *Go.*

Although what she really wanted to do was lie down and quit.

She reached the bank of fuel cells. As she grasped for the nearest, flames engulfed her.

SOMETHING clicked, and Tony's armor hummed back to life. His jets kicked in, just as the water was about to slap him in the face. It was too late to pull up entirely, so he briefly plowed into the sea before soaring upward. Making a turn so hard that all of the blood seemed to pool to one side of his head, he aimed at Scorpio again.

But someone had been paying attention.

A pair of figures sped toward him.

"These two again," he muttered. *Gemini?* That had to be who they were.

Lightning forked out from one of them, jagging through his armor without doing any real damage. Then the wind hit him, easily hurricane force. He fought free of it just in time to see the twins join hands.

It was like watching a sun being born. Even with the optical filters in his mask, the flash left spots in his eyes—but that was the least of his worries. The two men were growing, fast, merging into a single, two-headed being. A titanic hand reached out for him and he wasn't able to dodge in time. Colossal fingers wrapped around him and squeezed. Static electricity blasted through his suit, circuits whining as they started to overload. Again.

"Shunt!" he shouted.

The repulsor in his chest exploded, venting the excess charge built up in his suit. It hit one of the two heads, and he was happy to hear a basso profundo yelp of pain. Gemini let go of him, so he followed up by driving into them, hammering at the other head with his alloy-covered fists before thundering on toward his original target.

Scorpio was watching, however, and he waved the Key. Focused on that, Tony didn't see Capricorn until the goat-man caught hold of him. He felt his breath catch as the air in his suit went instantly bad.

"JARVIS!" he shouted.

Air reserves cut in and his recirculation system went into high gear, thanks to the modifications he'd made on the flight from Taiwan.

"That won't help you for long," Capricorn said.

"I know," Tony replied, blasting his chest beam again. It knocked Capricorn back just enough that the missile JARVIS had sent from the Quinjet caught him in midair. It grabbed Tony's foe in a magnetic lock, and yanked him off across the Salish Sea.

Then everything went white as he failed to dodge the next blast from the orrery. Once again he was plummeting downward, the ozone scent of overloaded circuits sharp in his nostrils.

"JARVIS!" he yelped.

"*Rerouting*," the computer told him.

"No time," Tony said, watching the ground come up, wondering if he could at least angle to hit one of the globes. Then something struck him from the side. He braced for whatever was in store, but the impact was almost—gentle.

It wasn't an attack—someone was holding him.

A guy with long, flowing blond hair.

TWENTY-EIGHT

"THOR!" he yelped. "Man, am I glad to see you."

"And I you," the thunder god said. He flung his hammer and did a flip in the air. The weapon struck the approaching Capricorn in the chest. Then they were touching down on the shore of the island, where Cap and Strange stood. Strange was in the midst of a conjuration; weird green light had formed a sort of cat's cradle between his hands. The light stretched out, split open, and the Hulk stepped out.

"Where mist-woman?" he raged.

"I have forced her from you," Strange said.

"Hang on there, big guy," Cap said, placing his hand on the Hulk's shoulder. "Let's just get our game plan together." He turned to Tony. "Sorry to be late to the party," he said. "What did we miss?"

"Ah, well—Nat's under the island, trying to shut down the orrery—sabotage it, or whatever. We're just trying to get the Key back from Scorpio."

"We haven't much time," Strange said. "The Shining Herd is descending."

"Scorpio has some kind of shield around him," Tony said. "My repulsors won't go through, and missiles just bounce off."

"No shield," Hulk said. "Hulk grabbed bug-man, but mist-woman let him go."

"Maybe it stops tech," Tony said, "but not living things."

"Noted," Cap said. "We have to go for the Key. We know the Hulk can get through, so big guy, this is on you, okay? The rest of us will clear the way. You just get the Key and go. In fact—Strange, whoever gets it, teleport them as far away as possible. We've got to keep it out of their hands. Without it they can't finish their thing, right?"

"That's correct."

"So when this conjunction is over, they'll power back down. We'll work out how to deal with them then."

"Your strategy is sound," Strange said, "but if we cannot get the Key from Scorpio, I must do what my predecessor did—overload the Key. If that happens, you must all be ready to flee this place immediately."

"Let's make that our final option," Cap said. "If what you said is true, that could cause a lot of collateral damage."

"Agreed," Strange said.

"Okay," Cap said. "Let's—"

"Hulk smash bug-man!" the Hulk hollered, charging away.

"I'll go left," Tony said, rocketing toward Taurus.

"Thor," Cap said, "take the right flank. I'll follow our boy up the middle. Strange, see if you can handle the beams from the orrery." Strange nodded and rose into the air, a pale yellow nimbus forming around each hand.

The Hulk was already in motion.

Thor took to the air.

Cap started his run.

The orrery kicked into overtime. The Hulk took the brunt of the blasts, and while they deflected him as a baseball bat to the head might an ordinary person, he kept moving forward.

The blue orb of Neptune brightened, and Steve dodged, just barely—although that took him into the blast from the next planet, which he took to be Jupiter. The beamz darted for him but resolved in a bright lens a few yards short. Strange was on the job. Steve leapt onto one of the armatures, positioning himself between Jupiter and the Sun.

Maybe if they fired at each other…

They did, and he managed to leap clear, but another beam flashed in his peripheral vision. Light and heat slapped him like the hand of a giant while he was midair. He clipped the spinning armature on the way down and then fell farther, landing roughly on a concrete slab, rolling aside as yet another planet tried to fry him. He took cover at the base of the orrery. There the turning arms shielded him from the sun, and for a moment none of the planets was in his line of sight.

Rolling to a crouch he peered out, searching for the best way through. Blood collected in his mouth. He saw Thor struck by two of the beams. Strange's shields stopped three others. The Asgardian fell along the arc of his last flight. At this distance, it was impossible to say if he was just stunned or out of the fight. Meanwhile, at least five members of the Zodiac converged on the Hulk.

Steve spit out the blood, chose a path, and bolted, determination hardening.

Vaulting over the first stellar blast he ducked under the next. The third he deflected with his shield, angling it so the kick of it sent him flying straight toward his target. The acceleration was dizzying, but he held onto his focus, his arm aching. Two, three, four of Strange's shields appeared to support him, and then he was there, slamming into Scorpio with his right shoulder and grappling around him with one arm.

The sting arced over, stabbing into his shield, then he slammed the disk into Scorpio's face. As they both began to fall, he sent the shield whirling toward a woman with crab claws coming out of her face, and changed his hold to the Key, trying to rip it out of Scorpio's hand.

The air turned into jelly, clogging his nose and mouth. He wrenched at the Key, but something hit him, hard, and everything bleached like an overdeveloped black-and-white photo.

Then he fell.

TWENTY-NINE

SOMETHING made Hulk feel heavy, so heavy his arms and legs didn't want to move, and he crashed to the ground, surrounded by enemies. *Covered* in them. The horse-man with the bright arrows kept shooting him. The crawfish woman kept trying to tear into his mind, and the lion was on his back, ripping at his flesh.

He was confused, and he was frustrated, and he was *angry*. It was like he had bees flying around inside of his skull, and he had had enough. But the weight—

Then the Iron Man came flying in. He hit the bull-woman, picked her up, and carried her into the sky. Suddenly lighter, Hulk slammed the ground with both fists, then launched into his enemies, right and left. He threw the lion into the horse with arrows. He butted the crawfish with his head, tore a lump of stone from the ground and clocked the Archer.

The bug-man came to ground.

Hulk swept his arms wildly, scattering them all, then pumped his legs and launched himself once more at the man holding the glowing thing. Mist-woman darted in front of him, but before she could touch him colorful bands of light appeared, freezing her in place.

He reached his enemy.

The bug-man was a lot bigger, now—bigger than an elephant— but Hulk didn't care about that. Nothing was too big for him to fight.

He grabbed the bug-man by his pinching hands and began to pull, trying to tear off his jointed arms.

The sting arced over and hit him between the shoulder blades. He felt it sink in, deep, and then his mighty frame spasmed with pain unlike any he'd ever felt before. But he wouldn't let go. He continued to pull, his rage mounting. He felt as if his bones were burning inside of him, but he didn't care. He doubled down, yanking on the claws. The bug-man screamed as one of his arms popped at the joint and then tore free. Hulk roared and hit him in the face with the severed limb.

But it wasn't the arm holding the glowing thing, the thing he was supposed to get, so he put both hands on that.

The pain inside of him grew, and for the first time since the fight had begun he felt... weaker. Inside. Scorpio loomed over him and pushed him down to one knee, and once again the sting dug into him on the side of his neck. He struggled to rise back up, but then the ground pulled on him again, hard, really hard, and he felt heavy once more. Only this time he kept getting heavier. The earth beneath him began to crack and shudder.

Then he fell through it.

○————————○

TONY drove his suit to full power, ramming Taurus into a rocky hillside beyond the orrery. His armor strained with effort; she was probably thirty feet tall now, and her mass had increased commensurately. Her humanity was fading; her back legs were bent the wrong way, and when she came up out of the hole, it was on all fours.

He blasted her in the face with his chest beam, but that hardly slowed her down. It must have temporarily blinded her, though, because when he stepped aside to avoid her charge she went hurtling past him, right into the stone façade of the hotel that stood near the orrery. He assumed it was abandoned; he hoped it was.

Twisting, he fired repulsors at another Zodiac freak show, the conjoined twins and the small hurricane that followed them around, but with little result. Then a jagged burst of colorful sparks from above got their attention. Strange was still in the fight.

So was Taurus. She lowered her head, but this time she didn't charge. Instead Tony was suddenly falling.

Up.

As he flew toward the bright, creepy stars, he engaged full thrust. That slowed him down a little, but his heads-up suggested that he was still moving upward with an attraction of about ten gravities. His systems, already strained, were beginning to approach their limits.

The "sun" was heating up below him, but the skyward pull was so strong he couldn't deflect from its path. He cut off his thrust and redirected all of his resources to defenses. While he didn't think it would be enough, he hoped to discharge the overload through his chest beam, passing the energy along as he had done earlier, but—

He got it, then. He understood.

If only he survived long enough to tell someone...

○———————○

NATASHA dove clear of the flames before they could do her serious harm, coughing at the scent of singed hair. The newcomer was built like a pro wrestler. His head seemed tiny compared to the massive coiled horns perched there. He was outlined in fire, and even as she dodged he hurled a gout of flame toward her.

"Not nice," she said. "Sneaking up on people. You can get in trouble for that."

Aries' only answer was a bestial bellow as he charged her, trailing flame behind him. Below, Virgo shook off her stupor and prepared her whip, which was no longer wrapped around Pisces.

Great, Nat thought. *I've got about four seconds before this becomes really* difficult. She stood her ground against Aries' charge, throwing out her palms to meet his fists, taking hold of them as she fell back, planting her feet in his breadbasket and transferring his own momentum beyond her and up.

Heat seared through her gloves and boots, and it felt as if she'd stuck her face into the mouth of an open furnace as he passed over her.

Without waiting for the result, she flung herself down toward the waters below as the flaming Aries crashed into the fuel cells. She had a glimpse of Virgo's empty eyes staring up, her mouth open, and then everything washed out as the cells ignited and an explosion filled the cavern just as her head hit the water.

She glanced back once. It was almost like staring at stained glass. Then she began swimming for the tunnel as the water above her began to boil.

That's it for the orrery, she thought. The burning batteries would make the chamber beneath the island a living hell for the near future. There was nothing she could do for Blonsky at the moment. Better see what she could do up top.

○————————○

STEVE arrested his freefall by catching one of the orrery's turning arms and swinging beneath it, tumbling so he hit the sphere representing Mars before continuing to the ground. He landed on his feet, albeit shakily, found his balance and prepared to leap aside when the globe began to incandesce. The ground beneath the contraption seemed to be swaying, as if in an earthquake.

It wasn't the movement of the orrery he was feeling; that had ground to a halt. The shaking sensation was in the concrete beneath his feet.

"Oh," he said. He leapt, springing back up onto Mars, then across to the armature supporting Uranus, and ran, even as the entire structure began to quiver violently. He leapt off the end as the center of the vast clockwork erupted, sending a dome of flame skyward and a shockwave that rushed out from the sun toward the outer planets.

Natasha, he thought. That must have been her doing. She'd destroyed the orrery; the blasts of energy from the planets had stopped. He hoped Nat was okay, but he didn't let it stick in him hard. She was a survivor.

And the way back to Scorpio was clear.

Off to the right, Thor rose up beyond the flames, whirling his hammer and hurling himself toward the Key. Strange was just behind him. The Hulk was nowhere to be seen.

Steve started to join them, but paused. It felt as if something was pressing down on him, as if the sky was literally falling. He looked up and saw the heavens ablaze. The stars, now blindingly bright, had begun to connect themselves with strands of light. He thought he heard distant music, weird and atonal, and whispers in a language he didn't know, in voices that were not human.

This has to end soon, he thought. Strange's predictions had always been somehow unreal. How could constellations "descend" from the sky? But they weren't so much coming down as pushing *through*, from a place more alien than anything he'd seen in his travels with the sorcerer. They were beating against a barrier that had protected the Earth since time began, and they were winning. The invisible wall began to crumble.

Thor streaked toward Scorpio, and half a dozen Zodiac members converged on him. The Key in Scorpio's remaining claw looked immense.

Then Strange was there.

"There is no time," he said. "I must overload the Key."

"Do it, then," Steve said. Though the very thought filled him with dread, he tamped it down. There was still too much to do.

"They will try to stop me," the sorcerer said. "If you could hold them off, that would be excellent."

Above, the combined might of half of the Zodiac sent Thor crashing to Earth.

○——————○

NATASHA pulled herself onto the island, eyes tracking the battle, trying to sort out where she was most needed. She picked out Scorpio and the Key, floating high in the air. Sprinting that way, she leapt atop one of the orrery arms and sped along it. Above she saw Thor crash into the half-a-dozen Zodiac members who had swarmed in to protect Scorpio. He went down, hard, but Natasha was behind the Zodiac leader and his protectors. Distracted by the others, they would never see her coming.

Something reached into her mind. Something familiar, something trying to take hold her arms and limbs from the inside.

She knew what it was, and she pushed back against it with cold fury. She saw Cancer coming at her, just a few yards away.

"Oh, no," she snarled. "You will *not*."

It made sense; the crab-woman wasn't a bruiser, like some of the others. Her powers were more insidious. She was using them to guard Scorpio's back. Of course, Cancer was now three times the size she had been, and the claws extending from her gigantic head were big enough to snip Natasha's limbs off.

Cancer lunged at her, trying to do just that, but Natasha shot a cable at a higher armature, using it to flip up and over the extended pincer. She came down behind her opponent and kicked her at the base of her neck, then followed that up with a ridgehand to the side of her armored head. Cancer spun, but Natasha leapt over her again, drawing her pistols and firing into the joint of arm and claw.

The crab-woman let loose an awful, whistling shriek as the claw fell away, and for a moment seemed paralyzed by pain or shock. Natasha took that opportunity to beat Cancer until she slumped over senseless.

○——————○

THOR struggled back to his feet. The orrery had fallen silent. The constant bursts of energy from the planets were finally subdued. He was preparing to fly back toward Scorpio when Aquarius appeared over him, taller than the greatest Jotun, a watery form bent on revenge.

"I've dealt with you before," the Asgardian said. "I can do it again."

He lifted Mjolnir and summoned the Bifrost.

A small spark of electricity flashed around his enchanted mallet. Then Aquarius smashed him with a watery fist.

And again.

"No Bifrost!" Heimdall's words vibrated through the water engulfing him. *"The Mulapin descend. Asgard cannot touch this place now—it is beyond my reach."*

That was unwelcome news. He struck with his hammer, sending lightning through Aquarius's watery form. Bubbles formed along its path. He struck again.

Aquarius lifted him and pounded him against the rocks, then hauled him up again. Thor leapt free, spinning his hammer at his side as his foe towered above him again. Then he hurled it.

It missed the giant's aqueous head by a handspan, streaking into the sky until it was lost from sight.

Aquarius laughed. "You cannot strike down water," he said. Then he swung his fists, battering Thor mercilessly against the stone foundations of the island. The thunder god fought back, but his opponent was right—one might as well seek to command the tides.

With every attack he struggled back up, but each time it was more difficult.

"So much for the might of Asgard," Aquarius crowed. "When the Shining Herd rules, your kind will not dare to come here."

Thor held up his hand.

"Do you beg for mercy?" Aquarius asked. "It is a useless gesture."

"No," Thor said. "I'm just waiting."

"Waiting…?"

There was a shrieking sound as Mjolnir returned from where he had thrown it, beyond the atmosphere of the planet. Its uru metal heated like a meteor, like the dying star in which it had been forged. The hammer struck the body Aquarius had formed from the Salish Sea, which instantly became a cloud of hissing steam. Continuing through, the hammer found rest in Thor's outstretched hand.

"Thor!"

The thunder god turned, to see Captain America standing with Doctor Strange. The Captain was gesturing toward the sorcerer, and Thor saw why.

Scorpio stood alone, holding the Key above his head. It was hard to see—not because it was too bright, but because its outline had begun to blur, to blend with the weird star shine from above. Scorpio's allies were charging toward Strange and Cap.

Leo was in the lead, alternating between two and four feet as he ran, and even on four he was as tall as a bison at the shoulder. Leaping into the fray, Thor hit him from the side and landed a solid blow, sending the big cat turning through the air to collide with the flaming ruins of the orrery.

His next target was Taurus; Mjolnir struck her just above and between her eyes, on the slaughtering spot. Lightning struck with the blow, and she toppled back.

Then Capricorn butted him, and he felt the cold pierce his bones, but he grabbed hold of the monster and dug his feet in, just as Cap's shield sailed past him and knocked back the now-conjoined Gemini twins.

Thor heaved Capricorn out toward the sea, then turned to face the momentarily stunned Gemini, calling to the storm that they had generated, struggling to turn it against them.

THIRTY

STEVE caught his shield and watched in appreciation as Thor knocked Leo and Taurus both down for the count, and then brought Gemini to a standstill. Libra was still bound in the magical prison Strange had summoned for her, which left Scorpio unguarded.

The Key seemed to be vibrating, pulling streamers of energy from the sky, but also from everywhere else.

One long, erratic coil of energy bridged the gap between Strange and Scorpio.

"Seek cover, Captain," Strange said. "Thor might survive this, but—"

He was cut off as something lunged from the burning orrery. Aries—but a bigger, stronger-looking Aries. Flame licked his flesh, and the breath from his nostrils was blue-white, like a pair of acetylene torches.

Steve charged to meet the burning ram, crouching behind his shield at the last instant, protecting himself as he put the full momentum of his attack into his shoulder. The blow numbed his arm, but he couldn't give Aries time to react. Jamming the edge of the shield into his adversary's jaw, he struck him again with the flat, and finally with an uppercut from his gloved right hand. He felt cloying heat all around him, but kept at it, driving Aries away from Strange.

Then the air seemed to crack in half. He looked up and saw the Key shine brighter than the sun, and for a full two heartbeats it went brighter. But then a flash of power shot from the Key into the heart of the ruined orrery, blasting into the Earth itself. An instant later, Strange lit up like fireworks. He trembled, and jerked like a marionette controlled by an overactive child. Flames burst from his eyes and mouth, and he gasped out an unearthly syllable.

Then the sorcerer was gone, leaving only a curling wisp of smoke where he'd been standing. Scorpio was still there, still holding the Key, and the constellations flowed as if the sky was made of syrup.

What the hell?

Aries, taking advantage of Steve's pause, came back at him, trying to engulf him in flame. Whatever damage Steve had done to him in the moments before, he seemed fully recovered.

Sweat leaked from beneath his mask and stung his eyes, and the skin of his face felt close to blistering. He landed a solid blow on his opponent, but it wasn't obvious which of them was more hurt by it. To make matters worse, Taurus and Leo were back in the fight, closing on Thor.

There was a gleam of gold and red in his peripheral vision, and he heard the familiar whine and *pow* of repulsors. Two of Iron Man's blasts hit Aries, knocking him back.

Stark came down next to him.

"I've figured it out," he shouted. "Heat sink. They didn't have one last time."

"Heat sink?" Steve said.

"Like when you're soldering old-style circuits, but the soldering iron is too hot for the transistors, or the fan in a computer—never mind. Give me about two minutes. Then blast that Key again."

"How? Strange is gone."

"Thor can do it," Tony said. "Maybe me, if I can get back in time. But tell Thor. You'll have to get the Key out of Scorpio's hand, though."

"Okay," Steve said. "I'm on it."

"You need some help?"

He spun to see Natasha, soaking wet but otherwise looking intact.

Her gaze twitched past him and she fired her Widow's Bite at Aries, who was getting back up. He dropped like a rock.

"Always," Steve said.

"Hill," he heard Tony say, "targets are painted. They're all yours."

Aries was getting back up *again*, but then something whizzed down from the sky, knocked him forty feet, and exploded. An instant later, Taurus, Leo, and Gemini suffered the same fate.

A little bit of cavalry never hurt, Steve mused.

"Thor!" he shouted. "New plan!"

Tony was gone, jetting toward the water.

○━━━━━━━○

HULK crashed through concrete and steel, some weird machines, through an inferno of smoke and flame and into water. There, his weight continued to crush him, pushing his last gulp of air slowly from his nose. The fire from Scorpio's venom burned hotter, too, turning his guts into jelly.

With enormous effort he managed to roll over onto his belly, and from there push himself up with his arms, folding up into a crouch and then, on wobbling legs, stand, so that his head came above the surface.

His first aching breath was polluted with smoke, but it was better than no air at all. He took a step, trying to find a shallower place. His strange weight was starting to fade, but everything else in him was beginning to fail. He felt tired; even blinking his eyes took effort, and strength was draining from his limbs.

He knew what was happening.

Banner was coming back.

Weak, puny Banner. And when he returned, the bug-man's poison would kill him. So he had to fight; he had to stay the Hulk, or neither of them would survive. But his rage and his strength continued to ebb. He felt his shoulders slump and darkness pool at the corners of his mind.

He fought to stay awake, to focus. What was he looking at? Something strange. A big glass jar, like a fishbowl, with someone in it. Someone who looked familiar. He was green, like Hulk—but he was asleep. Who was it? There was no other Hulk. Hulk was alone; there was nothing like him anywhere.

And yet he felt something. Like they had met before. Painfully he took a step forward, and then another. Then one of his knees buckled, and he sank below the water again.

What did it matter, anyway? Everyone hated the Hulk. It would be better if he was dead. Better for Banner, too. Banner hurt; Hulk wasn't sure why. He had been happier. Now he wasn't. Banner didn't even really want to be Banner again, which was strange. Maybe he should just let himself sink into the water and take a breath. Take a few breaths. Fill up with water until he couldn't breathe at all. Then everyone would be safe. No more innocent people would suffer because of Hulk or Banner. Let someone else worry about it all. Cap. Thor. Puny man with iron clothes. Let them fight, while he had peace.

Peace was all Hulk really wanted.

His other leg bent, and he knelt on the bottom.

Peace, he thought.

His eyes closed, but he saw light. He tasted it, felt it shine on his bones, felt it rinse the poison from his blood, fill him up with new strength. Banner shrank away.

And Hulk was angry again.

He broke from the water. Light was still all around him, pouring from the fishbowl, from the man in the fishbowl. Only green fishbowl-man was bigger now, much bigger, twice the size of Hulk. Still green, and ugly, and still asleep.

There was someone else there, the person trying to make him think sad thoughts. The person who told Hulk to breathe in water. He was still there, still trying to make Hulk think things. He looked weird, like a combination of a snake and a fish and a person.

"You!" Hulk shouted, and he leapt forward, fists pumping. The fish-snake-man fell back beneath the first few of his attacks. Then he dove into the water and didn't come back up.

Hulk stood in the water for a moment, panting, trying to remember what he was supposed to do.

Bug-man.

He looked up at the hole through which he'd fallen. Then he heard something come up from the water behind him. He turned around, roaring, ready to fight.

But it was the Iron Man.

"Whoa! Buddy!" Iron Man said. "Hulk. It's me."

"Hulk sees Iron Man," Hulk said. "Hulk goes to fight bug-man."

"Hang on," Iron Man said. "We've got work to do down here."

"What work?"

"That guy," he said. "The green guy in there. The Zodiac is using him for a heat sink. Or an energy sink. Whenever we try to overload the Key, the overflow spills back into him. He absorbs it."

"So?"

"So, we need to stop that from happening."

"Hulk smash green man?"

"No," Iron Man said. "We don't have to smash him. We just have to get him out of there. Away from here."

Hulk turned toward the fishbowl.

"Iron Man talks too much," he said. Then he swung at the glass.

It was harder than it looked. It took two hits to crack it, and after that it just kept splintering without really breaking, so it looked like a weird spider web. It quickly became frustrating.

Then the Iron Man blasted it with his chest thing, and the whole thing fell apart.

Hulk's next breath felt funny, and his head went all spinny. He stepped back.

"Gas," the Iron Man said. "Some sort of gas. Get back."

"Hulk knows gas," he said, shaking his head back and forth, trying to clear it.

The big green guy stirred. He opened his eyes and looked around, blinking, mouth open.

"*Šta?*" he groaned, jerking his arms, but the tubes in them pulled back. He seemed to notice his arms, then—and the rest of his body. He began screaming made-up words, words that meant nothing, ripping the wires and tubes from his body.

Then his eyes settled on Hulk.

"Banner!"

"Not Banner!" Hulk yelled back.

The green man was fast, and his punch was even harder than Thor's best hit with his hammer—so hard that Hulk was momentarily stunned.

"Hey, listen, wait," he vaguely heard the Iron Man say. Then there was a loud clanging noise. When Hulk's head was cleared, the other green guy was gone, and Iron Man was lying down.

"Ouch," Iron Man said.

"Where did he go?" Hulk demanded.

Iron Man sat up. "Not important right now, big fellah," he said. "We've still got to take care of Scorpio—the bug-man. You ready?"

"Hulk ready to smash something."

○━━━━━━━━━○

THOR beat back Taurus and Leo again, but each time they recovered more quickly. He saw Aries start after Cap, who was dodging the deadly arrows of Sagittarius and lightning strikes from Gemini.

The SHIELD missiles were helping, but the Zodiac monsters were shrugging them off now, just as his own blows were losing their effect. He caught a glimpse now and then of Nat, but the most powerful of the Zodiac were concentrating on him, trying to prevent him from reaching Scorpio. They were doing an excellent job… but that was the plan, wasn't it?

Because Thor was meant to be a distraction.

THIRTY-ONE

CAP dodged an explosion that knocked Sagittarius aside, leaping high and far over the broken orb of Neptune as Aries and Gemini were likewise struck. A wicked thread of light cut through where he'd just been running, and he realized that wherever Virgo had gone, she was back.

Scanning the battlefield, he spotted her. Virgo was bigger than she had been, but not gigantic as some of them had become. Yet her *presence* was greater. Something deep, deep down told him he ought to be bowing to her, instead of fighting her.

He knew that wasn't coming from him, so it just pissed him off.

So instead he leaped inside her guard and slammed his shield into her godlike face.

Once again, it was just him and Scorpio.

Closing the distance, he deflected the sting and punched his target, hard, noticing that the claw the Hulk had torn off had nearly grown back. No sense in giving it more opportunity—he piled it on, landing punch after punch, once again driving the Zodiac chief back.

Out of the corner of his eye he saw Virgo flick her whip. So he caught Scorpio's arm and jerked it aside, and the energy lash wrapped around it. He grabbed the other end of the knout, gripping it with his gloved hand, and *yanked*.

It hurt like hell. It hurt so much he wasn't even sure he had a hand left, but the whip-line contracted, slicing through the chiton of Scorpio's arm.

The Key fell free.

Dropping his shield he caught the Key with his good hand, leaping away, holding it in the air.

"Thor!" he shouted. "Now!"

○————————————○

THOR dropped lightning all around him and took to the sky, breaking free of his foes. Focusing on Cap, holding the Key aloft, he felt the lightning build in him, preparing to discharge it and overload the Key. He didn't know if Stark had succeeded in his mission, but the moment was here and they had to trust that Iron Man had done his job.

Yet he paused.

If the Key exploded while Cap was holding it, the Avenger would surely die. Cap was prepared for that, was always ready to give his life.

But Thor couldn't be the one to take it.

So he whirled his hammer and streaked toward him. He could take the Key himself, fly high above the world...

Leo snatched him from the air and hurled him to earth. Thor punched the foe with the butt of his hammer and jumped back up in time to see Scorpio rise up behind Cap, and strike him down.

○————————————○

NATASHA peppered Scorpio with Bites, to no effect—then shot a line to wrap around his arm as he reached for the Key. Cap was down; she couldn't tell if he was dead or not, but he wasn't moving.

Yanking on the line to gather momentum, she put both of her heels into his arachnoid face. Then she did a backflip, picked up the Key, and ran like hell as Sagittarius tried to skewer her with energy arrows. At this point they were more like spears, each one as long as she was tall, and left smoking holes in everything they hit.

The Archer was full centaur, too.

Natasha put a flying kick into Virgo's face, not holding out hope that it would do too much damage. But she just had to keep them guessing, get the Key to Thor, help him break free long enough to supercharge it...

Twisting to avoid the back-cut of the whip, she dropped straight into the path of one of the Archer's bolts. She struck it away with the Key, but that numbed her arm, her shoulder, and most of her right side. She stuck the landing, but another bolt shattered the stone at her feet and sent her flying.

She hit the ground rolling, but when she came up, Scorpio was almost on her. She tumbled aside, then launched herself up, atop the arachnid foe. Her arm was still numb, but she managed to pull her pistol and pump five shots into his chiton-covered head before his convulsions threw her off.

Above, the stars looked as if they were starting to *drip* from the sky, melting like they were in a Dali painting.

She had to do something more than continue this game of keep-away. Someone had to break free and get the Key away, far away, from any human population, and then destroy it. Scorpio looked a little dazed, but he was coming around, and she guessed at any moment he would be back in the fight. She couldn't see Thor or the Hulk, but Tony was scorching by, tied up with Virgo and her whip, arms strapped to his side, showers of sparks flying where her weapon wrapped around his suit.

Launching herself straight into their path, she caught Virgo's neck in the crook of her arm, and slammed the Key into the woman's face with everything she had in her. It felt like hitting a tank, but Virgo's head snapped back, and her whip uncoiled just a little, enough for Tony to wrench an arm free and blast Virgo with his repulsors. Virgo twisted, dislodging Natasha's one-armed grip, sending her spinning into the void. Then she glimpsed Tony, coming out of the whip's coils.

"Tony!" she shouted, and hurled the Key at him.

She saw him catch it, then switched her attention to the long fall below her. Fortunately Scorpio was there, so she could break her fall by kicking him in the face.

———◦————————————◦———

STILL recovering from Virgo's attempt to cut him in half with her whip, Tony managed to hold onto the Key for about three seconds before one of Sagittarius's bolts hit him dead on. The fireworks were impressive, but the result was that he dropped the Key. He hit the ground next to it and started for it again, but then something crashed into the ground right next to it.

"Bruce," he gasped. The Hulk towered over him, reaching for the Key.

"Hulk do this," he snarled. "Hulk fix." But he didn't see Scorpio behind him, the sting that came down and jabbed him in the back and emerged through his belly.

The Hulk raised his head and screamed up at the falling sky. He grabbed the sting protruding from his stomach, and slashed it off with the Key. Then, as Scorpio reeled away, he leapt toward the zenith, quickly dwindling with distance.

Lightning struck, and Tony saw Thor break from his pack of attackers, following the Hulk. The Zodiac went after him.

All of them.

———◦————————————◦———

THIS time, no flash of weird light came to revive Hulk. Instead, the scorching pain from the bug-man's sting gave way to numbness, starting in his toes and shooting through his body. He looked down and saw Thor following. Behind him all the animal monsters, growing bigger as they flew.

He closed his eyes, and saw lights exploding there. He was angry, wanted to crush the bug-man, knock all of his friends down, wreck the whole place, everything in sight. They had done all of this, caused him pain, attacked him when all he wanted was peace.

He recognized Banner's thoughts creeping into his own. He usually hated that, but this time they agreed. It felt like Banner was proud of him. Which was stupid, because Banner was stupid, and weak, and Hulk didn't care what Banner thought of him.

Not usually.

Opening his eyes, he shook his head to stay awake. He could see the shadowed ocean, the little lights below, and far off in the distance the gleam of the sun. He was very high up. Soon he would begin to fall.

That was okay.

He had done what he could.

Hulk cocked his arm, and with the last of his strength he threw the Key as hard as he was able—outward. Away.

Then his eyes closed again.

○──────────────○

MOMENTUM carried Thor forward, but it wasn't enough. The Shining Herd was lapping at his heels. He'd twice been struck by the arrows of Sagittarius, each inflicting a grievous wound. He would heal, given time, but he couldn't take many more such insults without succumbing to oblivion.

There was a tug stronger than Earth's gravity.

Taurus. She was the last in the line of his pursuers, but her powers had grown. In a few moments she would be close enough to stop his flight and bring him back to Earth. Then this would all be over.

He hurled Mjolnir down with all of his might, aimed straight at the beast, and followed the trail of his weapon with his gaze. It bent aside from its target.

He swore a curse that had been ancient when his grandfather, Bor, had been young. The tug against him grew stronger. But then he saw a missile of gold and red hit Taurus and knock her from the sky.

"Thank you, Stark," he muttered.

He continued to rise, but his momentum was waning. Another

of the flashing arrows struck him, and then a burst of heat from the flaming Aries, who was nearly on him. He gauged the distance.

The Hulk still had the Key.

Aries grabbed his ankle with his flaming hand. Capricorn was close behind.

"Come on!" Thor grunted.

Then Mjolnir returned, traveling in a straight line that put Aries in the way. The hammer's haft slapped into Thor's palm, pulling him along.

Looking up again he saw the Hulk throw the Key, and in that instant he knew he must act. Thor mustered the full power of the storm, unleashed its fury, and watched through blurring vision as the bolt arced out. It connected with the golden ankh.

The Key shivered, growing bigger, brighter.

Then it filled the heavens with blinding light.

○──────────────○

BRUCE was floating. He opened his eyes.

He was on his back, weightless, looking up at the night sky. The constellations were strange, larger than usual, and in the midst of them was a star that didn't belong there—a new star, far brighter than any other. A supernova?

Then he realized he wasn't lying on anything. He was falling, the rushing wind filling his senses. Hulk's last few memories bubbled up into his waking mind.

Well, crap, he thought, but at least it looked like they had succeeded. The Hulk had done something right. Bruce didn't want to die, not really, but if he had to go…

He hit something hard, yelped, and hit it again. Suddenly his weight returned—and more. The rush of the wind decreased; he was decelerating.

Then he saw why.

"Tony!" he gasped. Iron Man had him cradled in his arms.

"Yeah," Tony's amplified voice replied. "Hang on. I'm on reserves. This could still get rough."

———○━━━━━━━━○———

AT first Thor didn't know when or where he was—he only knew it was cold, that he had saltwater in his nose and mouth, and that he felt like he'd fought an army of Jotuns on his own and done poorly...

As he lifted his head above water, identified land, and began to swim, memory returned. The Key exploding, the retreat of the constellations into the night, his long plummet to the water.

He heard the others calling for him now. Captain America. Natasha. They were on the island, on the rocky north side, away from the destruction of their battle. The Quinjet was there, too, settled on the stone.

"Thor," Cap said as he walked up. "Nice to see you."

"Sorry for the delay," Thor managed. "How are they?" He nodded at Banner and Stark, who were laid out. Stark was still in his armor. Natasha was with Bruce, injecting him with something.

"JARVIS says Tony is fine," Natasha said. "Bruce—I think he'll make it, but the Hulk took a beating. It didn't all go away when he changed."

"And the Zodiac? Has the world ended?"

Cap looked up. "I think you did it," he said. "After you blew up the Key, the Zodiac guys whittled back down to size. I guess they still had their teleportation bracelets, though, because they've all gone."

"Ah, that's too bad," Thor said. "I had some words for them."

"I think we'd all like to have a word or two with them," Captain America said. "I intend to get around to it, anyway, but right now I think we have to go back to work."

"What's happening?" Thor asked.

"JARVIS has been filling us in," Natasha said. "Earthquakes, big ones, all up and down the coast. Massive blackouts. Riots. Fires."

"I failed, then," Thor said. "Your notion was to get the Key far enough above the Earth to prevent what happened last time. How many have died because I didn't do better?"

"Listen," Cap said, "the real question is how bad it would have been if you hadn't tried. Based on Strange's accounts, JARVIS estimates the explosion only affected a tenth of the area it devastated way back when, and not nearly as badly." He laid a hand on Thor's shoulder. "You did good."

"As you say, but damage was done." Thor nodded. "Is there any sign of the mage?"

"None," Cap replied. "As far as I can tell, we'll just have to wait for his return. Guys like that operate in a place that's way above my pay grade."

"Indeed he is a mystery, even to me," Thor said. "With your permission, I would like to fly ahead and see the extent of the damage."

"I was going to suggest that," Cap said, "but first, help me get Tony aboard. That suit is really heavy."

"Aye," Thor said. "I can help with that."

THIRTY-TWO

MONICA took a sip of her coffee.

"I've missed this," she said.

"Yeah," Bruce replied. "Me too. But there's been a lot to settle up. The move from New York, cleaning up the mess in Seattle. But, a few loose ends aside, I think I'm done for a while. I'm here now."

"I'm holding you to that," she said.

"You won't have to hold very hard," he said.

She nodded, then gazed at something beyond him. Bruce turned, following her gaze to the half-finished tower rising against the San Francisco skyline.

"Tony Stark thinks big," Monica said.

"Just wait until it's done," Bruce said.

"I'm in no hurry," Monica said. "I already have what I want." She reached across the table and laced her fingers in his.

"You mean the new mass spectrometer they just installed in your lab?" Bruce asked.

"Of course," Monica said. "What else could I mean?"

They sat for another moment, quietly, holding hands.

"This is all because of you, you know," she said. "Great things have come of this, and more will come."

"More you than me," he said. "But great things, yes."

There couldn't be any doubt about that. The Terrigen Crystals were yielding up their secrets to Tony and Tarleton. The two scientists were so certain of their usefulness that Tony had already drawn up specs for a new Helicarrier, one powered entirely by the crystals. Construction was supposed to start within the week.

If she meant great things for the two of them, he couldn't argue with that either. He hadn't felt so content—no, not content, *happy*— since before the Hulk showed up. Maybe not even then; youth was a mess, even in the best of circumstances. There was some truth in the maxim that it was wasted on the young. He finally felt like he was in a place to accept the good things life brought him, while keeping the downsides in perspective.

It wasn't so bad being Bruce Banner these days. Not perfect, but not bad at all.

"How *are* things going up in Seattle?" she asked.

"Nearly done," he said. "The fallout wasn't as bad as we feared. The Key was *way* up there when it exploded. The effects were minimal." He frowned. "Still," he muttered.

"You'll find them," Monica said. "They can't hide forever."

"The Zodiac is good at hiding," he replied. "They've been doing it for millennia. They may not even be on Earth."

"Let them hide," Monica said. "I'm sure they have no wish to challenge the Avengers again. Not even the West Coast Avengers."

"Aghh," he said.

She laughed. "I only say it to torment you, of course. I know how you feel about the name."

"It's growing on me," Bruce said. "Shall we go?"

"Yes," she said, setting her empty cup aside. "I'm done."

They had paid at the bar, but he left a tip on the table.

"Do you think the Zodiac took him with them? Blonsky?" she asked, as they walked up the street toward the new, improved AIM building and the skyscraper-in-progress just beyond. It was a lovely morning, all golden sun, turquoise sky and slight breezes.

"I don't know," he said. "We're still not sure what happened there. Blonsky got away while we were still fighting the Zodiac, but there's been no sign of him since. He might revert to—you know, a regular guy, the way I do. But the trouble is, we don't know exactly what he *is*."

"But you must have some idea," she pressed.

He shrugged. She looked away.

"Are you still worried you had something to do with it?" he said. "You shouldn't be."

"He left behind a gamma ray signature…" she began, then stopped.

He shook his head. "The Zodiac needed something to absorb excess energy, in case we tried to overload the Key. After fighting me, they knew the Hulk could absorb the stellar energy that gave them their power. So, they came looking for me to use as their energy sink. I wasn't around, so they took Blonsky instead. But he's not another Hulk. There is gamma in his radiation signature, but there's also the Zodiac stellar energy, and possibly a dose of Terrigen Crystal.

"Maybe he injected himself with your gamma cell experiment. Maybe he thought it would make him stronger. But you and I both know that what you had wouldn't have resulted in what he became. It might have been a start, but it couldn't account for what I saw."

"I only had the best of intentions," she said. "I've destroyed everything the fight didn't, including my notes—"

"I know," he said. "Let's put it aside, okay? I'm more interested in what we're going to do today than what we did yesterday."

"Of course," she said, brightening. "On to better things."

"Better things," he agreed.

Together, they went into their labs.

EPILOGUE

IT had already been an exciting day for Kamala Khan. She had never flown before, and watching the entire breadth of America unfurl below her was amazing. She'd pressed her face to the window for so much of the trip she now had a slight crick in her neck. And that had been on a regular airplane.

After they had landed at the airport in San Francisco, a woman with her name on a placard—*her* name—had led her and her father to a special gate, to board not just another plane but a *Quinjet*, where a bunch of other kids and their parents were also boarding. They'd had to wait there while flights from other parts of the country arrived, but she hadn't been bored in the slightest. How could she be? The controls and displays were the same ones the Avengers used. One of them might have been in the very seat she was sitting in at the moment. But which one? Thor? Captain America?

Captain Marvel? But that was silly. She didn't need a Quinjet. She could fly. She could do *anything*.

Whatever. That wasn't important. She—Kamala Khan, eleven years old—was in a Quinjet, headed to "Avengers Day," the celebratory grand opening of the Avengers' West Coast base. It was just so cool.

Her father didn't seem as excited. He fell asleep almost as soon as he was in his seat.

And then came the takeoff. Not like the plane earlier, zooming down a runway and tilting into the air, but jumping straight up, like a helicopter, then rocketing off toward their destination. The airport was south of downtown San Francisco, and she had a great view of the city, the ocean, the bay. They turned out to sea, and then back, and ahead she saw the long orange-colored span she had seen in a hundred movies and television shows.

"I can see the bridge, Abu," she said. "Look!"

Her father snorted, rousing from his nap. He groaned, shifting in his seat.

"Uh," he grunted. "It's about time. Oh! These seats don't recline."

"It's so beautiful," Kamala said.

"Huh," he remarked. "Why call it the Golden Gate Bridge if it's not golden?"

Typical Abu, she thought. Sometimes she wondered if anything really impressed him. She glanced around at the other passengers. About half of them were kids around her own age, the other finalists in the contest.

Worry crept into her excitement. She had been ecstatic when her fan-fiction was chosen for the A-Day contest finals. No one else she knew had been chosen—no one else from New Jersey, in fact. But now she was looking at the competition and feeling a little deflated. They all looked so formidable. She was suddenly, acutely aware of the Captain Marvel t-shirt she had on. Everyone else she saw just had on regular shirts. Was she too geeked-out?

"There are so many other kids," she sighed. "I bet their stories are all amazing."

"Competition is what makes us strong," Abu said, calmly.

"What if they don't like my story?" she said, thumbing through her manuscript, eying each page critically. "What if it doesn't fit in? It's gotta be perfect, y'know?"

Her father looked at her.

"When you were born," he said, "your brother said you had googly eyes."

She looked up at him. That sounded like something Aamir would say—the jerk—but why was Abu bringing it up now?

"What?"

"But I thought your eyes were the most beautiful things I had ever seen," he went on. "We are all unique, Kamala. You should be proud of who you are."

She felt a little smile spread on her face.

"I love you, Abu," she said.

"I love you more," he said. He leaned a little closer, and spoke more confidentially. "And I'm pretty sure you're gonna win this thing."

"Oh! Could you imagine?" she said. "And the winner! For best fan fiction *ever* is… 'The Avengers versus the Evil Sewer Lizards' by Kamala Khan! And the crowd goes wild! *Ahhhh! Ssshh!*"

"That's the spirit!" Abu said.

Kamala giggled.

"Promise me something," Abu said, a little more seriously. "Win or lose—"

"Oh," she said. "I'll always be good, Abu."

"No, *beta*," he reproved. "Good isn't a thing you are—"

"—it's a thing you do," she finished.

"That's my girl," Abu said.

"Folks," the pilot said. "We're approaching the Avengers' West Coast headquarters on the left, and we'll be touching down in three, two…"

Kamala didn't hear the rest of it. She was too busy staring at the skyscraper with the giant "A" on it—and then the Helicarrier below, festooned with banners and balloons.

She felt her heart lift. Abu was right: win or lose, she was here. Nothing so exciting had ever happened to her before and for all she knew might never again.

She promised herself she would make the best of it.

ABOUT THE AUTHOR

GREG KEYES was born in Meridian, Mississippi, on April 11, 1963. His mother read to him early and often, until he learned to read—and soon after that, to write. To his delight, he discovered that writing books was actually a job, and so he decided he should do that. He wrote, he listened to the oral traditions of his family, he studied, he went to college. He earned degrees in anthropology; travelled; played strange, violent games; learned to play music; associated with interesting people. In 1996 he managed to get the job he'd been working toward when his first novel, *The Waterborn*, was published.

Since that time Greg has published over thirty books, including the original series Children of the Changeling, The Age of Unreason, and The Kingdoms of Thorn and Bone, as well as the standalone books *The Hounds of Ash* and *Footsteps in the Sky*. He has also had the great fortune to be asked to contribute to other universes, writing books for *Babylon 5*, *Star Wars*, *Planet of the Apes*, *Pacific Rim*, *The Elder Scrolls*, *X-COM* and *Independence Day*, and to novelize the films *Interstellar* and *Godzilla: King of the Monsters*. He is currently finishing the third book in his newest trilogy, The High and Faraway. He lives, writes, fences and cooks in Savannah, Georgia, with his wife Nell, son John (formerly known as Archer), daughter Dorothy (formerly known as Nellah), and a small pack of wiener dogs.

ACKNOWLEDGEMENTS

AT Titan, thanks to my editor, Steve Saffel, London editors Craig Leyenaar and Davi Lancett, Hayley Shepherd, Nick Landau, Vivian Cheung, Laura Price, George Sandison, and Natasha MacKenzie. Thanks also at Marvel to Loni Clark, Isabel Hsu, Sven Larsen, Dakota Maysonet, Becka McIntosh, Eric Monacelli, Caitlin O'Connell, Bill Rosemann, and Jeff Youngquist. Thanks to Uroš Perišić for his help with the Croatian language.

SPIDER-MAN
HOSTILE TAKEOVER

The official prequel to MARVEL'S SPIDER-MAN, the PS4 exclusive video game from Marvel and Insomniac Games, that leads directly into the game narrative itself

Wilson Fisk—the so-called Kingpin of Crime—has returned to New York, establishing himself publicly as an altruistic entrepreneur and philanthropist. Spider-Man knows better, but he can't uncover Fisk's scheme that, if executed, will make the crime lord "too big to fail."

When a new threat—a deadly doppelganger with Spider-Man's suit and abilities—wreaks havoc in the streets, can the real wall-crawler prove his innocence? With the clock ticking and lives on the line, can Spider-Man stop the brutal rampage of the Blood Spider? Will Spider-Man fall to his fears and foes, or will he rise and be greater?

X-MEN AND THE AVENGERS
GAMMA QUEST OMNIBUS

When the Scarlet Witch of the Avengers and Rogue of the X-Men both disappear under mysterious circumstances, each team's search leads them to more questions than answers. Desperate to recover their missing teammates, they must join forces to uncover the truth. But their efforts will bring them up against a foe with the deadliest power of all: to make them turn on each other!

SPIDER-MAN
THE VENOM FACTOR OMNIBUS

Collecting all three of Diane Duane's fan-favorite Spider-Man novels in a brand-new omnibus, featuring *The Venom Factor*, *The Lizard Sanction*, and *The Octopus Agenda*. Venom is out of control, murdering one of the innocents he swore to protect. The Lizard is rampaging through the Everglades in search of a cure. Doctor Octopus is masterminding a plan to rain nuclear bombs down across the globe. Not all is as it seems as Spider-Man fights his fiercest enemies in this action-packed trilogy.